MOVING ON

He halted abruptly in the darkness when the cold muzzle of a gun met his ribcage and he heard a throaty voice whisper, "Welcome, Taylor. I've been expecting you."

The graceful shadow moved from his side and turned up the lamp. Vida stood in the dim light of the room. Her dark hair was loose against her shoulders and she was wearing a diaphanous nightgown that outlined her womanly curves clearly. She evinced little discomfort with her revealing appearance as she said, "Did you have fun at the Last Chance tonight, Taylor? I did."

Taylor responded with a touch of irritation he could not conceal, "I figured you were having fun since every man in the saloon was falling all over you."

"Yes, but I did deserve the attention." A smile lifted the corners of her lush lips as she said offhandedly, "I was magnificent tonight."

Taylor responded tightly, "You're magnificent in every role you undertake, Vida…but you didn't come to Lowell to hear me say that. What are you doing here, and why are you pretending to be an entertainer?"

"I don't know. Why are you pretending to be a drunk?"

"That's my business."

"Well, it's my business, too."

ELAINE BARBIERI

TEXAS TR★UMPH

LEISURE BOOKS NEW YORK CITY

To my new grandson,
Albert Benjamin Barbieri.
I love you, little fella.

A LEISURE BOOK®

May 2005

Published by

Dorchester Publishing Co., Inc.
200 Madison Avenue
New York, NY 10016

ISBN 0-8439-5409-4

The name "Leisure Books" and the stylized "L" with design are trademarks of Dorchester Publishing Co., Inc.

Printed in the United States of America.

Visit us on the web at www.dorchesterpub.com.

TEXAS TR★UMPH

Prologue

The glittering New Orleans ballroom came alive with the lilting strains of a waltz. Fashionably dressed couples danced, laughing and conversing as they circled the polished floor to the gradually accelerating swell of music. No one appeared to notice as a handsome couple swept through a doorway, then slipped into the seclusion of a darkened room.

Taylor Star closed the door behind him, not bothering to turn on the light as he released his beautiful partner and began hastily removing his clothes. He stripped off his evening jacket and tie as his partner loosened the neckline of her crimson gown. They conversed in soft, tense tones.

"Did you get the information you were looking for?"

She whispered, "Of course I did. Did you doubt me?"

"I never doubt you, Vida."

"It's Lisette this time, remember?"

"How could I forget?"

1

"We don't have much time. Pierre won't take lightly having someone steal the woman of his choice out from under him. He'll be on my tail like a hawk."

Stripping down to her undergarments, Vida lay down on the couch. She groaned when Taylor flopped on top of her.

Not a moment too soon.

There was a sound at the door.

Taylor covered Vida's mouth with a passionate kiss as she mumbled, "You're crushing me, dammit!"

The door snapped open to reveal Pierre Maison standing in the opening. His lean, aristocratic figure rigid with subdued anger, he deliberately ignored Taylor as he addressed Vida haughtily.

"I thought you had better sense, Lisette. I assumed a young woman of your breeding would be impervious to the attentions of an infamous rake like Taylor Star, but it appears I was wrong. However, you will soon learn that you were the one who was made a fool of tonight, not I."

Allowing a moment for the import of his words to linger, Pierre continued, "You will both leave immediately. Neither of you are welcome in my home any longer. I will personally see to it that from this evening on, you will no longer be welcome anywhere in New Orleans where polite society meets."

Not waiting for a response, Pierre snapped the door closed behind him.

Taylor moved immediately to his feet. He pulled Vida up behind him, noting that she disregarded her partial nakedness as she reached for her clothes. Unable to resist an appreciative, purely male glance at the white swells of her breasts, he urged, "Make it quick, Vida. Our carriage is waiting."

Stepping out into the hallway minutes later, he guided Vida politely as they walked with heads high. He ignored the shocked whispers following them as they headed toward the doorway.

Taylor returned Vida's amused glance as their carriage pulled away. Vida Malone. His smile lingered as he silently scrutinized the gleaming black of Vida's upswept hair, her flawlessly fine features, her dark, fathomless eyes, and the womanly proportions that turned men's heads—all inherited from a Spanish mother who had impulsively married a fast-talking Irish lad. That volatile combination had produced a woman of unusual beauty, sharp intelligence, keen sensitivity, and an adventurous spirit that was a match for any man.

A match for any man . . .

Impulsively brushing her warm lips with his, Taylor whispered, "You're beautiful, Vida. There wasn't a woman at the ball tonight who was your equal. It's no wonder poor Pierre was smitten."

"Yes, poor Pierre." Vida's smile dimmed. "Poor Pierre who grew wealthy on the blood of innocent seamen."

Withdrawing a sheaf of papers from the lining of her dress, she continued, "But poor Pierre will have much more than our perceived dalliance on his mind when we deliver this information to Allan Pinkerton and it becomes known that Pierre is responsible for the criminal activities that have almost brought New Orleans shipping to its knees."

"Another job well done, Vida, my dear partner."

Vida replied in a faintly caustic tone, "And since Pierre will never learn how the authorities became aware of his criminal involvement, you'll escape our scandalous episode tonight completely unscathed—*as usual*."

The clear blue of Taylor's eyes sparkled with amusement. "Actually, tonight added another layer of polish to my already sterling reputation as a womanizer. After a few days, I'll be more in demand at these society soirees than ever before."

"Of course, while I—"

"While you, my poor, unfortunate dear, will probably be banned from polite New Orleans society forever."

"It's a man's world!"

"Yes, it is."

Her expression suddenly tight with irritation, Vida exclaimed, "I believe you're actually enjoying this, damn you!"

"I am, to an extent."

"Taylor!"

"Vida, you know my reputation in New Orleans is valuable to the agency."

Vida's caustic smile returned. "What would Allan do without you?"

"Or without you?"

Halted by his unexpected compliment, Vida stared at Taylor for a silent moment, then said, "You mean that, don't you?"

"Of course I do. I've never had a more competent partner." He added more softly, "Or a more appealing one."

Vida replied instinctively, "Your reputation is going to your head, Taylor."

"I meant every word!"

Hesitating again, Vida then responded, "You probably did, considering that I'm the only female partner Allan ever assigned to you."

4

"That's true, too, but—"

"And don't think you'll be getting rid of me so easily. With a change of hair color, dress, and demeanor, I'll be able to slip back into New Orleans without anyone giving me a second look."

"I'm counting on it. I'd miss you sorely."

"Taylor . . ."

The slowing of the carriage at his lodgings averted Taylor's gaze from the unexpected softening of Vida's expression. When he turned back, all trace of familiarity was dismissed from his tone as he instructed, "I'll pack up my things and leave New Orleans tonight for our meeting with Allan. Make sure you wait at least a day before following. We can't chance anyone becoming suspicious of collaboration."

Resignation heavy in her tone, Vida responded, "I'll endure the hypocritical whispers, properly chastised—*as usual*. Then I'll leave the city humiliated, never to return—*as usual*."

"Vida . . ." Hesitating, Taylor linked Vida's gaze soberly with his. Then appearing to think better of his intended response, he pushed open the door and whispered in farewell, "Allan and I will be waiting for you."

Taylor stepped down onto the sidewalk, then turned when the concierge appeared unexpectedly beside him. The balding man handed him an envelope as he said anxiously, "This arrived for you a little while ago, Mr. Star. It's marked urgent."

Apprehension moved up Taylor's spine as he opened the envelope. He unfolded the single sheet.

It read: *Have you forgotten Bonnie? It is time to go home.*

Taylor went still as vivid, painful memories flashed

across his mind. He was still staring at the letter when Vida asked, "Is it from Allan? What does it say?"

Volatile emotions suddenly overwhelming him, Taylor crushed the sheet in his hand.

Uncertainty rang in Vida's voice as she inquired, "What's wrong, Taylor?"

Taylor responded enigmatically, "Tell Allan not to expect me in Baton Rouge. I won't be coming."

Taylor did not wait for Vida's response as he tossed the coachman a few coins and ordered, "Take the lady home."

"Taylor!"

Vida's exclamation trailed away as the coach jerked into motion and Taylor walked into his quarters without a backward glance.

Chapter 1

Lowell, Texas—1869

The biweekly stagecoach rolled to a halt on Lowell's deeply rutted main street. The door snapped open and a well-dressed, middle-aged gentleman exited the conveyance, muttering under his breath as he turned to assist an overweight matron down the steps behind him.

Deliberately waiting for the driver to finish tossing down the baggage, the gentleman approached the gray-haired, heavily mustached driver and said irately, "You may rest assured, my dear fellow, that neither my wife nor I will ever use this stage line again if drunken degenerates continue to be allowed to travel with decent passengers."

A veteran of countless years at the reins, the driver eyed the gentleman, then replied as politely as he could manage, "I ain't your 'dear fellow,' mister. My name's Pete Sloan, and I'm sorry to tell you this, but as long as a man pays his fare and don't cause me no trouble, he can ride in my stage."

The gentleman continued speaking angrily as Pete strode toward the open door of the coach and looked inside at an unkempt, unshaven drunk snoring noisily with an empty bottle of red-eye tucked in the corner of the seat beside him. Shaking his head, Pete said loudly, "Wake up, fella! Lowell is the destination you paid for, and that's where we are. It's time to get up and on your feet."

The man barely stirred.

Taking two steps up into the coach with the spring of a man years his junior, Pete grasped the other man by the shoulder and shook him hard. The drunk's eyes opened into slits of brilliant blue.

"You heard me, fella. Get up!"

The drunk unfolded his tall, spare frame slowly and glanced around him as he said, "We're in Lowell?"

"That's right."

"Well, I guess it's time for me to get out."

Hardly waiting for Pete to touch down on the dusty surface of the street, the drunk staggered down the steps behind him. He stood, swaying unsteadily as he looked around him.

Pete stared at the fellow, noting his unexpected height and breadth of shoulder and the brilliant, presently bloodshot blue eyes under dark brows. He studied the thick, unruly dark hair that hung against the fellow's shirt collar and searched the even features hidden underneath the unshaven stubble of a week-long beard. He said, "Seems to me I've seen you some-place before, fella."

"Maybe." The drunk turned to stare back at him. "What's your name?"

"My name's Pete Sloan. What's yours?"

"Hell, now that would be telling, wouldn't it?" The drunk laughed, then spotting the saloon at the end of the street, he said, "There it is, the Last Chance Saloon—just like I remembered it."

The drunk staggered away as the gentleman and his wife walked toward the hotel in disgusted silence.

Pete stared after the drunk. He raised his hand to scratch his head, then froze in mid motion with eyes widening before turning in the direction of a storefront halfway down the street.

When he burst through the doorway minutes later, the buxom, middle-aged woman inside jumped and said, "Dammit, Pete, you just about scared the life out of me!"

"I didn't mean to scare you, Doc, but . . ." Pete lowered his voice as he said with a touch of incredulity in his tone, ". . . but I'm thinking I just brought an old friend of yours back into town."

"An old friend?" Doc asked impatiently, "What are you talking about?"

Pointing out onto the street at the tall drunk staggering toward the saloon, Pete responded, "Unless I'm mistaken, and I don't think I am, that big fella is . . . *Taylor Star.*"

Taylor paused at the swinging doors of the Last Chance Saloon. His slow, unsteady approach had allowed him time to covertly scrutinize the changes the years had wrought on the small Texas town that had once been his home. It hadn't taken him long to realize that the changes were few. The necessary businesses still lined the street behind false-fronted facades worn by time, and the most prominent business establishment of all was still the saloon that occupied the greater portion of the street at the far end. He wondered if Miss Ida's fancy house was still located around the corner—a place he had come to know early on when searching out his pa after his mother's unexpected death.

Harsh memories of the past returned as the saloon's inevitable aroma of stale beer met his nostrils. His mother, dead at the age of thirty-six from an unexpected heart attack; his father whoring away his sorrow; his beloved little sister, Bonnie, killed in an accident only weeks later; his brother's departure from the ranch in the middle of the night. The tragic progression of events had come to a stunning climax a few months later when his father married a widow young enough to be his daughter.

Have you forgotten Bonnie? It is time to go home.

No, he hadn't forgotten Bonnie. He hadn't forgotten any of it. His outrage still haunted him in the dark hours of the night, burning a hole inside him that he had never been able to fill.

It had taken him a few days to achieve enough distance from the emotion the letter had aroused to be able to study it like the Pinkerton professional he had become. The cryptic message had been unsigned. That fact had made him wary. He had not been in contact with anyone in Lowell in recent years.

Realizing he could neither shrug aside the letter nor the nagging images it had stirred to life, Taylor had known he needed to find out who had sent it and exactly what was intended by it. The deliberate tone of the cryptic message had led him to believe that discovering the answer to those questions would not be easy;

and to his mind, there was only one way to handle the situation.

No one watched his tongue in the presence of a drunk.

Suppressing the anxiety within, Taylor pushed open the swinging doors and staggered up to the bar. He was not surprised when Bart, the graying bartender, failed to recognize him. He had been too young to be a customer years earlier, although his father had not been. Bart's summons to take his father home became familiar to Taylor in the early days after Bonnie's death. Pa's drinking had stopped after he remarried; but, strangely, Taylor truly believed he would have preferred to see his pa still sagging against the bar, rather than married to Celeste DuClair, the woman who had so quickly turned Buck Star against his remaining son.

Taylor downed his drink, then tapped the bar for another as he glanced casually around the room. It was early in the day and the saloon had few customers. In addition to three weary saloon women lounging in the rear, he saw two wiry cattle-punchers seated at a table in the corner in laughing conversation. He didn't recognize them, but they appeared harmless. The dark, hairy man with coarse features at the end of the bar was also a stranger to him. He also seemed harmless at the moment, but Taylor reserved judgment on that one. Then there were Jake Colt and Barney Wiggs, both engaged in emptying their glasses a few feet away. They did not give him a second glance, and he was glad.

Taylor noted that Bart assessed him silently before saying, "You've had enough to drink, fella. It's time for you to move on."

11

Taylor smiled. Same old Bart, a saloonkeeper with a wary eye.

Emerging onto the street a few minutes later, Taylor continued his affected, wavering stance as he scrutinized the town. He turned toward a familiar voice as a robust, middle-aged woman appeared unexpectedly beside him and said, "I'll be damned, it's true. It is you, Taylor Star!"

Suddenly enveloped in an enthusiastic hug, Taylor felt his throat tighten as Doc Maggie released him just as abruptly, and with an uncharacteristic display of emotion brushed away a tear and said, "Welcome home." Her smile faded when she added soberly, "You look like hell, boy. What's happened to you?"

Regretting the deception he felt forced to maintain, Taylor put on a lopsided smile as he replied, "I'm glad to see you, too, Doc." He added with a wink, "So, where do we go from here?"

"I'll tell you where we're going."

Back in Doc's office with a third cup of steaming black coffee half consumed, Taylor eyed the frowning, motherly woman in front of him. Apple-cheeked and full-figured, she still wore her graying hair in a tight bun and obviously still dismissed the importance of fashion, but Taylor felt a swell of warmth at the sight of her. His mother's friend and confidante, Doc had delivered him and his brother, Cal, into the world. She had remained as close to the family as a blood relative. He had kept up an erratic correspondence with her during the lonely years spent back East in the military school where his father had banished him after marrying Celeste. With Cal gone and his father so wrapped up in his new wife, Doc had been Taylor's only contact with home. She had been his lifeline, the only warmth remaining when other memories were too painful to recall. He loved her dearly, but with that acknowledgment came recognition that telling her the truth might not be in her best interests.

Interrupting his thoughts, Doc asked abruptly, "Are you ready to talk to me now, Taylor?"

"I'm always ready to talk to you, Doc."

A smile flickered briefly on Doc's lips. "Still the same silver-tongued devil, aren't you?" Sobering, she added, "But you're not going to wangle your way around me this time. I want to know what in hell you've been doing to get yourself in the condition you're in!"

"Doc—"

"Don't 'Doc' me! The last thing I expected was to see you like this. The Taylor I remember was handsome, smart, headed for a future that would make us all stand up and take notice." Her voice thickened as she asked simply, "What happened to you, darlin'?"

"Nothing happened, Doc. I graduated school back East and I've been finding my way ever since."

"Finding your way . . ."

Taylor took Doc's callused hand in his. Seeking to provide her some kind of consolation, he said, "Maybe coming back to Lowell like this wasn't the best way for you to see me again after so many years, but . . ." Taylor took a chance and continued soberly, "But I got an unsigned letter that mentioned Bonnie. It shook me up pretty badly. It forced me to come home, and coming home wasn't easy."

"A letter?" Doc's rosy cheeks paled. "You got a letter about Bonnie, too?"

Taylor's attention sharpened. "Too?"

"Cal came home a few months ago. A note about Bonnie also brought him back."

Silent at the mention of his brother's name, Taylor remembered the closeness Cal and he had shared while growing up. The memory of their harsh parting twisted tightly inside him.

He asked bluntly, "Did you send those letters, Doc?"

"No."

"Do you know who did?"

"No. Cal doesn't know, either."

Taylor remained silent as Doc continued hesitantly, "Cal married a fine woman he met here in town a few months back."

Cal . . . married.

Doc frowned, and Taylor was suddenly wary. The years had not dulled his memory of that expression. She had something else to say that she was reluctant to add.

He prompted, "And?"

"And . . . you've got a sister."

Standing up abruptly, Taylor responded, "Bonnie's dead."

"You're right. Bonnie is dead."

Taylor waited for Doc to continue.

"Your other sister's name is Honor. Her ma was your mother's friend, Betty Montgomery."

The knot inside Taylor twisted tighter as he muttered, "That damned old man!"

"Honor's a fine young woman."

Taylor would not reply.

"She lives in town. You can meet her anytime you want."

"I don't want to meet her."

14

Doc shrugged. "That might be best, considering the way you look right now."

"I don't ever want to meet her."

"Don't talk like that, Taylor. Your ma wouldn't want—"

"Don't tell me what Ma would or wouldn't want, Doc. I know what she'd want, and she wouldn't want the proof of Pa's infidelity parading around the streets, reminding everybody of her shame."

"It isn't *her* shame, Taylor. It's your pa's."

"I don't want to talk about it."

Doc continued determinedly, "Buck's sick, you know . . . damned sick, but the truth is it hasn't changed him none. He's still the same, hardheaded, stubborn old man—"

Doc halted abruptly when Taylor turned toward the door. She said as he reached for the knob, "Are you going to see Buck now?"

Taylor did not respond.

"Don't go off half-cocked, Taylor."

"Don't worry about me, Doc."

Taking the few steps to his side, Doc grasped Taylor's arm and whispered, "You were always such a bright young fella. I figured you could do anything you wanted to do with your life."

"Are you trying to tell me something?"

"I'm trying to tell you that the saloon isn't the right place for you to be. You're better than that."

Taylor's voice softened as he whispered, "I told you, don't worry about me. I'm fine."

Her eyes moist, Doc replied, "And damned handsome underneath all that dust and scratchy beard, would be my guess."

15

"Right."

"Don't waste all you got going for you, you hear? And don't go too far before we have more time to talk."

Unable to reply, Taylor turned and walked out the doorway.

The sunny knoll was achingly familiar. Feeling driven after his conversation with Doc, Taylor had approached it steadily, while unwilling to admit where he was headed even to himself until his destination came clearly into view.

Dismounting in a shaded spot, Taylor tied up his horse and turned toward the small, fenced-in graveyard. He halted beside the two gravestones, the ache inside him deepening as he read the inscriptions:

EMMA ELIZABETH STAR   BONNIE EMMA STAR
Beloved Wife and Mother   Beloved Daughter
Born January 10, 1824   Born May 3, 1853
Died June 12, 1860   Died June 29, 1860

The inscriptions were sadly inadequate.

The text on his mother's stone did not speak of her endless capacity for love, of her patience, understanding, or the gentle guidance she had extended to her children. Nor did it express the agony her passing caused for those she left behind.

Bonnie's inscription did not deal with the laughter or the celebration of life the dear child had brought to each day. It did not speak of the joy she shared so easily, nor of the aching gap she left in the hearts of those who loved her when her brief life ended so tragically.

16

Taylor surveyed the small, carefully tended plots more closely. Freshly cultivated and raked, they were free of the weeds and spidery undergrowth that covered the surrounding area. Newly planted flowers bloomed on the fenced expanse, a glorious burst of color that would surely have warmed the hearts of the two buried there, while a bouquet that had long since faded rested between the twin stones.

Doc's hesitant revelation a short time earlier returned to his mind, and Taylor felt again a wrench of pain. He whispered, "I've been away too long, and I'm sorry, Ma. A lot has changed in the time since I was here last. The living proof of Pa's infidelity now walks the streets of Lowell for all to see—another thoughtless cruelty Pa dealt you. But you always forgave him, although I never could. I was young when everything happened all those years ago. I handled things poorly. In the time since, I've settled longstanding accounts for others, while I still wasn't able to face the unfinished business in my own past. I suppose that's part of the reason why that unsigned letter made me so angry, why it made me so determined to find out who sent it. But now that I'm here, it looks like learning who sent it is even more important than I realized."

His hoarse whisper continued after a moment. "The truth is, I never forgot either you or Bonnie. I never will, but I've come to realize that I can't avoid the past any longer. I don't know who sent those letters to Cal and me, or why, but I'll find out. And I promise you this: When I leave, you and Bonnie will rest peacefully."

Taylor's whisper faded into silence, but he felt reluctant to leave as he stared down at the weathered gravestones. The aching void inside him remained, but a peacefulness and calm that had long escaped him seemed to envelop him. He wished that he—

Taylor turned abruptly at the sound of footsteps behind him. He did his best not to reveal his reaction to the sight of the tall man approaching.

Taylor was the first to speak as his brother drew near. "Hello, Cal. I don't have to ask how you knew I was back. Doc sent somebody out to tell you, didn't she?"

Halting close enough so that Taylor could see the dark flecks in his brother's honey-colored eyes, Cal replied in a voice deep with maturity, "Yeah, she did. I suppose she thought I should know."

"How did you know where to find me?"

Cal shrugged. "Where else would you be?"

Yes . . . where else?

Taylor remarked, "You look more like Ma than ever."

"And you look like hell."

A smile touched Taylor's lips at his older brother's comment.

Cal scrutinized him more intently. He said abruptly, "Why the act, Taylor?"

"The act?"

"Others might be taken in, but you can't fool me. You're not the drunk you're pretending to be. What's going on?"

"I don't know what you're talking about."

"You forget, I know you. You may not smell right or seem to be in good shape right now, but I've seen that look in your eyes before. You've got something going on inside your head that you don't want anybody to know about."

Taylor inwardly smiled. Yes, he *had* forgotten.

Suddenly solemn, Taylor replied, "The truth is, there's only one thing I'm thinking about right now, and what I have to say has waited too long already." Taylor took a breath before continuing slowly, "I need to apologize to you, Cal. I'm sorry. I was wrong that last day when I said it was your fault Bonnie was killed. It was an accident. Nobody could've seen it coming, not even you."

The impact of Taylor's words registered hard in Cal's expression. Taylor saw the difficulty with which his brother swallowed before he responded, "I'm not so sure about that."

"Dammit, Cal." Taylor took an aggressive step. "I've spent countless sleepless nights going over that last day in my mind, and the answer is always the same. We both know Bonnie had gotten water from that well many times before. However the accident happened, however she lost her balance and fell in, you couldn't have anticipated it."

"I was supposed to be watching her."

"But Pa got in the way—him and that floozy he was spending his 'grief' with."

"Yeah . . ." Cal frowned, "Speaking of Pa—"

"He's sick. I know. Doc told me."

"He's not the man you remember."

"Is that supposed to be good or bad?"

Cal replied simply, "He's dying, Taylor."

Cal's statement sucked the wind out of Taylor, leaving him suddenly wordless as Cal continued, "But you need to know he's still the same bastard he always was . . . maybe more so, now."

His breath returning in a caustic laugh, Taylor

shook his head. "Somehow I wouldn't expect anything different." He asked, "How are things going with him and Celeste?"

"She's got him wrapped around her little finger."

"So that hasn't changed, but she must have some good in her, the way she's been taking care of Ma's and Bonnie's graves."

Responding with unexpected heat, Cal snapped, "Celeste couldn't care less about those graves. My wife's been taking care of them."

"Your wife."

"Pru says the graves are her responsibility now that Ma and Bonnie are her family, too."

After long seconds, Taylor commented, "Pru . . . your wife's name is Prudence, huh? That's one helluva moniker."

Truly smiling for the first time, Cal replied, "Yeah, but she does it proud. You have to meet her. We have Old Man Simmons's place now. It was left to Pru when the old man died."

"Settled in, are you?"

"In some ways."

Attuned to the cautious note in his brother's voice, Taylor said abruptly, "Doc told you what brought me home. I need to know . . . truthfully. Do you know who sent the letters?"

"No."

"Pa?"

"He didn't send them. He still blames me for Bonnie's death. If he never had to see me again, it would be too soon. I expect your reception won't be much different."

"Doc?"

"She didn't send them, either. She'd own up to it if she had. And it wasn't Honor." He added cautiously, "Doc told you about Honor, didn't she?"

"I don't want to talk about her."

"Taylor, she—"

"I said, I don't want to talk about her!"

Cal shook his head. "Same old Taylor . . . won't give an inch."

"That's right, 'same old Taylor,' so I'm going to be honest with you and tell you exactly why I came home." Realizing he was defining his reasons for the first time, Taylor said, "The first reason was to find a way to apologize to you. I shouldn't have said what I did, and I've regretted it. It was my fault that you turned your back on all of us at the Texas Star."

"No, it wasn't."

Not bothering to argue the point, Taylor continued, "My second reason was to find out who sent me the letter, but I have the feeling now that there's more behind that letter than either of us knows. Someone wants both of us back here, Cal. I need to find out why."

"So do I."

The realization that they were united in that cause kept Taylor and Cal briefly silent as they stood eye to eye. Taylor severed the silence to say, "So we know where we stand, but I need to warn you: As far as everyone else is concerned—*everyone else*—when we met today, you took me at face value and our meeting wasn't pleasant."

"Taylor, what are you—"

"And from this point on, believe only a quarter of what you hear about me, and even less of what you see. That's all I've got to say right now."

Cal studied Taylor's expression. He said abruptly, "Take care, brother."

Taylor shook the hand Cal extended toward him. He was unsure who took the first step when they embraced suddenly and heartily, and Cal said, "Let me know if you need me."

Taylor was mounted when Cal's horse disappeared back through the trees.

About to leave, Taylor glanced back at the two headstones, somehow suddenly certain that Ma was smiling.

Chapter 2

She didn't like the way he was looking at her.

Celeste stepped down from her buckboard in the familiar isolated glade, her expression stiff. Blonde, with exquisite features and a delicate stature, she was meticulously groomed—in sharp contrast with the man awaiting her in the doorway of the dilapidated shack to which she had been summoned.

Celeste felt an inner swell of revulsion at the sight of Derek Beecher. Dark, unclean, hairy, uncouth, lecherous . . . those negatives that so aptly described him had once conversely raised a wild, sexual heat inside her—but times had changed. Derek had been an effective ally in her scheme of vengeance against her husband, Buck Star, but the association that had previously reaped great financial rewards for them both had been brought to an abrupt halt by Cal Star's return. It had deteriorated further after the appearance of Honor Gannon. Derek was the only member of his gang of rustlers to have escaped Cal both alive and unidentified—which

Celeste was beginning to conclude was an unfortunate circumstance.

Keeping her distance from Derek, Celeste stood beside the buckboard as she inquired, "Why did you signal me to come here, Derek?"

Derek's oily face twisted into a sneer as he responded, "What's the matter, Celeste? Afraid to come into the cabin?"

"Afraid?" Celeste's gaze was cold. "I'm not afraid of anyone or anything. You should have learned that by now."

"Come inside, then."

Celeste asked more sharply, "What do you want, Derek?"

Derek raised a hairy brow.

Contemptuous, Celeste responded, "Are you telling me you brought me here to satisfy your . . . *needs?* Because if you did, you made a mistake. I left that occupation behind me a long time ago."

"I've got something to tell you. You was always happy to express your appreciation when I showed how I was looking out for you."

"Out with it, Derek!"

Derek responded flatly, "Somebody arrived in town that you might be interested in."

"Really? Who's that?"

"Taylor Star."

Celeste went still.

"I said Tay—"

"I heard you!"

Celeste struggled to maintain a calm facade. Things had been going so well. Her cautious, systematic destruction of Buck's health with the aid of her longtime servant, Madalane, had been enormously successful. Doc Maggie was totally baffled by Buck's "sickness," and Buck was so grateful for Celeste's "devotion." She had been certain she would finally be able to convince Buck to write his two sons out of his will—a step she had been unsuccessful in achieving despite her husband's estrangement from both men.

Then Cal Star had returned to Lowell unexpectedly. He became a hero in the eyes of the town by overwhelming the rustlers that had devastated the area, but she had made sure Buck did not share in the adulation. She had also manipulated his emotions so that father and son remained alienated.

Victory had again been at her fingertips when Honor Gannon came to town. Honor Gannon . . . so clever, so insidious. The young woman had wormed her way onto the Texas Star ranch and had become established there before revealing the devastating truth that she was Buck's illegitimate daughter. Celeste congratulated herself that she had overcome that setback as well.

Now, with final retribution so close at hand . . .

Celeste accused hotly, "You're lying, Derek! Taylor Star turned his back on the Texas Star ranch years ago. He has no reason to return to Lowell."

"Well, either Taylor Star is the fella who got off that stage this morning or Doc Maggie made herself one helluva mistake."

"Doc Maggie?"

"The old lady welcomed him back like a long-lost son in front of the whole town. It didn't seem to matter to her what he looked like."

"What do you mean, 'what he looked like'?"

"Hell, he was drunk as a skunk when he staggered off that stage and made his way to the Last Chance. He didn't waste no time getting himself thrown out of the saloon just like Pete had to throw him off the stage."

"Where is he now?"

"Nobody knows. He rode off after Doc sobered him up a bit. I figured I'd warn you in case he was headed your way. I wanted to remind you I was here in case you needed me to handle anything for you."

Celeste's expression was tight. "You're here if I need you, huh?"

"We always did work real good together."

Celeste stared at Derek silently. He was correct. Their association had been mutually advantageous for an extended period. It was only Derek's ineffectiveness against recent problems that had turned her against him. If Taylor Star had come home, she might indeed have good use for Derek again. Any information he provided could become crucial, and she knew she could trust Derek to do whatever she asked, because he hungered for what only she was able to give him.

It kept him her virtual slave.

That thought gave Celeste a familiar rush. Greed and lust were the only two emotions she indulged— and Derek, foul degenerate that he was, had a way of raising both emotions to a sudden, overwhelming boil inside her.

Celeste walked toward Derek. Stopping a hairsbreadth away, she whispered, "I have to get back to the ranch in case Taylor shows up, but I figure you've got something coming to you for bringing me this information."

Celeste hooked an arm around Derek's neck and

pressed her mouth against his wet lips. The heat inside her flared red hot as he clasped his arms around her, dragged her inside the cabin, and slammed the door shut behind them. Her trembling hands reached for the buttons on his pants as he pulled up her skirt and dragged down her undergarments. She gasped as his hard heat nudged the delta between her thighs and he jammed himself inside her. She surrendered to the sexual frenzy of grunts and rutting motions that followed, then joined Derek in the loud groans of climax that quickly echoed in the dank confines of the cabin.

Still struggling to catch her breath as Derek withdrew, Celeste whispered, "You're correct, Derek. We do work very well together."

Vida looked at the neatly bearded man who stood unsmiling across from her in his small Baton Rouge hotel room. He was average in height and appearance, but Vida knew the assumption that he was an "average" man was far from the truth.

Appearances were deceiving. Allan Pinkerton was a legend, an icon, a man whose determination, moral sensitivity, keen intelligence, and highly developed deductive powers had already made him the most renowned detective in America. The founder of the Pinkerton Detective Agency, "The Eye That Never Sleeps," he was also one of the most far-reaching thinkers of the time. He even believed that women were as intelligent as men, and that they were possessed of abilities exclusive to their sex which could be used beneficially in many lines of work.

In short, Allan Pinkerton was a man after Vida's own heart.

Allan was one of a kind, not unlike her father, the Irishman who had wooed her beautiful mother with his charm, only to surrender his life early on to a barroom brawl and a bullet meant for someone else.

Constancia Malone had never forgiven fate for taking her husband so cruelly, while Vida had never forgiven the lawlessness that had been the more direct cause. She had been determined to do something about it.

And she had.

Vida remembered the day she'd walked into Allan Pinkerton's office and told him she wanted to be a detective. She had noted his initial hesitation, but she had also noted the moment when her persuasive arguments began to register with him. She had not lost a step since.

Vida also remembered the day when Allan partnered her with Taylor Star. She recalled that upon seeing Taylor for the first time, she was struck with the thought that she had never met a more handsome man.

Minutes later, she was sure she had never met a more charming or intelligent man.

At the conclusion of the first half hour, however, she was certain she had never met a more *arrogant bastard*.

Taylor had protested being partnered with a woman. He had been certain she could not be professional, nor quick of mind. He had reluctantly admitted that she was beautiful—a concession which had only angered her more, since he had insisted her beauty was a detriment, that no man who saw her would ever forget her face.

But Allan had been resolute, and she had been just as determined. She had proved herself to Taylor each step of the way. She had earned his respect, while he had earned her—

"Did you hear me, Vida?"

Brought abruptly back to the present by Allan's question, Vida responded, "Sorry, my mind was drifting."

"A dangerous exercise."

Allan's Scottish burr was thickening, a sign that he was annoyed, and Vida felt contrite. In her concern about Taylor, she had dispensed with the usual precautions and had not waited the customary few days after her partner's departure to leave. She had arrived in Baton Rouge a day earlier, had turned over the evidence she had collected with Taylor in New Orleans, and had delivered Taylor's message that he would not be coming. When she had nothing more to offer about Taylor's whereabouts, Allan had dismissed her with a frown. He had called her back to his hotel room that morning, displacing her from her hotel quarters where she had been waiting hopefully for a message from Taylor—a message that she somehow knew would not come.

Yes, her mind had been drifting.

Vida responded regretfully and with total honesty, "I'm sorry, Allan. I know you're anxious to get on to the next case, but I was thinking about Taylor."

"If you had been listening, you would have heard what I was telling you about him."

Immediately alert, Vida asked, "What about Taylor? Do you know why he left New Orleans so mysteriously, or where he went?"

"He went . . . home."

Vida unconsciously shook her head. "To Texas? That's impossible. He wouldn't do that."

"I would've thought your association with the agency has proved that no situation is impossible."

Vida remained silent.

Allan repeated, "Taylor went home."

"Why?"

"Since we both have only a sketchy knowledge of his personal history, the answer to your question remains a mystery to me, but it's not a mystery the agency is meant to solve. I'm satisfied to know where Taylor has gone. I can only assume he'll return when he's ready." Allan continued, "In the meantime, I have a new assignment for you, Vida, and a new partner."

"A new partner . . ."

"Yes. He's not as handsome as Taylor, but he's an extremely capable investigator who is anxious to work with you. He's on his way to Baton Rouge as we speak. You'll do well together, I'm sure."

Vida was uncertain exactly when she made the decision that turned her toward the door. She heard Allan's voice trailing after her, asking where she was going.

Vida did not think she needed to respond.

"Oh, hell . . . that can't be him!"

That startled comment traveled clearly in the afternoon silence as Taylor guided his horse on the approach to the Texas Star ranch house. He glanced in the direction of its source and saw two men watching from beside the bunkhouse.

Randy and Big John.

Taylor's throat momentarily tightened. Those two men had been standing in almost the same spot years earlier when he'd left the Texas Star. They had been frowning then, too, in obvious disapproval of his father's decision to send him away. He remembered thinking they were the only persons left, aside from Doc, who really cared what happened to him.

Taylor was briefly tempted to cast aside his drunken guise and forget the tactics he was using to uncover the *who and why* of the cryptic notes he and Cal had received. That thought ended abruptly, however, when the screened porch door opened and Celeste stepped into view.

Taylor went cold inside. Strangely, Celeste appeared even younger and more lovely than she had been when he left—in direct contrast with his father, who stepped into sight behind her.

Taylor struggled for composure at the extent of Buck's physical deterioration. Cal had warned him. So had Doc, but he was momentarily speechless at seeing Pa so gaunt that he was emaciated, so pale that he looked as if he had not a drop of blood left in his veins, so shriveled that he appeared to have shrunk in size, and so old beyond his years that the few gray strands left of his formerly thick, dark mane stood up like wiry stalks on his bony head.

"I should've known you'd end up this way." Buck ended Taylor's pained reaction to the sight of him by continuing in a voice startlingly strong and harsh despite his obvious decline, "Celeste met Joey Marsh on the road when she took old Blaze out for some exercise earlier. Joey told her you were back in the area. We was half expecting you'd come here—just like your brother did when he came back—but I have to say your brother had more sense than to show up looking like you do."

Taylor stepped down onto the ground without waiting for an invitation to dismount. He stood swaying unsteadily as he responded with a half smile, "I gotta say that you look like hell, too, Pa—so I guess we're even."

"No, we're not!" His haggard face flaming, Buck snapped, "You're proving just by standing there that you'll never be half the man I was—not in a hundred years. Look at you! You're a bum—a *drunken* bum! Wouldn't your ma be proud of what I'm seeing now."

Taylor tilted his hat back from his forehead as he replied, "Funny that you should be remembering Ma now, when you forgot her so easy after she died."

"I never forgot your ma."

Shrugging half-heartedly despite the anger he concealed, Taylor replied, "Is that so?" He turned to Celeste, who had remained strategically silent, and said, "Did you hear that, Celeste? I bet you didn't know Ma's been sharing the bed with Pa and you all these years."

Buck's growl of rage turned Taylor back toward him as Buck took a feeble forward step and rasped, "If you came back here to prove to me that I wasted my money when I tried to make a man of you by sending you back East to school, you've succeeded."

"You didn't send me to school back East in order to make a man of me, Pa." Digging his hand into his un-buckled saddlebag, Taylor withdrew a half-empty bottle of red-eye and took a fortifying drink before continuing. "You sent me back East to get rid of me so you and Celeste could be alone."

"Put that bottle down!"

Taylor laughed aloud.

"I said—"

"I heard you, but I'm all grown up now. And not only am I the man I want to be, I'm the man *you* made me."

Buck took another shaky step. "You heard me, boy."

"My name's Taylor, in case you forgot."

"Put that bottle down!"

Taylor took another drink, and Buck took a lurching forward step.

Grasping Buck's arm to steady him, Celeste said, "Let him be, Buck. He told you. He's the man he chooses to be."

"Look at him. He's a drunk! He puts the Star name to shame!"

"No, Pa." Taylor's lopsided smile was devoid of mirth. "You did that all by yourself."

Taylor took a deep drag on the bottle, acutely aware that he was carrying his facade too far when the world began shifting around him and he heard himself say in a voice that appeared to come from somewhere outside himself, "But I've come home, and this is where I'm going to stay."

"No, you're not!" Celeste's outburst turned Buck and Taylor toward her as she continued, "You turned your back on the Texas Star years ago when you graduated from school and dropped out of sight without so much as a word to your father in the time since."

Taylor looked back at Buck. "Oh . . . were you waiting to hear from me, Pa? That's funny. I figured you'd be glad if you never saw me again."

"Don't try to blame your father for what you've become," Celeste responded in Buck's stead as Taylor took another drink. "He never missed a payment at that school."

"That's right. He wanted to make sure I stayed away." Taylor hiccuped before continuing, "But I surprised him. I came home after all."

33

Celeste responded tightly, "This isn't your home anymore."

"Celeste . . ."

Responding to Buck with a suddenly apologetic expression, Celeste whispered, "I'm sorry, Buck. Maybe it isn't my place to say that, but you know it's true."

"Are you going to run me off, Pa?" Taylor took another swig, then looked at the bottle. It was nearly empty. Suddenly realizing that he was no longer *pretending* to be drunk, he said, "I think I'm done talking. I'm going to have to rest for a little while." He started unsteadily up the porch stairs. "I'm going to my room."

"Your room?" Celeste looked up at Taylor as he stood towering over her. She turned back at Buck and said, "Do something, Buck! Tell him he doesn't have a room here anymore."

The world reeled eerily as Taylor attempted to focus. He grasped the doorframe nearby, then said in a voice that sounded unlike him, "Damn . . . I think I'm going down."

Hurried footsteps sounded on the stairs behind him before Taylor felt strong hands grip his arms to hold him upright. Turning toward Big John and Randy, who were supporting him silently, he mumbled, "Hello, boys. I ain't seen you in a dog's age."

"Take him to the storage room and put him on the cot in there."

Taylor smiled when Celeste gasped at Buck's gruff order. He chuckled as Big John and Randy steered him inside, then asked when they turned him toward the rear of the house, "What happened to my old room?"

"Madalane took that over a long time ago."

Celeste protested behind them, "Buck . . . you can't mean to let him stay here."

"Just for a while until he sobers up, Celeste, darlin'. I can't let him wander around like that. I don't want the Star name blackened by him."

"You can tell just by looking at him that it's too late to worry about blackening the Star name!"

Silence.

"I'm sorry, Buck. Forgive me, darling."

Celeste's voice faded . . . or was it his own consciousness that was fading?

Taylor was uncertain until the two cowhands dropped him unceremoniously onto a hard cot, and Big John said with a reluctant smile, "Well, you did it, boy. You got the old man to go against his darlin' wife's wishes for the first time that I can remember. You may be drunk, but Randy and me have to salute you for that. Welcome home."

The two men were chuckling when they walked away.

The room was spinning around him, but Taylor was inwardly smiling. His mind was clear enough to realize that he had accomplished his first purpose. His drunken guise had succeeded in situating himself on the Texas Star ranch—where he was certain he wouldn't otherwise have stood a chance of being allowed to remain.

The second part of his plan was playing out nicely, too. Yes, people did speak freely in the presence of a drunk. He had already learned that Celeste was still adept at manipulating Buck, and Randy and Big John could not have made their positions clearer. He'd soon find out everything else he wanted to know. It was just a matter of time.

In the interim, another point was becoming increasingly clear. He would have one helluva headache when this was all over.

Taylor's stomach turned, nearly revolting. Raising a hand to his mouth, he closed his eyes. It appeared, that his hangover had just begun.

Vida swept into the dimly lit Last Chance Saloon and Dancehall with a practiced flourish. All heads turned in her direction, and she smiled broadly, satisfied at the impact of her entrance. She paused a few feet inside the swinging doors to prolong the moment.

Confident that the gawking patrons of the saloon had a lot to look at, Vida raised a hand to the upward sweep of her luxurious black hair. The hat perched securely atop the gleaming mass was trimmed in gold satin, the exact shade of the gown fitting her so precisely that her womanly proportions were clearly revealed. The dress plunged at the neckline, then nipped in at her minuscule waist, before flaring out to her ankles to tease male imaginations with the thought of the long, slender legs underneath.

Holding the mesmerized gazes, Vida fluttered long, dark lashes downward toward the creamy rise of delicately sculpted cheekbones, then looked up seductively to reveal startlingly dark eyes often described as mysterious . . . fathomless . . . heart-stopping. She was aware that some said the slender bridge of her nose was perfect, almost regally fine; that others said her lips and straight, even teeth formed the perfect smile.

Only a few knew that Vida considered her undeniable beauty—a gift from her mother's side of the family where such beauty was common—nothing more than a useful tool, a distracting mask behind which her keen mind functioned with great efficiency in her chosen profession.

Her keen mind.

Vida's smile momentarily faltered. It annoyed her that so few believed a beautiful woman could also have a *brain*. Her greatest pleasure had come in proving to the skeptical that they were wrong.

Well . . . it was *almost* her greatest pleasure.

The silence that had greeted her appearance turned into low mumbles of appreciation as Vida approached the bar and said to the bartender in a voice calculated to carry well over the hushed conversation, "Hello there! My name's Vida Malone. What's yours?"

Bart responded with obvious appreciation, "My name's Bart Childs, and I'm glad to meet you, ma'am."

"Glad to meet you, too, Bart." Vida winked at the mustached bartender as she continued, "My driver and I arrived in town only a few minutes ago, and I spotted this place right off."

Vida allowed a few moments for her statement to be absorbed. No common arrival on a stagecoach for her. Her entrance into town with the buggy and driver she had hired at a previous stop was well calculated, as was the multitudinous luggage stacked in the rear of the vehicle. It would be talked about for days.

Vida continued, "I'm an entertainer. I decided to travel northward when I got tired of Baton Rouge, so I'm looking for a job. Can you direct me to the right fella to talk to here?"

"That would be me, ma'am."

"Well, then, Bart . . ." Vida swept the fellow with a sultry gaze before continuing, "Along with my more

37

obvious attributes, I sing." She glanced at the silent piano and added, "I guarantee that I'm good, but if you can find somebody to play that thing, I'd be glad to sing a song so you can decide for yourself."

Bart replied without hesitation, "Harvey won't be in here to play for another hour yet, but I don't need to hear you sing. I figure if you sing half as good as you look, that'll be good enough. Besides, I have a feeling the fellas here won't care none if you're a bit off key."

"Just for the record . . . I'm *never* off key." Vida added candidly, "But I need to make something clear first. I'm friendly, but not *too* friendly, if you get my drift. I don't mind mingling with the customers, but I don't do any backroom work."

Bart did not immediately reply, causing Vida to say without a flicker of compromise, "My personal time and the 'friends' I make are my own choice."

"Just so you know, we don't have a backroom here. The fellas around here know where to go to take care of that kind of business."

"As for what you pay . . ."

"Since the Last Chance is the only saloon in town, I figure the pay don't make much difference if you're intending to stay in Lowell for a while, but we can work something out that's fair after you start."

Vida studied Bart's expression for a moment, then responded, "I expect we can . . . so I guess I'm hired."

Bart smiled, a genuine smile that Vida had a feeling was rare. "Ma'am, you were hired the minute you walked through that doorway. You can start any time you want."

"My name's Vida . . . and you can be sure your customers will get their money's worth. I'll see you tomorrow."

Vida sauntered back toward the swinging doors. She whispered a few words to the other saloon women in passing, effectively forestalling any possible future friction as she left them chuckling in her wake.

Pausing at the doors, she turned to blow a kiss to the male patrons, who had followed her exit intently, then laughed aloud at the cheers she received in return.

Out on the boardwalk in the bright, late-afternoon sunlight, Vida assessed her progress as she signaled her driver to proceed to the hotel. She had made an entrance into Lowell that would soon have the town talking. She had secured a job in a location where cowpokes would speak freely in an attempt to impress, providing all the information she would need about the town and its inhabitants without any obvious effort on her part. She had established an instant connection with the bartender, who could become her greatest ally.

Next?

Situate herself in the hotel where she would be easily accessible. Then contact Taylor Star.

Vida's smile briefly faltered as her buggy approached. She was aware that Taylor might not be pleased to discover she was in Lowell. As confidentially as Taylor and she had conversed in the past, he had never revealed why he did not communicate with his family. Yet the mysterious letter that had caused him to abruptly reverse that decision had obviously drawn fresh blood. Taylor had reacted uncharacteristically, and her professional instinct had flashed warning signs that she'd been unable to ignore.

All eyes again turned in her direction when she entered the hotel, and Vida made her smile brighter. One thing was sure. Whatever Taylor's reaction to her appearance in Lowell would be, she wouldn't have to wait long to find out.

"Things are starting to look up around here."

Bart turned toward the rear of the saloon, where Derek Beecher stood with a half-empty glass in front of him on the bar. Bart responded with caustic amusement, "If you're meaning that woman who just walked out the doorway, something tells me you're setting your sights kinda high. Vida Malone is going to have fellas lining up to buy her a drink when she starts working here tomorrow."

"Maybe, but she'll single out who she wants to spend her time with soon enough."

"And you're thinking that fella's going to be you?" Bart said with a laugh.

"What's so funny?" Derek's thick features turned suddenly hard.

Bart stared back at Derek Beecher without responding. He didn't like Derek much. If there was one thing more than a decade behind the bar had taught him, it was that there were some fellas you couldn't turn your back on, no matter how long you knew them. Derek was one of those people.

"Have you looked at yourself in the mirror lately?" Bart asked.

"What's that supposed to mean?"

"If you need to have me explain it to you, I figure it would be a waste of my time."

"You figure a fine-looking woman like that won't think I'm good enough for her, is that it?" Derek sneered. "Just so's you know, good-looking women are partial to me. I could tell you some stories you wouldn't believe about . . ." Derek cut himself short but he was unable to keep himself from adding, "Hell, some of 'em can't keep their hands off me."

"Right."

Derek snarled, "Laugh if you like, but we'll see tomorrow. I know what women want, and no matter what you think, I've got it. I'll have that sweet little tart eating out of my hand."

"Sure."

"You think I won't?" Derek was beginning to boil. "I got me a woman who's got ten times the looks of that Vida Malone, and she can't do enough to please me."

"That's why you spend so much time here in the Last Chance."

"I spend my time here in the Last Chance because I know how to keep a woman begging for more."

"That's what this beautiful woman of yours does, huh . . . beg for more?"

"All I have to do is snap my fingers."

Bart eyed Derek. A summons at the opposite end of the bar drew him away, saving him from an intended response that he realized probably would not have been wise. Grateful, Bart turned his back on Derek.

"Is it true? Tell me, Doc. I need to know."

Honor stood inside Doc Maggie's office door, awaiting a reply. She had been to the mercantile store and had heard the whispers that had started the moment she walked through the doorway. It had only been Agnes Bower, however, who'd had the courage to tell her what the whispering was about.

Incredulous, Honor had felt the need to turn to Jace,

but her husband had gone to San Antonio to deliver a prisoner. She had then gone to the only other person in town she could trust for the absolute truth.

"Doc?" Honor swallowed, anxious as she pressed for an answer. "Did Taylor Star really come back to town today?"

Honor noted Doc's hesitation before she replied, "He was on the morning stage."

"Did you talk to him?"

"Yes."

"What did he say?"

"We didn't get a chance to do much talking. He was . . . under the weather."

Honor took a shaky breath, then managed, "Where is he now?"

"I don't know."

"Did he go to the Texas Star to see Buck?"

"I don't know."

"Does Cal know he's back?"

"I sent somebody out to tell him."

"Did . . . did you tell Taylor about me?"

"Yes."

"What did he say?"

Doc did not reply.

"Oh."

"He wasn't expecting to hear he had a sister he didn't know about, Honor. It was a shock to him. Bonnie was special to him, and he—"

"That's all right, Doc." Honor halted Doc's attempted explanation with a forced smile. "It's not his fault. If I were Taylor, I'd be shocked to find out about me, too."

"It's not like you think, Honor. Taylor's a fine man

down deep. He was under the weather and not think-ing clearly, that's all."

"That's the second time you said 'under the weather . . . ' "

The door opened unexpectedly to reveal Cal stand-ing in the opening. Responding in Doc's stead, Cal said, "Doc means Taylor was *drunk*, Honor."

"Drunk?"

"Staggering drunk and looking like hell."

Honor shook her head, unconsciously negating Cal's statement as he closed the door behind him and con-tinued, "I came to town as soon as I could. When you weren't home or at Jace's office, I knew you had to be here. I wanted to be the one to tell you about Taylor."

"To tell me what? I don't care if Taylor was drunk. Maybe he had to get that way to get up the courage to face Buck again. But that isn't what you meant, is it? What you meant was that you wanted to be the one to explain why Taylor doesn't want to meet me." Honor's smile grew unsteady. "The funny thing is, I under-stand how Taylor feels, and I don't really blame him. If it had been my mother that Buck had been unfaithful to, I'd resent a bastard sister, too. I might even wonder why she showed up in Lowell—if maybe she came here looking to get a portion of the Texas Star for herself."

"It's not like that. Taylor doesn't care about the Texas Star—and even if he did, we all know who's go-ing to get the ranch if anything happens to Pa."

"How do you know what Taylor's thinking?" Honor hesitated. "You talked to him, didn't you, Cal?"

"Yes."

Doc interrupted, "He rode off without a word. How did you find him?"

43

"I knew where he'd be."

Doc's round face sobered. "He went to visit the graves, didn't he?"

Cal did not need to reply.

Honor brushed away the tear that slipped down her cheek. She whispered, "I wish . . ."

"What do you wish, Honor?" Sliding his arm around his sister's shoulders, Cal continued gently, "You can't mean you wish you hadn't come to Lowell. You belong here as much as we do."

"Maybe."

"No 'maybe' about it."

Honor took a breath, then said, "Please do something for me, Cal. When you see Taylor again, tell him I understand how he feels, that neither Jace nor I . . . that we realize—"

"I'm not sure when I'll see Taylor again."

"What do you mean?"

"Just that." Cal shrugged. "I'm not sure what Taylor was thinking when we parted."

"But—"

"Taylor's my brother, but as close as we once were, a part of him has always been a mystery to me. I'm not really sure of anything about him now."

"Oh, Cal . . ." Honor whispered, "I'm sorry. If I could do anything to make this situation better—"

"You are doing it, just by being who you are . . . my sister."

Cal slid his arms around Honor and held her comfortingly close. He did not see the tear Doc brushed from her wrinkled cheek before she silently slipped out the doorway to allow them a moment's privacy.

* * *

Vida swept along the boardwalk toward the restaurant a few doors down the street. She had taken a room in the hotel, told her driver to deliver her luggage upstairs, and paid the old man with a generous tip and a flirting smile.

A look out the window of her room had revealed the thirsty driver making a beeline for the Last Chance Saloon, but her intentions were different. She hadn't eaten since breakfast and she was hungry. After dinner, she looked forward to a cooling bath and a quiet evening during which she would think out her plans more clearly. She knew the importance of her initial appearance at the Last Chance. She needed to make sure the impression she made—

Vida's thoughts came to an abrupt halt when she saw a woman step out of a storefront a few feet away. She was middle-aged, full-faced, and full-figured, with gray hair in a tight bun at the nape of her neck, but with a look about her that set her apart from the average matron.

Vida glanced at the script on the storefront window. *Margaret Beamer, M.D.*

It was Doc Maggie.

Vida struggled to retain her composure. Taylor had spoken very little about his past, but the warmth that had entered his voice the few times he mentioned Doc Maggie's name had filled her with a spontaneous affection for the woman she had never met. But Doc Maggie seemed upset. Her expression was tense, and her eyes were suspiciously bright.

Impulsively, Vida halted and inquired, "Are you all right, Doc?"

The old woman looked up and swept her with a glance. She replied, "Do I know you?"

45

"No." Vida forced a practiced smile. "But you came walking out of that office like you owned the place, and I figured you must be the Doc Maggie I've heard so much about since I came to town."

"New in town, are you?"

"Yes. My name's Vida Malone. I just arrived today."

"And you heard about me already?"

"I took a job at the Last Chance."

"Oh, that explains it. Those women all know me pretty well." The old woman continued professionally, "Well, pleased to meet you, Vida. Is there something I can help you with?"

"No, I was just worried that you looked upset." Marveling at the woman's quick recovery, she added, "But it looks like I was wrong."

"Maybe you were and maybe you weren't," Doc responded evasively, "but I'm fine now and I'm here if you need me. You can keep that in mind."

Aware that Doc had managed to reverse the tone of their conversation, Vida replied, "I'll remember, and I'm pleased to meet you, too, Doc . . . really pleased."

Vida looked back as she reached the restaurant to see Doc in complete control as she pushed open her office door and walked back inside.

The significance of the moment struck Vida in a flash. Taylor's tone had indicated a true affection for the old woman, and Doc Maggie probably couldn't help loving him.

Vida paused at that thought.

Damned if she didn't know the feeling.

Chapter 3

Taylor awoke slowly. Briefly disoriented, he glanced around the darkened room. There was a hard cot underneath his back, and boxes stacked nearby. Oh, yes, he remembered. His plan was progressing successfully and he had been temporarily installed in the storage room behind the Texas Star kitchen so he could sleep off the bottle of red-eye he had consumed.

A full bottle.

Taylor shivered in remembrance. He grimaced at the sour taste in his mouth and the feeling that this was not the last time he would awaken similarly affected in order to maintain his guise of drunkenness.

The sounds of a meal being consumed in the kitchen beyond his doorway and voices in whispered conversation interrupted his thoughts. He listened as the conversation continued.

". . . and there ain't no telling what Buck will do when Taylor's back on his feet." Taylor recognized Mitch's voice as the cowhand then asked, "Did you get a chance to talk to him?"

"No. Taylor was too drunk to talk sensible. Randy and me just dropped him onto the cot like Buck told us to and got out of the house as soon as we could. Celeste was madder than a hornet that Buck told us to take Taylor inside. We figured there'd be hell to pay soon, and we didn't want any part of it."

Taylor heard the warning in Randy's voice as he interjected, "Quiet. Here comes Madalane."

Madalane.

Taylor's mouth tightened in remembrance. He wondered belatedly why the men were allowed to eat in the house, when he last remembered Celeste banishing them to the bunkhouse for their meals so that "we can have some privacy at our meals."

Taylor controlled a contemptuous snort as he drew himself to a seated position. He had known that Celeste's desire for privacy was just another ploy to place a barrier between Buck and the men who supported him.

Taylor stood up gingerly. Granted, the aromas wafting from the kitchen were a bit exotic for his tastes, but he was hungry. He was also keenly aware that he needed to eat something in order to settle his stomach.

With a few unsteady steps, Taylor arrived in the kitchen doorway to see the cowhands silently consuming their meal while Madalane stood near the stove, supporting herself with a cane. Taylor concealed his surprise at the sight of Celeste's Negro servant. The woman had aged. Lines marred her formerly handsome features; her erect, womanly stature was noticeably bent, and a shadow of pain dulled her dark eyes. Yet the hatred he remembered so clearly was still visible in those dark eyes when Madalane turned to look at him without a word of greeting.

He hadn't expected more.

Taylor looked toward the table when Mitch mumbled, "Damned if Taylor don't look even worse than you both said he did."

Responding to the cowhand's remark, Taylor approached the table with a caustic smile and said, "Glad to see you too, Mitch. As a matter of fact, I'm glad to see all three of you boys again." He asked bluntly, "Where are the rest of the ranch hands?"

"There ain't no more." Randy explained expressionlessly, "We're the only hands left on this spread."

Momentarily stunned, Taylor replied with a lopsided smile, "Well, I guess my pa will be happy to have me back to help out, then."

Waiting until Madalane carried yet another platter into the dining room, Randy responded, "I wouldn't count on it. Your pa already ran Cal off when he came back and volunteered to help. Then he ran off Honor . . ." Randy paused and glanced at the dining-room doorway before whispering, "You know about Honor, don't you?"

"I know."

"So, I wouldn't be expecting any more than the others got, if I was you."

Taylor casually shrugged his broad shoulders. "I don't care how it worked out with the others. I'm back at the Texas Star now, and I figure on staying here as long as it suits me."

Big John gave a subdued hoot. "It looks like you haven't changed so much after all, Taylor."

Big John's smile drained away as his gaze flicked to the doorway and Taylor turned to hear Buck growl, "Like Randy said, I wouldn't count on staying, *boy*."

Taylor's innards twisted tight as he replied with feigned amusement, "Are you saying you'd turn out your own son, Pa?"

"That's what I'm saying."

He taunted, "I can see Celeste has given you a good talking-to."

"Celeste doesn't have a thing to do with it!" Quaking beset his gaunt frame as Buck continued, "I don't keep anybody on this spread who doesn't earn his keep, and from the look of you, that means you."

Realizing he'd never have a better opportunity, Taylor replied, "Well, I can't rightly say it was my idea to come back in the first place. Fact is, I got an unsigned letter in the mail telling me it was time to come home."

"Well, *I* sure as hell didn't send it," Buck retorted.

"Hmmm . . . Who could've sent it, then? Doc Maggie didn't."

"You saw her already, did you?"

"I did." His smile again grew caustic as Celeste appeared in the doorway behind Buck. "And I'm thinking Celeste didn't send it to me, either."

"That's for sure," Buck grated.

Turning to the three ranch hands who remained silent at the table beside him, Taylor asked unexpectedly, "Did any of you fellas send me that note?"

The men exchanged glances before Randy responded flatly, "What note?"

Turning toward Madalane, Taylor said, "What about you? Did you send it, Madalane?"

The malignant heat of Madalane's gaze burned hotly

in reply as Buck snapped, "Are you trying to be funny, Taylor? Because I'm not laughing."

"Well, you can thank whoever did send me that note for bringing me home . . . and since I'm here, I figure to stay awhile."

"Do you?" Buck took another shaky step. "Well, if you do, it's going to be on *my* terms."

"I can see that hasn't changed, either."

Ignoring Taylor's remark, Buck stated, "You're going to have to clean yourself up and start walking the straight and narrow if you expect to stay on this ranch."

Taylor laughed. "Oh, that's all you want?"

"No more drinking!"

Taylor did not reply.

"You're going to have to work right along with the rest of the fellas here, and that means you follow Randy's orders. He's in charge until I get back on my feet—not you! Do you get that?"

"Sure, I understand. Randy's the boss."

"No, *I'm* the boss. I give the orders, and everybody else on this spread follows them, including Randy and you. Remember, if you expect to stay on, you're not the boss's son. You're just another cowhand. *Comprende?*"

"Things haven't changed as much around here as it first seemed. But now that you've had your say, Pa, it's time for me to have mine." Turning toward Madalane, Taylor said, "I'm hungry. Fill up a plate for me so my stomach will stop growling."

Buck glared. "Is that all you got to say?"

"No. I figure Madalane will need to clean up that storage room a bit, too, if you expect me to sleep there."

51

At Celeste's gasp, Buck grated, "Clean it up yourself!"

Taylor noted that Celeste grasped Buck's arm as he swayed, but the old man shook off her grip to repeat, "Get yourself cleaned up, Taylor. If you don't straighten out, you won't last long here—son or not."

Buck turned abruptly back toward the dining room as Taylor glanced down at the plate Madalane had placed in front of him. Madalane left the room haughtily when he stared at the plate and grumbled with a frown, "What in hell . . . ?"

Mitch waited until Madalane had cleared the doorway before responding, "She says it's island food. The boys and me say it just plain ain't good. We ain't had a decent meal around here since Honor left."

Taylor glanced up sharply at the mention of Honor's name.

"Your sister worked here while Madalane was off her feet—you know, before she told Buck who she was."

"She's not my sister."

The men went silent.

"I only had one sister, and she's dead."

The silence stretched long as Taylor picked up his fork and started to eat.

Taylor looked up from the fencepost he was setting. He had risen before dawn so he might "clean himself up," more a favor to himself than in compliance with Buck's directive. A quick dip in the ice-cold stream and the feeling of clean clothes against his skin had done almost as much to raise his spirits as scraping off his annoying, week-long beard. He had almost forgotten what it was like to be out of bed at dawn and working while the sun was still rising, in a silence broken only

52

by the chirping of birds and the buzzing of bees in the wildflowers, and with the blue Texas sky stretching out as far and wide as the eye could see . . .

"Taylor."

. . . and with the sound of Randy's voice barking orders.

"Make sure you set that post deep. Some of them wily cattle got used to the old fences. They learned real fast that if they leaned against a post enough, they could push it down. I don't want to waste no more time chasing those critters."

No doubt.

Taylor glanced around him. Fencing wasn't the biggest problem on the Texas Star. It had taken no more than a glance to see that the ranch house itself was in disrepair, that the outbuildings suffered a similar plight, and that the barn and tack were in a sorrowful condition; but it was the herd that had suffered the most. Their numbers were depleted, and the condition of the cattle was less than ideal. It was obvious that the men were putting in a full day of hard work, but the shortage of help on a spread the size of the Texas Star made their efforts a losing proposition, no matter how hard they tried.

He couldn't understand it.

Taylor jammed his shovel into the earth to stand it upright, then raised his hat and wiped the perspiration from his forehead with the back of his shirtsleeve as he said, "You sure do drive a man hard, Randy. So how come the ranch is in such damned bad shape?"

Randy turned toward him without a trace of a smile. "You can thank your pa for that. Celeste started giving the orders on the ranch when he got sick. She didn't know what she was doing, but she wouldn't take no advice from any one of us. Your pa wouldn't hear a word against her, even when things started falling apart with the rustling and all. Somewhere along the way, most of the fellas got disgusted and quit, and things just went downhill from there."

"But Mitch, Big John, and you didn't quit."

"Damned right! I was here when your ma and pa first started this place. I remember what the Texas Star brand meant to your ma, and there's no way I'm going to let a pampered little. . . ."

Randy halted, choosing not to continue.

Taylor responded soberly, "I remember what the Texas Star meant to Ma, too. I thought it was just as important to Pa."

"It is, and he near to killed himself trying to get it back on track after Cal came home and nailed them rustlers down."

"Cal did that, did he?"

"He sure enough did, even though Sheriff Carter had been on their tails for months without even coming close. One of them fellas got away from Cal without being identified, but everybody figures that fella hightailed it out of this part of Texas in order to save his skin."

"So?"

"So the damage was already done. Them rustlers had whittled down all the herds hereabouts, but the greatest damage was done to this spread. Your pa was too sick by then to be much help no matter how hard he tried. And since Celeste had already driven off most of the cowhands and your pa's finances was bad, he couldn't find any hands willing to work for what he could pay—except Jace."

"Jace?"

"Jace Rule, a real fine fella and a hard worker."

"What happened to him?"

"He married Honor. He's the sheriff in Lowell now, since Sheriff Carter retired and moved to be closer to his daughter and her family."

Taylor said, "But Cal's still around."

"Your pa won't let him near this place. Buck's so damned stubborn. He still blames Cal for . . ."

Randy hesitated, and Taylor supplied in his stead, "For Bonnie's death."

Randy waited, and Taylor responded to his unvoiced question, "I've grown up since that day. I look at things differently now." He asked abruptly, "So what's happened to Madalane? She used to be a handsome woman, and now she just looks old and mean."

"She broke her leg, and things ain't been going well since. I expect there ain't nothing like pain to change a person's looks. But to my mind, the outside of her just matches the inside now."

"Her personality sure hasn't improved."

"Face it, Taylor. That woman don't like any one of us because we don't cater to her darlin' girl."

"And my pa's blind to it all."

Randy did not reply. Instead, he turned with a frown as Mitch approached and said, "I'm fixing on getting into town right after supper tonight, Randy. Big John's going with me. You two are invited to come along if you like. I figure a good time will be had by all."

"Not that woman again?" Randy's scowl tightened.

"You did nothing but talk about her in the bunkhouse last night until I was sick of hearing you."

Amused, Taylor interjected, "So Mitch has himself a woman."

Turning toward him, Randy snapped, "Not *his* woman. He's talking about the new saloon girl who arrived in town late yesterday afternoon. He saw her when he was picking up some lime for Buck. She says she's a singer, and she's starting at the Last Chance tonight. To hear Mitch tell it, word spread so fast that there ain't a fella within a hundred miles who ain't going to be waiting to hear the first note that comes out of her mouth."

Taylor withheld a smile as he addressed Mitch. "A real fine-looking woman, huh?"

"I saw her when I was in town, and I'm telling you, she's really somethin'. I ain't never seen nothing like her, is the truth. She came strutting down the street in that bright yellow gown, with all that black hair piled atop her head, all dark eyes and fluttering lashes, and with her female parts moving so smooth that it made a man feel good just to watch. She seemed real friendly, too. She gave me a real big smile."

"Mitch—"

"All I can say is she's the best-looking woman to hit this town since . . . since . . ." Mitch halted, at a loss for words before continuing abruptly, "Jake Colt said her name means 'life' in Spanish."

Taylor went still.

"And she sure brought this town to life."

Could it possibly be . . . ?

"Jake said she came up from Baton Rouge, that she just decided to travel north on a whim. I figure that's this town's good luck."

It *had* to be a coincidence.

Taylor heard himself say, "I'll go into town with you tonight, Mitch."

"Your pa won't like it, Taylor." Randy was frowning. "He expects you to settle down to work, not go gallivanting off to the saloon after your first day on the ranch."

Mitch interjected, "Hell, there ain't no harm in it, Randy. We ain't expecting to stay out all night."

Randy turned sharply. "Keep out of this, Mitch."

"It's not Mitch's decision." Taylor shrugged. "Besides, my pa can expect all he wants, but what he's going to get is up to me."

"I'm telling you—"

"I'm going with Mitch."

Taylor turned back to his shovel, abruptly ending the discussion—with the thought that the day could not pass quickly enough.

Vida smiled provocatively as she sauntered past the cowhands lined up at the bar. She had arrived at the Last Chance an hour earlier, just as the sun had slipped below the horizon, and she had spent her first hour at the Last Chance getting acquainted with the customers. It had amused her when Bart whispered that it seemed every cowhand in the county had shown up to hear her sing.

To hear her *sing?*

She doubted it.

Vida was well aware of her effect on men, and she had planned very carefully how she would capitalize on it. The gown she wore was a part of her strategy. Red was her color. It contrasted vividly with her dark hair and fair skin. She did not truly need the kohl she had used to accentuate her sultry gaze. Her naturally vibrant coloring made lip paint another unnecessary tool, but Vida also knew that such excesses were expected in a place where men wanted their women to be brighter and more exciting than the norm to which they were accustomed.

She had purchased her gowns specifically for that purpose before coming to Lowell, and she was wearing her favorite. The red garment hung off her shoulders to a tantalizing degree. She knew the brilliant gold trim dangling from its revealing neckline would appear garish to some, but she was also aware that it would have the same titillating effect as the miniature gold bells sewn inconspicuously into the narrow waistline of the garment—bells that teased the imagination with sound at each swish of her hips.

Vida winked at Harvey as he approached the piano. She leaned back against the rickety instrument when he sat down and indicated he was ready to begin. A short conversation with the pleasant, gray-haired man, and a few minutes spent watching his nimble fingers as he played, had convinced her that he was capable of anything she needed from him.

Vida scrutinized the crowded saloon as it grew silent with anticipation, but her mind was far from the bars of the song she prepared to sing. She had already accomplished part of her purpose by familiarizing herself with the faces staring back at her—images her keen mind burned into memory for future reference. She knew that before the evening was over, she would have gained valuable background information about the town and the surrounding ranches.

Yes, as Allan Pinkerton had acknowledged years earlier, an intelligent woman possessed abilities exclusive to her sex that could be used beneficially in so many ways—and she knew how to implement every one of them.

Vida scanned the room again, this time searching for a certain, familiar face. Disappointment nudged her when she did not see him, but a true smile spread across her lips when a few loud chords from Harvey's fingers were met by a round of whistles and applause.

Raising her hand for silence, Vida said, "Thanks for the welcome, boys! I know you're waiting to hear me sing, and I was thinking about what would be the best way to say hello tonight, and to tell you how glad I am to be here. I finally figured the best way to do that would be to start off by singing the same song my Irish father used to sing for me when I was just a little lass. It's my favorite."

Vida paused as Harvey played elaborate introductory chords, and then she started to sing:

"Believe me if all those endearing young charms
Which I gaze on so fondly today
Were to change by tomorrow and fleet in my arms,
Like fairy gifts fading away.
Thou would still be adored, as this moment thou art,
Let thy loveliness fade as it will,
And around the dear ruin each wish of my heart
Would entwine itself verdantly still.

"It is not while beauty and youth are thine own,
And thy cheek unprofaned by a tear,
That the fervor and faith of a soul can be known,
To which time will but make thee more dear.

No, the heart that has truly loved ne'er forgets,
But as truly loves on to the close,
As the sunflower turns on her god when he sets,
The same look which she turned when he rose."

Vida's sweet alto rose to rebound in the otherwise silent room with the final, poignant chorus:

Thou would still be adored, as each moment thou art,
Let thy loveliness fade as it will.
And around the dear ruin each wish of my heart
Will entwine itself verdantly still."

Utter silence met Vida's final note. Embarrassed sniffles sounded on the crowded floor and callused hands reached up toward unexpectedly damp cheeks. A small smattering of applause swelled to an enthusiastic roar, bringing a true tear to Vida's eye for the gruff, lonely men who still revered the ideal of true love.

Halting the applause, Vida said, "Thanks again, boys. Your welcome has touched my heart, but now I want to hear what *you* want me to sing. Come on, fellas, and make the songs lively!"

The response was instantaneous.

"Sing 'Oh, Susannah!,' darlin'."

"How about 'Camptown Races'?"

"'I Dream of Jeannie' . . ."

Behind her, Harvey played the first chords of "Oh, Susannah!" and Vida knew the choice had been made.

"Ain't she somethin'?"

Taylor barely heard Mitch's question as the opening strains of "Oh, Susannah!" filled the saloon.

Unconsciously nodding in reply as he stood inside the saloon doorway within a crush of wranglers out for a night on the town, Taylor allowed his gaze to rest for silent moments on the woman in red as she sang the lively tune.

Vida.

He should have known it could be no one else.

Questions shot through Taylor's mind as he followed Big John and Mitch toward the bar. Strangely, his first thought was to wonder if the touching introduction Vida had made to her song was true, if her Irish father had indeed sung that song to her when she was a child. He realized suddenly that as well as he had believed he knew Vida, his only certainty was that she was not above using emotion to gain a desired effect. In this case, she was terrifically successful.

The men loved her.

Taylor picked up the whisky glass that had been placed in front of him and drank it dry. Truth was, he didn't wonder why the crowd loved her. She was somethin', all right. He had always known Vida was beautiful—and had perhaps been a little too keenly aware of her womanly attributes at times. He had also always known she was quick of mind, that not only did she react instantaneously to danger, but she seemed actually able to anticipate it in many ways. Nor could he count the number of times when he had silently acknowledged that she was intelligent, that not only were her deductive powers acute, but she was bright enough when sensing danger to quickly discern ways to avoid it.

Unfortunately for him, he had belatedly discovered that she was *too* smart to fall for the casual technique he had used successfully on so many women in the past.

Vida had proved herself to be invaluable to Allan Pinkerton. Taylor had no doubt that Allan had had another case waiting for the two of them when she'd arrived in Baton Rouge—a case she would be able to handle just as flawlessly with one of Allan's other experienced agents as with him.

So his next question was, what was she doing in Lowell?

Still standing at the crowded bar as "Oh, Susannah!" drew to a close, Taylor felt a physical jolt when Vida first saw him. The silent contact reverberated deep inside him, raising a strange resentment when she glanced away casually and walked into the diverse crowd of her admirers.

The moment seemed to freeze into motionlessness when the swarthy fellow Taylor had seen at the bar the day before grasped Vida's arm and jerked her to a halt. Taylor restrained his impulse to stop the man. He knew Vida. She had set up her introduction to Lowell well, and experience had taught him that she was capable of handling all the contingencies.

Of course, if she was not . . .

"How about you let me buy you a drink, sweetheart?"

Vida resisted the impulse to shake off the fellow's sweaty grip on her arm. Her destination was the section of the bar where Taylor was standing, where she hoped to make casual contact with him. She didn't appreciate being deterred by a fellow who was not only crude but also unclean—and whose leering glance indicated he wanted to buy more than a drink.

Aware that her handling of this situation would set

the tone of the evening to come, she said coyly, "What's your name, fella?"

The man leered. "My name's Derek."

"Well, Derek, I figure there's a whole passel of fellas waiting to buy me a drink right now. I guess the only fair way is to start off at the far end of the bar and work my way down, if that's all right with you." She winked. "I'll be sure to see you later."

His responsive smile was a hideous sight. "Maybe I don't feel like waiting until later," Derek responded.

Vida sensed rather than saw Bart move into action behind the bar as he reached down unobtrusively to a shelf underneath. She halted him boldly by saying, "Wait a minute, Bart. Derek wants to buy me a drink, but the fact is, I'm going to buy him one instead. I figure it'll keep him company until I can take him up on his offer later." When Derek looked at her with surprise, she said in a mock whisper, "And you'd better do some heavy thinking, fella, because I'm going to let you pick out my next song."

Derek glanced at the bar when Bart slapped a drink down in front of him. Taking advantage of his momentary distraction to deftly dislodge his grip, Vida said, "I'll see you later."

Vida glanced casually at the spot where she had last seen Taylor. He was leaning against the bar conversing with the big cowboy beside him. He knew her well. He had confidence in her and had waited to see if she could manage the situation on her own. He had also worked with her long enough to know he should not make any moves without first seeing what she had in mind.

She wondered what he was thinking.

As she neared the far end of the bar, a young saloon girl named Ellie stepped up next to Taylor and leaned casually against him. Stunned at her own heated reaction to the sight, Vida stopped and turned in response to a young wrangler beside her who offered, "Anything you want to drink is on me, Vida, honey." He patted his pocket. "And there's plenty more where that's coming from."

Recovering, she responded with a practiced flutter of her eyelashes, "You're a man after my own heart."

Vida downed the drink Bart set in front of her in a gulp, then silently cursed when a flush of unnatural heat suffused her. She knew better than to allow emotion to make her act unwisely.

Vida restrained the inclination to glance back again in Taylor's direction.

Yes, she knew better.

Randy stood opposite Buck in the parlor of the Texas Star. He was frowning, and Buck knew instinctively that was a bad sign. He had signaled Randy in from the yard when Celeste walked into Madalane's room. Knowing there would never be a better time to speak to the wrangler candidly, he asked, "How did Taylor do today? Did he put in a full day's work?"

"Is that why you called me in here, boss—to report on Taylor?"

"You're in charge while I'm off my feet, aren't you?" Buck fought off the urge to sit down in the nearest chair. It was dark and he was tired. He was *always* tired of late, and that fact exasperated him further as he snapped, "I need to know. I don't intend to carry any dead weight on this ranch."

"Taylor never was 'dead weight,' and he ain't now."

"Meaning?"

"He worked just as hard as any of the men did, if that's what you're wanting to know."

"And?"

Agitated, Randy snapped, "And he doesn't like what he sees around here."

"He doesn't, huh? I'd say it's a little late for his opinion to count."

"Whether it is or it isn't, I figure that's something you should be discussing with Taylor, not me."

"Is that so?" Buck restrained his annoyance. He'd had a bad day. The latest recurrence of his sickness hadn't been so easy to beat. His bouts of purging had stopped a while back, but it was obvious even to Doc Maggie that he wasn't rebounding like he had in the past. He was starting to get the feeling that he couldn't beat the sickness this time—and Taylor's return wasn't making things any easier.

Buck continued harshly, "Maybe I *would* discuss this with Taylor if he was around—but he isn't. He took off after supper without even stopping in to talk. Where in hell did he go, anyway?"

Randy's frown tightened. "He's in town with Big John and Mitch."

"In town?"

Randy did not reply, forcing Buck to prompt, "What did they go to town for?"

"I don't know."

"You damned well do!"

"Ask Taylor when he comes back."

"Spit it out, Randy! I'm going to find out sooner or later."

Pausing, Randy replied, "There's a new entertainer at the Last Chance. They went in to see what she's like."

"*What?*"

"They went in to see—"

Buck's harsh laughter cut Randy's response short. Surrendering to his weakness, Buck sat abruptly in the soft chair behind him and said, "I saw the way Taylor looks. I should've known."

"Taylor looked damned good this morning." Randy took a step forward as he continued more softly, "He cleaned himself up and worked hard all day. He was the old Taylor except for the chip on his shoulder, and if you don't mind my saying it, boss, you're the one who put that chip there."

"Is that so?" Buck felt a familiar agitation taking hold as he continued, "Well, *I* think Taylor got that chip on his shoulder when his mama died so unexpectedly, when his sister got killed right afterwards because of his brother's carelessness, and when his brother took off in the middle of the night without even bothering to see his sister buried or to say good-bye."

"You don't figure that his pa marrying a young woman right after his mama died had anything to do with it?"

Momentarily silent in the face of that hard truth, Buck replied, "If Taylor was the man he was supposed to be, he would've understood."

"He wasn't a man. He was a boy."

"Well, he's a man now, and look at him!" Shaking with an ever growing sense of futility, Buck continued, "He's a drunk . . . a waster!"

"No, he ain't. He's a man who's got a reason to—"

"What are you trying to do to my husband, Randy?" Entering the room unexpectedly, Celeste rushed to Buck's side. She turned back toward Randy to continue accusingly, "You know he's a sick man!"

"He asked me a question, ma'am."

"He didn't ask you for a sermon—especially when you don't know what you're talking about!"

"Celeste, darlin', I can handle this."

Celeste looked down at Buck, her eyes moist. "I won't let him do this to you, Buck. I won't let a hired hand try to make you feel guilty because we love each other."

Rising unsteadily to his feet, Buck slid his arm around his young wife and whispered, "Don't cry, Celeste. Randy didn't mean anything. He was just—"

"He was just trying to make you feel sorry for Taylor, when you have no need to feel sorry. You did the best you could. We *both* did. Taylor's gone bad, Buck, just like Cal. That's all there is to it, and it's not your fault."

"Begging your pardon, ma'am, you're mistaken," Randy interrupted firmly. "Cal hasn't gone bad, and neither has Taylor. Taylor worked hard today, and he was sober."

"How dare you contradict me? As for Taylor being sober—you mean like he probably is right now?" Celeste rasped, "He's at the Last Chance—you said it yourself—and he's probably already stumbling-down drunk!"

"He went in with Big John and Mitch to see—"

"He went in to get drunk, and I won't have you trying to make my husband take the blame for either of his sons' weaknesses."

67

"Ma'am—"

"I think you've said enough." Celeste continued with the rasp of tears in her voice, "If it was up to me, I'd throw you off this ranch right now and see to it that you never came back!"

Buck interrupted, "Celeste . . . wait a minute."

"We're better off without this man, and you know it, Buck."

"No, we aren't." Turning to Randy, Buck said, "My wife's upset, Randy. She doesn't mean what she said."

"I meant every word of it. He hates me! He has always hated me!"

"No, Celeste. You're not thinking clearly right now."

Randy asked unexpectedly, "Do you want me to leave the Texas Star, boss?"

Buck stared at the graying ranch hand on whom he leaned so heavily, then looked back at his tearful wife. His response was soft and concise.

"No."

Buck said no more as Celeste fled from the room.

Celeste pushed open the door to Madalane's room without knocking, then slammed it shut behind her. The Negress sat up in the bed where she had already retired.

She did not have long to wait before Celeste approached the bed and whispered in a hiss, "So . . . what are you waiting for? Aren't you going to say 'I told you so'?"

"What are you talking about?"

"What am I talking about? Didn't you hear what just

went on in the parlor? Are you deaf? My husband took Randy's side over mine!"

"Tell me what happened."

Celeste paused, her breast heaving. "Why should I? What good would it do me? You've been of little use to me since you broke your leg. You limp around the house like an old woman and take the first opportunity to go to your room, where you sleep, totally dead to the world."

"I have been ill."

"You broke a bone and it has healed!"

"It has not sufficiently healed for me to take up my chores without tiring."

"What is that supposed to mean? Do you expect me to take over your chores, to work around this house like a common housemaid while you *recuperate*? Perhaps you would like me to cook the meals, or wash the dishes. Or would you prefer that I clean the house and do the laundry? Well, I will do none of it!"

"I have asked nothing of you since I resumed my tasks."

"And you will *get* nothing from me! You are *my* servant. I am not yours."

"I know what I am in this household."

"And what is that, Madalane? Pray, tell me."

Her dark eyes growing intense, Madalane whispered, "I am a woman who loved your mother as she would have loved her own child. I am a woman who swore allegiance to you, her daughter, when my dear Jeanette was stolen from me by the heartless act of the man who is now your husband. I am the woman who shares with you a solemn vow to wreak vengeance against Buck Star and all who carry the Star blood. For this vengeance I would give my life."

"That is the woman you *were*."

"That is the woman I *am!*" Madalane's dark eyes flared open wide. "Do not let my present feeble appearance deceive you. My leg is weak, but my resolve is strong. I tire and sleep, but I dream dreams of vengeance that will allow me little rest. I am your ally—an ally who will never betray your trust despite your selfish and callous behavior. Now, tell me what happened in the parlor to make you so angry!"

Her breast still heaving with agitation, Celeste rasped, "I told you! My husband turned against me. He chose to heed Randy's opinion about Taylor instead of mine, and when I pressed him to fire Randy . . . he refused."

Madalane's gaze grew pensive. She responded, "Randy stands up for Taylor, and Taylor is Buck's son. A man and his son—a difficult bond to break."

"Taylor is a drunk!"

"He proves the weakness of the Star blood that father and son share. Where is he now?"

"He went to town with the other ranch hands—to the Last Chance Saloon."

"The drunk has gone to the saloon." Madalane's full lips twitched into a fleeting smile. "You do not seem to realize how great an opportunity has been provided to you. You will be able to prove to your husband how understanding you can be when his son comes home and repeats his drunken performance—when he proves to your husband he is unable to fulfill his duties on the ranch."

"I will laugh in Buck's face."

"No, you will not! You will be gentle and understanding. You will forgive your husband for his brief disloyalty to you—and you will use the incident to convince him he must write his sons out of his will."

Celeste slowly smiled. "Yes . . . my husband does not realize it, but he has provided me with a valuable tool. How clever of you to realize it, Madalane."

"My body may be lagging, but my mind is not."

Her smile quickly fading, Celeste snapped, "I am sick of hearing about the handicap you claim, Madalane. It would be far better if your body and mind *both* performed as they should."

"In time."

"Time . . . time . . . I tire of waiting!"

"As do I."

"My patience wanes!"

Madalane replied sharply, "Control yourself, Celeste. Go back to the room you share with your husband. Lie in his bed. Let the tears fall. Appeal to his weaknesses, and he will not be able to resist you. It is your gift."

Celeste sneered. "You flatter me in the hope of gaining my favor. I recognize your ploy, yet you speak the truth. Bending men to my will *is* my gift. I have used that gift well in the past, and dear Buck . . . dear weak, dying Buck . . . does not stand a chance against me."

Renewed, Celeste strode back toward the door. She turned back to Madalane to add, "Be on your feet early tomorrow morning, Madalane—without excuses. I want breakfast ready on time so that when Taylor fails to show up at the table with the other hands, Buck will see his son for what he really is."

When Madalane returned her gaze coldly, Celeste rasped, "Did you hear me?"

"I heard you."

Celeste pulled the door closed behind her.

Taylor walked softly up the rear staircase of the hotel. He paused, squinting in the dim light of the hallway, then moved silently down the corridor. It had not been difficult to obtain the room number he sought. The hotel clerk was a braggart who had drunk liberally at the Last Chance bar; and Taylor, unlike most others, had listened to every word the man said.

Taylor paused outside Room #11. He listened but heard only silence inside. He tried the knob. Locked. But locked doors had never been a problem for him.

Moments later, Taylor pushed the door open a slit, then slipped inside. He halted abruptly in the darkness when the cold muzzle of a gun met his ribcage and he heard a throaty voice whisper, "Welcome, Taylor. I've been expecting you."

The graceful shadow moved from his side and turned up the lamp. Vida stood in the dim light of the room. Her dark hair was loose against her shoulders, and she was wearing a diaphanous nightgown that outlined her womanly curves clearly. She evinced little discomfort with her revealing appearance as she said, "Did you have fun at the Last Chance tonight, Taylor? I did."

Taylor responded with a touch of irritation he could not conceal, "I figured you were having *fun* since every man in the saloon was falling all over you."

"Yes, but I did deserve the attention." A smile lifted

the corners of her lush lips as she said offhandedly, "I was magnificent tonight."

Taylor responded tightly, "You're magnificent in every role you undertake, Vida . . . but you didn't come to Lowell to hear me say that. What are you doing here, and why are you pretending to be an entertainer?"

"I don't know. Why are you pretending to be a drunk?"

"That's my business."

"Well, that's my business, too."

Taylor stared at the beautiful woman standing in front of him. Despite the fact that they were totally alone in what would be considered an intimate situation, Vida remained completely at ease. It occurred to him belatedly that he wasn't sure whether to be insulted or flattered.

Yet he was certain of one thing: *Vida drew him like a magnet.* She was a constant challenge to him and so much more.

Taylor said irritably, "It's late and I have to be back to work at daybreak. So out with it. What are you doing in Lowell? Did Allan send you here?"

"No."

"Then why—"

Vida interrupted by taking a tantalizing step closer as she said, "You left me puzzled when we parted, Taylor. We had concluded a very successful assignment—one of many, I might add. We were both feeling very mellow when we rode back to our respective quarters in the coach. We intended following the assignment through to the end by meeting up with Allan in Baton Rouge."

"I know all that."

"And then the concierge handed you a letter."

Taylor went still.

Vida took another step closer. "You had the same reaction just now as you did when you read the letter. I knew before you looked up at me that something was wrong, but I didn't expect you to shut me out."

"It's personal, Vida."

"Too personal to share with your partner?"

"It has nothing to do with business."

"Oh." Vida took a step that brought her breathlessly close. "We're only friends when it comes to business, is that it?"

"Vida—"

"Tell me what it's all about, Taylor. We're partners. I feel responsible for you."

"Respon—" Incredulous, Taylor stared at her. "*You* feel responsible for *me?*"

"Yes."

"Well, I'll be damned!"

"I came here to make sure that wouldn't happen."

"Don't worry about me, Vida. I can take care of myself."

Silent for a moment, Vida placed her palm against his chest. Her touch started his heart pounding as she whispered, "Tell me something, Taylor . . . truthfully. If you thought I was in some kind of trouble, would you help me whether I wanted help or not?"

"That's not a fair question."

"Why not?"

"Because you have your hand on my chest and you can feel my heart pounding like a hammer. If I say no, you'll call me a liar, and if I say yes, there's no way I'll be able to get you to leave."

Vida moved closer. "So answer me truthfully."

Taylor reached up to grip her hand as he said with a sincerity that came from the heart, "I'd never be able to turn my back on you, and you know it."

"That's all I wanted to hear."

Sliding her arm around Taylor's neck, Vida drew him flush against her and pressed her mouth to his. Reacting with a spontaneous groan, Taylor crushed her close, deepening the kiss. He had kissed Vida before while holding himself back, but this time her body was soft and warm against his and his hunger was—

Vida drew back from him unexpectedly. Speechless, Taylor heard her say, "All right, so tell me. What was it about that letter that made you change your plans and take the chance of throwing away everything you've worked for? I want to know, Taylor."

"Vida . . ."

Backing up as she pulled Taylor toward her, Vida sat on the bed and pulled him down to sit beside her. She repeated softly, "Tell me."

Vida's leg was pressed warmly against his. He could smell her womanly scent and feel her heat. The taste of her lingered in his mouth as those eyes as dark as obsidian smoldered with heat.

"Damn." Taylor suddenly laughed aloud. "You're a formidable woman, Vida."

"I know."

Sobering when Vida's expression did not change, Taylor asked, "Why do you care what was in that letter?"

"Because I do."

Unable to resist, Taylor pressed his mouth lightly to hers. She was as sweet as honey, but she was frowning when he drew back.

"The letter was unsigned," Taylor said. "It asked me if I had forgotten Bonnie."

"Your sister."

Momentarily silent, Taylor asked, "You know about Bonnie?"

"You were quite the topic of conversation at the Last Chance tonight."

"My father and me, I assume."

"Among others."

Taylor's throat tightened. "I loved Bonnie, you know. We all did. She was the apple of Pa's eye, and she was so much younger than Cal and I that she was like a gift to us when she was born. She was sweet and loving, and so damned innocent. She followed Cal and me around and tried to imitate everything we did. I tried to act annoyed sometimes, but I couldn't resist her. None of us could." He paused for a breath. "She didn't deserve what happened to her."

"Your brother—"

"It wasn't Cal's fault. When my mother died, everything fell apart at the ranch. Pa started whoring away his grief in town, and Bonnie never seemed to stop crying. Cal and I were left home to run the ranch. Bonnie was feeling really bad one day, and Cal took her into town to raise her spirits. When they got there, Cal saw Pa and one of his whores staggering down the street. Cal didn't want Bonnie to see Pa like that so he chased her off to play with one of her friends before he faced Pa down. A few minutes later, Bonnie was dead. An accident. She fell into a well."

Taylor swallowed and cleared his throat before continuing resolutely. "When Pa and Cal came home and told me Bonnie was dead, I didn't want to believe it.

My father said Bonnie was dead because of Cal, because he hadn't watched her closely enough. I blamed Cal, too. I yelled at him. I told him it wouldn't have happened if he'd let me go into town with him. Cal was too broken up to defend himself. When I woke up in the morning, he was gone. I found out he had ridden off in the middle of the night, without waiting for Bonnie to be buried and without saying good-bye."

"Then your father met Celeste and married her."

Taylor made a soft scoffing sound. "It didn't take him long. My mother wasn't even cold in her grave."

"And his new wife turned your father against you."

Taylor frowned. "Who've you been talking to?"

"There wasn't a fella at the Last Chance who didn't know the whole story." Vida paused. "So who sent you the letter, and why?"

"I don't know. I've talked to Cal. He got a letter, too. He came back home before I did, but he hasn't been able to find out who sent it."

"You and your brother obviously never intended to return . . . so why did the letter bring you both back?"

"I don't know." Responding honestly, Taylor continued, "The accusation that I had forgotten Bonnie hit me hard. I would never . . . *could* never forget her. It would be like losing a part of me. All I know is that I wanted to face the person who sent me that letter."

Taylor paused.

Vida asked pointedly, "And?"

Silent for a few moments, Taylor responded, "And there was something about the letter that struck me wrong somehow."

"Professional instinct."

"Maybe."

"But you came back pretending to be a drunk. Why?"

"If you knew my father, you wouldn't have to ask."

Vida shook her head. "I don't understand."

"The old man always was ornery, and I figured he hadn't changed. He would've run me off if he'd had a choice—just like he ran Cal off when he came home. With me coming home the way I did, he didn't have any choice but to let me stay for a while. His pride wouldn't stand for having somebody find me lying on the side of the road, dead drunk."

"So what have you found out?"

Taylor gave a hard laugh. "Nothing, except that the ranch is in debt, Pa is dying, and Celeste is primed to collect what's left."

"I'm sorry."

Taylor shrugged. "I suppose I should be feeling sorry, too, but that cantankerous old man makes it hard."

"Did he send the letter?"

"No."

"Are you sure?"

"I asked him, and he was insulted that I might've thought for a minute that he did. Besides, he has Celeste. She's all he wants."

The shadows of the room fell on the exquisite planes of Vida's face as she whispered, "What can I do to help?"

She was beautiful, all right.

A half smile playing at his lips, Taylor replied, "I could think of something that would make me feel real fine right now."

"I'm serious, Taylor."

"So am I."

"Taylor . . ."

Taylor's half smile faded. "I appreciate the offer, Vida, but I can handle this myself. Allan is probably expecting you back."

"I'm not leaving yet."

"Yet?"

"Until everything here is settled."

"That could take a while."

"Not with both of us working on it."

"Vida—"

"I'm staying. Men talk freely with a glass in hand, a bottle of red-eye nearby, and a pretty woman beside them. There's no telling what I can learn."

"No, I—"

"I'm staying."

"But—"

"Just tell me what your plans are."

"I don't have any plans."

"I know you better than that."

"I told you. I'm going back to the ranch, and I'm going to find out who sent those letters, and why."

Vida stood up unexpectedly. "So, I'll learn what I can here. You know where I'll be if you need me."

"If I need you?"

"We're a team."

"A team . . ."

Taylor stood up slowly and walked to the door. Turning back toward her, he said, "If we're such a team, why didn't you ever tell me you could sing?"

"There need to be a few mysteries left between us, Taylor."

He pressed, "What about that song you said your

Irish daddy used to sing to you when you were a little lass. Did he?"

Vida smiled.

"Damn it, Vida, did you even *have* an Irish daddy?"

Vida fluttered her lashes.

"Oh, hell."

Sliding his arms around Vida, Taylor crushed her close and covered her mouth with his. The kiss was slow and sweet, and he indulged it with a hunger that had gone long unsated. It started feelings uncurling down deep inside him that made him step back warily to whisper, "Well, that was real, anyway."

In a minute he was out the door.

Chapter 4

Pierre Maison's narrow face was lined with fury as he glanced at Gasper Bouchet, then at the prison cell surrounding them. Cold, dank, and unclean . . . abominable. It was *she* who had put him there.

Addressing the man who was his confidant and legal counselor, Pierre whispered, "I missed my record book the day following my soiree. At first I thought I had misplaced it. I searched endlessly for it, but when the police came to arrest me and I was faced with the evidence they had against me, I knew where they had gotten their information. I also realized that no one else but Lisette could have stolen it. When you informed me she had disappeared from New Orleans the night of the ball, I became even more certain it was she."

Gasper whispered in response, "I did as you asked and had her traced. When she left New Orleans after the ball, she went directly to Baton Rouge where she met with Allan Pinkerton himself."

"Allan Pinkerton!"

"Obviously, Pinkerton's agency was hired to investigate the shipping disruption in New Orleans, and she is the detective Pinkerton dispatched."

"What about Taylor Star?"

"Lisette and he parted shortly after they left your house that night, and then Star departed the city. He was not present at the meeting between Pinkerton and Lisette in Baton Rouge. It appears she simply used Star to make her exit from your house."

Pierre demanded, "Where is she now?"

"I don't know."

"Find her."

"Pierre—"

"Find her!"

Gasper nodded stiffly, then added, "There's something else, Pierre. Her name isn't Lisette Tordeau. It's Vida Malone."

"Vida Malone . . . a name as common as the woman she turned out to be." Pierre stood up abruptly. "She used me, but she will not gain from that deception. How quickly can you have me released from here?"

"Pierre . . ." Perspiring profusely despite the cell's damp chill, Gasper whispered, "The evidence against you is monumental—complete with names, dates, places, and amounts received for each illicit cargo."

"I asked, *how soon?*"

"I have a friend in the court who is sympathetic if the price is right, but I can make no guarantees."

"Pay whatever price he asks."

"You must understand, Pierre. Your release from prison in no way guarantees that the charges against you will be dismissed."

"Pay whatever price he asks! I'll take care of the rest."

"The rest?" Gasper stood up abruptly. "I hope you are not anticipating any unwise actions that might reflect unfavorably on your case."

"The only time I was unwise was when I lusted after Lisette Tordeau—a woman who never truly existed." Pierre's smile was tight. "But she and I *will* meet again, and I will not make that mistake a second time."

"Pierre . . ."

Pierre faced the uncertain lawyer squarely. His tone rang with resolve as he whispered, "She will pay."

Well, that was real, anyway.

The din of the Last Chance reverberated around Vida as Taylor's words of the previous night returned to mind.

Yes, that kiss had been real.

Vida forced a bright smile as she strolled along the saloon bar. Taylor had been full of questions about her presence in Lowell when he had come to her room, and she had answered them truthfully . . . as truthfully as she had dared.

Vida smiled at the image of how Taylor had looked when she first saw him standing at the saloon bar the previous evening. He'd been wearing trousers and a shirt that had seen much wear, boots so old they had conformed to the shape of his feet, and a stained hat with a brim obviously curled by his hand to suit his taste. With a faded neckerchief tied around his neck and an aged gun belt worn low on his hips, he had been dressed more commonly than she had ever seen him, yet he had still been so damned handsome that her heart had skipped a beat the moment she saw him.

The problem was, *as truthfully as she had dared* left

much unsaid. She had conveniently left out of her explanation the profound sense of loss she had experienced after that evening in the New Orleans coach when Taylor read the mysterious letter and sent her on her way without any explanation. Her precipitous departure from New Orleans was more revealing than she cared to admit. The same could be said for the endless time spent in Baton Rouge waiting for a message from Taylor that she knew would not come.

Taylor was gone, and her uncertainty whether he would return to the life they had shared had left her shaken. She had told herself she was disturbed because they had worked so well together, that she could never have the same rapport or trust in another partner. She had even tried to convince herself that her success as a Pinkerton was partially due to Taylor's brilliance as a detective; yet she had known those were only partial truths. Taylor was an astute detective, but so was she, and she was more than capable of adjusting to another partner.

The problem was, she didn't want to.

Vida had sensed that Taylor felt the same . . . until he received the letter. She had wondered belatedly why she should have been so surprised. Taylor was a man accustomed to living life on his own terms, accustomed to having women lay their hearts at his feet. He was also a man who knew how to make a graceful exit.

Yet between them it had always been different. They—

"What are you thinking about, sweetheart?" Vida turned toward the familiar raspy voice as Derek continued, "I'm thinking by the smile on your face, it has to be me."

Facing the fact that some parts of her job would always be more unpleasant than others, Vida looked at the unclean fellow lounging against the bar and made her smile brighter. "Of course I was thinking about you, Derek . . . you and all the other fellas I'm planning on singing for tonight. That's why I was looking for Harvey. He said he was going to meet me here this afternoon so we could go over my songs."

"Maybe Harvey don't appreciate you like I do."

"That could be, but . . ." Never more grateful to see the aged piano player walk through the swinging doors, Vida said, "But it looks like Harvey does appreciate me after all."

Leaving Derek with a wink and an unspoken promise, Vida moved immediately toward the piano. She breathed a sigh of relief when Harvey smiled a greeting and sat down on the piano stool. His comment was unexpected.

"Looks like Derek's been leaning on you pretty heavy, darlin'." He did not wait for her reply as he continued, "I figure you're used to handling fellas like him, but I gotta say, you don't seem like the kind of woman who'd sit still for it."

Vida gave a short laugh. "You've got a pretty keen eye, Harvey. I'd probably be handling him a little differently if it wasn't obvious that Derek is one of the Last Chance's best customers. I figured setting him straight right off wouldn't be the best way to start out working here."

"Don't you worry your pretty little head about that one." Harvey motioned with his chin toward the bar where Bart kept a cautious eye on the saloon floor. "Ain't you never noticed the way Bart looks at Derek?

Bart don't like him, and no matter how much money Derek spends in here, that ain't going to change."

"Derek does seem to have pretty deep pockets. Does he work on one of the ranches around here?"

"Work? I got a feeling that fella don't know the meaning of the word."

Vida asked offhandedly, "What's that supposed to mean?"

"It means he spends too much time here to hold a regular job, and he's such a blowhard that most fellas don't believe half of what he says."

"Like?"

"Like he says he works for an outfit that travels through here periodically, and that they pay him good enough to set him up until their next trip."

Vida raised a skeptical brow.

"Yeah . . . and then there's all his bragging about how great a ladies' man he is."

Vida's skeptical brow tilted cynically.

Harvey's thick mustache quivered with amusement. "Derek almost made Bart laugh out loud when he boasted that good-looking women couldn't keep their hands off him. I suppose that's why Derek figures you won't be able to resist him."

"Why, Harvey." Vida's smile warmed. "I believe you paid me a compliment just then."

"I'm supposing I did." His face reddening, Harvey continued determinedly, "The truth is, you're the best-looking woman Lowell has seen in a dog's age."

Succumbing to impulse, Vida leaned forward and kissed Harvey's wrinkled cheek before whispering, "That's the best compliment I've had in a dog's age, too."

Harvey's face flushed more darkly. He was about to speak when he glanced at the bar and mumbled, "Don't look now, but if looks could kill, I'm thinking I'd be a dead man right now, and you'd be lying right beside me."

"Who—"

"Don't turn around, darlin'. That's what that Derek fella is looking to have you do. Like I said, he's a blowhard." Pausing briefly, he added, "But I gotta warn you, I've seen him in action a couple of times, and he can get real nasty. Besides, he don't hang out in the best company."

"What are you saying?"

Harvey shrugged. "Nobody else seemed to have thought much of it, but Derek looked to have a lot in common with that Bellamy fella who ended up causing so much trouble at the Texas Star."

Coming to full alert at the mention of the Texas Star ranch, Vida nudged, "Bellamy?"

"That Bellamy fella who tried to kill Jace Rule when he was working at the ranch. When things started going bad, he kidnapped Honor Gannon and—"

"That same Honor Gannon who is Buck Star's illegitimate daughter?"

Harvey grunted his surprise. "It looks like it didn't take you long to hear about Buck Star."

"But what did Bellamy have to do with Derek?"

"Hell, Bellamy came in here one day, by all accounts a perfect stranger. He sidled up to the bar and before the hour was out, him and Derek was thick as thieves. They spent the next few nights drinking and visiting the ladies together as if they was old buddies."

"Maybe they were. Maybe—"

"No, they wasn't. I overheard enough of their conversation to know they was strangers when Bellamy walked through the door. I'm just saying they hit it off real fine, like they was two peas in a pod—until Bellamy said something that sent Derek riding off like the devil was after him. We didn't see hide nor hair of Derek for a while after that; and after Jace Rule sent Bellamy to meet his maker, Derek made out like he didn't even remember who Bellamy was."

Harvey halted his recollection to whisper, "Speak of the devil and here he comes walking toward us."

The words had hardly left Harvey's mouth when Vida felt a damp palm on her shoulder and heard Derek say, "You two look real chummy all of a sudden, Vida, honey. I thought you was supposed to be working on a song."

Effectively dislodging Derek's grip by turning to face him, Vida responded with a smile, "We're doing just that. Harvey here is amazing. It looks like I'll have my choice of songs to sing."

"Just as long as you remember who's waiting to buy you a drink when you're done."

Turning back to Harvey as Derek walked away, Vida mumbled, "And he smells bad, too."

A flourish of chords covered Harvey's words as he warned, "Watch him, darlin'. He can be bad news."

Harvey continued playing an introduction as Vida reviewed in her mind the information she had learned since arriving in Lowell:

The Texas Star, once the biggest and most successful ranch in the area, had been brought to near ruin by a series of disastrous circumstances.

Cal Star, Taylor's older brother, was nearly killed bringing down the rustlers who had devastated it.

A killer called Bellamy had conspired to use Taylor's half-sister in order to kill Jace Rule while they both worked at the Texas Star.

Taylor and Cal had both received anonymous letters that someone knew would bring them home.

And Derek was somehow in the middle of it all with a pocketful of money that never seemed to run out.

The conclusion was clear: Something underhanded was going on, and Taylor and Cal Star were its focus.

That thought sent a chill down Vida's spine as she started to sing.

"You aren't still mad at me, are you, darlin'?"

Their bedroom was revealingly silent as Buck grasped his young wife's arm, halting her as she attempted to brush past him for the fifth time since they had awakened. He had heard her sobbing during the night, but his attempts to console her had failed. He knew she believed he had sided with Randy against her.

Buck looked at Celeste's pale, faultless countenance. It was still a wonder to him how a woman as young and lovely as she could continue to love him so desperately when he was only a shadow of the man he had been when he married her. She was so determined that his health would be restored, so intent on bringing the Texas Star back to the ranch it had once been—not for herself, but for him. The only problem was, she didn't have any idea how to go about accomplishing either of those goals.

Buck unconsciously sighed. He knew everyone

thought he was blind to the mistakes Celeste had made on the ranch since becoming his wife, but that was because no one understood Celeste the way he did. He knew Celeste's concern for his health was the reason for her ongoing conflict with Doc Maggie. Celeste couldn't seem to accept the fact that he trusted Doc's judgment, that he knew Doc would always do her best for him. Celeste was so possessive of his affections that she unconsciously sought to keep him apart from everyone else, even the ranch hands whom he depended upon so heavily. No one seemed to realize that Celeste had tried to take up the slack while he was unable to handle daily affairs at the ranch; unfortunately, she had accomplished nothing more than to drive off most of the hands. He had attempted to explain those things to her, to no avail, but when she demanded that he fire Randy the previous day, he had known he could not allow her mistakes in judgment to further jeopardize the ranch's solvency.

Certain he'd never be able to make Celeste understand that Randy was the backbone of the ranch, Buck whispered, "Celeste, darlin', please answer me."

Celeste turned toward Buck slowly. A supreme actress, she allowed Buck to feel the full impact of her feigned distress as she whispered, "I'm not angry with you, Buck. I could never be angry with you. I love you. It's just that I feel . . . hurt."

"Celeste . . ." Buck's voice grew hoarse at the sight of her sadness. "I didn't mean to hurt you. Please try to understand. I need Randy's help on this ranch, especially while I'm still ailing."

"But he's arrogant—and he hates me!"

"No, that isn't true." Celeste inwardly smiled at

Buck's agitation as he slipped his arms around her. She trembled effectively as he consoled, "Randy just sees what needs to be done on the ranch better than most, and he wants to get it accomplished."

She whispered with torment in her tone, "He sees what needs to be done on the ranch better than I do . . . that's what you're saying, isn't it?"

"Celeste . . . Randy's been a ranch hand all his life."

"And I'm only your wife."

"Not *only*, Celeste. You know how much you mean to me."

Summoning tears with the ease of long practice, Celeste said, "I don't know if I do anymore."

"Celeste, how can you say that?"

"Because you've changed since Cal and Taylor came home, Buck, and since that. . . . person, Honor, came back to claim she's your daughter."

"No, I haven't changed. I see them all for what they are, and their return galls me."

"Yet Cal and Honor are now living nearby, and Taylor is living and working right here on the Texas Star."

"I can't control what Cal and Honor do, but Taylor is on the ranch only temporarily."

"That isn't the way he sees it."

"That's the way *I* see it."

Affecting the adoring gaze she employed so well, Celeste whispered, "It . . . it's just that they don't love you the way I do, Buck. I don't want them to take advantage of you, as they obviously intend on doing. I couldn't bear that."

"Don't worry. I won't let that happen, Celeste, darlin'. Honor and Cal know how I feel about them, and Taylor does, too."

"They're trying to worm their way back into your affections so they can separate us. They want to turn you against me."

"I'd never let them do that."

"Is that true, Buck?" Celeste inched closer and pressed herself against him. "You'd never choose them over me?"

"Never!"

Managing a restrained sob, Celeste mumbled against his chest, "I wish I could depend on that—that I'll always be first with you, just like you've always been first with me. That's all I've ever wanted."

"I'll do anything I can to prove it to you, darlin' . . . anything."

Sensing victory, Celeste murmured, "I hope with all my heart you mean what you're saying, Buck."

"I do, darlin'. Just tell me how to prove it to you."

Silently elated at Buck's ardent plea, Celeste allowed a few wordless moments to elapse as she savored her impending triumph.

Just tell me how to prove it to you . . .

Yes, she had him now, just where she wanted him.

"She sure is somethin', ain't she?" Riding beside Taylor as the ranch hands returned to the Texas Star after a long day in the saddle, Mitch pressed, "Come on, boys, admit it. That Vida Malone is just about the best-looking woman you've ever seen."

Somehow annoyed by Mitch's endless praise of the "new saloon girl," Taylor responded gruffly, "Maybe."

Mitch replied, "I don't care how many good-looking women you've known. There ain't a one of them who could compare with her and you know it."

A low grunt his only rejoinder, Taylor stared into the distance ahead. He had stayed in town hours longer than the rest of the hands in order to talk to Vida the previous night. Yet despite only a few hours' sleep, he had been awake at dawn, certain that his father would be waiting at the breakfast table, looking for an excuse to send him packing.

Weak as a kitten, pale as a ghost, and swaying like a lily in the wind, Buck had not disappointed him. He had been standing in the kitchen doorway when the hands came to the house for breakfast. The sight of that old man waiting for a chance to show his younger son up for the drunken bum he believed him to be had infuriated Taylor. That anger had strengthened him during the day, driving him through the long, wearying hours of work; but the sun was setting, the long day was over, and he was tired—too damned tired to argue with Mitch about his obvious infatuation with the image Vida had concocted.

"I'm going into town again tonight." Mitch looked at the men riding beside him as he asked, "Who's coming with me?"

"Count me in." Big John's response was surprisingly quick.

"I suppose I should go in to see what all the talk is about," was Randy's reply.

Taylor did not respond.

Mitch prompted, "What about you, Taylor?" He grinned at Taylor's fatigued glance. "I guess that'll teach you to come dragging yourself in after responsible cowpokes like us were already asleep for hours."

Taylor snapped, "How do you know what time I got in?"

"We would've had to be deaf not to hear you stumbling around." Mitch added with an amused twist of his lips, "I hope that sweet little Ellie was worth it."

Sweet little Ellie?

Taylor raised a brow in Mitch's direction. He had no idea if Ellie was worth it—but Vida definitely was.

"Oh, hell." Big John's expression dimmed as the group neared the ranch house and the smell of supper reached them. He grumbled, "It looks like Madalane's cooked up another one of her island dishes. The only chance we'll have of getting a good meal tonight will be if we buy one in town."

Grunting their concurrence, the men sat down at the kitchen table a few minutes later. Taylor sensed silent groans of dismay when Madalane placed a platter of hardly recognizable beef in front of them. He spooned the first forkful into his mouth, then looked up at Madalane's glowering countenance as she stared directly at him. He returned her gaze boldly as he said in reply to Mitch's earlier question, "I guess I will be going into town with you boys tonight. There're a few things I need to do."

"What would that be, Taylor?" Speaking unexpectedly from the kitchen doorway, Buck continued aggressively, "Other than needing to spend some time in the saloon?"

"Don't go condemning Taylor, boss." Big John spoke up in Taylor's defense. "Taylor didn't do much drinking last night. He was the last man back here because he's got himself a little chickadee at the saloon."

"One excuse is as good as another," Buck grated.

"What would you like me to do, Pa?" Taylor's smile was sarcastic. "Maybe you'd like me to spend the evening here with you and Celeste, talking over the good old days."

"I don't expect anything of the sort from you."

"I'm glad, because I'm going to town where—"

"—where you can get staggering drunk and forget your responsibilities to this ranch and to your father, and that's the truth of it!"

Celeste stepped out into view as she concluded her vicious diatribe. She stood belligerently at Buck's side as Taylor replied, "You may be right, Celeste, but I'm thinking that getting drunk to avoid responsibility isn't any worse than marrying an old man with the thought of outliving him and inheriting whatever he leaves behind."

"How dare you speak to me like that?" Livid, Celeste gasped, "Buck, are you going to let him say things like that to me?"

Buck's face flooded with color. "Apologize to your stepmother, Taylor!"

Taylor's lips twisted into a sardonic smile as he pushed back his chair and stood up, replying, "She may be your wife, but she'll never be my stepmother."

"Make him leave, Buck!" Celeste ranted. "Throw him off this ranch right now!"

"Apologize, Taylor," Buck demanded.

"I'll apologize, Pa"—addressing Buck directly, his tone soft and final, Taylor concluded—"when you can tell me truthfully, without any doubt on your part, that what I said about the reason Celeste married you isn't true."

Buck's brief hesitation was revealing. Taylor felt the acrimony in his father's gaze when Celeste gasped and fled the room in tearful dismay.

Buck turned to follow Celeste, his step so unsteady that Taylor walked behind him, uncertain if Buck would remain upright. He stopped in the parlor when Buck turned resolutely into the bedroom doorway through which Celeste had disappeared. His smile bitter, Taylor was about to leave when he halted abruptly at the sight of the paperwork piled on the desk nearby. The words DELINQUENT PAYMENT stamped across the top invoice caught his eye. Walking closer, he skimmed the pile briefly, noting as he shifted the papers that the invoices underneath were similarly marked. He went suddenly still at the sight of a legal document halfway down the stack.

It was Buck's will.

Taylor scanned the provisions set forth. Stunned, he glanced at the date the document had been signed.

"What are you doing?" Startled, Taylor met Madalane's fierce gaze as she limped into the room and demanded, "Get away from that desk! Your father's affairs are no longer your business."

"Neither are they yours."

Unintimidated by Taylor's response, Madalane ordered, "Get out of this room or I will call your father back here now—and I will not be responsible for what might follow."

"Don't waste your breath, Madalane. I'm still as immune to your threats as I ever was."

"Immune?" Madalane continued harshly, "Or too stupid to know when to take a threat seriously?"

"I have been accused of many things, but never of being stupid. There are others presently living in this ranch house who are far more worthy of that description than I am."

Madalane limped a few menacing steps forward to rasp, "Get out!"

"I don't take orders from you." Taylor's smile was cold. "But I have better things to do right now, so it looks like you'll be getting your wish anyway."

Taylor felt the heat of Madalane's gaze burn into his back as he walked through the kitchen. He did not speak a word to the men watching as he left the house.

The ceaseless din of the Last Chance continued around them as Vida smiled into Derek Beecher's oily, unshaven face. Inwardly groaning, she said with a raised brow, "So, women can't keep their hands off you." She gave a gentle shrug of her shoulder to hide her disbelief at the man's monumental ego. "Does that mean I can expect to find myself fighting for your attention?"

"Don't worry about that, sweetheart." Derek glanced down at the ample bosom bulging at the neckline of her gown. "You got a lot more to offer than most women I know."

"I like to think that compliment includes all of me, not just what I have to offer from the neck down."

Derek laughed aloud as he slapped a damp hand onto her shoulder. "You sure are quick-minded, I'll give you that."

Restraining her instinctive response to punch him in the face, Vida shook off Derek's hand as she reached for her glass. She had arranged to have Bart water down her drinks so she would remain "quick-minded," but the "pleasure" of Derek's company almost made her wish she hadn't.

"So, tell me more about this attraction good-looking women have for you."

His smile falling, Derek grated, "Don't believe me, huh?" He stared at her silently, then said, "I could tell you some stories—"

"Go ahead. I might enjoy them."

"Oh, you'd enjoy them all right. Hell, there ain't a red-blooded man or woman in this place who wouldn't."

"They're that good, huh?"

"Yeah, but I ain't dumb enough to queer what I got going on the side to impress any woman."

"Any woman . . . meaning me?" Vida moved closer to Derek's sweaty body as she whispered, "Who knows? It might turn out to be worth it." When Derek looked at her with a hint of suspicion, Vida moved back. "But maybe my type doesn't appeal to you."

"Oh, it appeals to me all right." Vida noted that Derek's chest began a slow heaving. Practically salivating, he said, "I like dark-haired women a helluva lot better than blonde females who act like they're better than I am until they fall into bed with me."

"Blonde women do that?"

"One in particular, maybe. But she changes her mind when I start giving her a taste of what she wants."

"I know the type." Vida sneered, subtly egging Derek on. "They act like they're doing you a favor when they're getting as much out of it all as you are."

"That's right. I'm getting sick of it, too, especially now, when she tries to play hard to get because she thinks she don't need me no more."

"But she had good enough use for you in the past, huh?"

Derek said gruffly, "Yeah, well, she learned her lesson all right the last time we was together. All I had to do was touch her, and she was ready for me."

"All this talk about blonde women . . ." Vida glanced around the saloon, then smiled. "Ellie's blonde. Is she the girl you're talking about?"

"Ellie? That trash?" Derek gave a harsh laugh. "I'm talking about a 'quality' woman . . . a woman as proper and refined on the outside as any woman you've ever seen, but who knows just how to make a man feel good."

"She's an older woman . . . one with experience who appreciates a man like you—is that what you've saying?"

"She ain't old. She's young, a year or two older than you, maybe, but as hot as they come."

"But she saves it all for you."

"That old man she's married to don't satisfy her, that's for sure."

"She's married?" Vida raised her brows. "And her husband puts up with it all?"

"He don't know. Hell, he thinks butter wouldn't melt in her mouth."

"Sounds too good to be true." Vida smiled. "So what are you doing standing here beside me at the bar when you could have that woman any time you want?"

"Maybe I'm sick of blonde women."

"You don't sound like you are."

"Maybe I'd like a taste of something different for a change."

"Sorry, darlin', I don't give out free samples."

"You don't, huh?" Derek leered. "Maybe you won't be able to resist me."

"I'm going to try damned hard."

99

His expression abruptly hardening, Derek grated, "Why the sudden change?"

"You're quite a man, Derek. I don't have any doubt that everything you told me about that blonde woman is true."

"It is true . . . every word of it."

"But I'm thinking that woman's still pulling the strings and making you dance to her tune, and I don't want any part of that."

"We had a business arrangement that worked out right for both of us. That's all. She don't have no long-range hold on me. Actually, I know for a fact that she's got plans of her own that are going to keep her around here for only a little while longer. Then she's going back where she came from—to the high life of New Orleans, to hear her tell it."

"And she's going to leave you behind?"

"Maybe . . . if I let her."

Feigning annoyance, Vida said abruptly, "Who is this woman, anyhow? If it was me, I wouldn't let her get away with it, no matter how good she is in bed."

Derek responded quickly, "No names."

"What do you mean?"

"I already told you more than I should've."

"You're loyal to her," Vida mocked. "Is that it?"

"Loyalty ain't got nothing to do with it. Keepin' quiet is as much to my benefit as it is to hers."

"Because?"

"It ain't none of your business!"

"Oh! I thought you were making it my business."

"Well, you was wrong."

"But you're still looking for samples, is that it?"

Derek did not reply.

"Well, you're not going to get any from me, that's for sure."

Derek's demeanor darkened. "Wait a minute."

Vida responded in a lowered tone, "You might have a lot to offer, but I don't want any part of it if that blonde woman can get you at her beck and call anytime she wants."

"She's at *my* beck and call! She needs me now more than before, and she knows it."

"Why does she need you more *now?* Is there something going on between you other than what happens between the sheets?"

"Getting kinda nosy, ain't you?"

Vida's smile was confident as she responded, "Well, the fact is, I know what I've got to offer, and it's plenty. I figure I can be choosy, so come back and see me when you're ready to put that blonde woman aside. Maybe we can talk then."

"That's crazy! You ain't—"

An elaborate flourish of the piano interrupted opportunely, and Vida said, "No, I ain't. So if you'll excuse me . . ."

A thread of apprehension tightened inside Vida as she turned her back and strode toward the piano to the rising sound of applause. She had sensed there was more to Derek's story than he had been willing to reveal, that his ego was the key to unlocking it, and she had deliberately provoked him.

Turning toward the crowd when she reached the piano, Vida surveyed the room for a familiar face. A combination of experience and female intuition had set red flags waving as her conversation with Derek had progressed, but she needed to know more.

Vida took a deep breath.

Where in hell was Taylor tonight anyway?

Taylor drew his mount to a halt as he scrutinized the Rocky W ranch house from a wooded copse nearby. An aching knot twisted tight inside him as he surveyed the familiar lay of the land. He remembered Old Man Simmons, recalling the time so many years earlier when the old man had given him a puppy from his bitch's litter. Ma showed her appreciation to Simmons with one of her pecan pies, but Taylor had never forgotten the old man's kindness.

Taylor scrutinized the ranch house and outbuildings more closely. They appeared to be in better shape than he had ever seen them. Cal's work, no doubt. Cal was a good man and a good cattleman. His wife was lucky to have him for a husband. It had taken Taylor a long time after Bonnie's death to admit to himself that he was lucky to have Cal for a brother, too.

All those wasted years . . .

Taylor raised his hands to his lips and whistled a long, warbling call. Almost amused, he remembered Cal's comment the first time he had proudly demonstrated that talent to his brother as a boy. Cal had said he wasn't sure what kind of bird call he was trying to imitate, but there was no way anybody could copy that sound even if he tried.

He hoped Cal remembered.

Taylor had whistled for the third time when Cal walked out onto the ranch house porch to scan the nearby foliage. Noting Cal's expectant posture, he whistled again. Cal turned immediately in the direction of the sound, then strode to the horse tied at the hitching post, mounted, and began riding toward him.

Cal burst through the undergrowth a few minutes later, drew his mount to a sharp halt, and said, "Damn! I knew it was you! What in hell are you doing hiding here in the woods? Why didn't you come up to the house?"

Dismounting along with Cal, Taylor said, "I figured this wasn't the best time for family introductions since I'm not sure yet how I want to play things out with Pa about you."

"I hear you're working at the Texas Star." Cal shrugged. "It looks like you got farther than I did with the old man. He wouldn't even let me in the house."

"Pa let me in, but he's looking for an excuse to throw me out again. I just may have given it to him tonight." At Cal's frown, he said, "Like you said, Pa's still a fool for Celeste, and I'm not."

"And you told her as much?"

"I let her goad me into saying more than I probably should have."

Cal's expression was tight. "What's going on, Taylor?"

"That's what I want to know." Uncertain how to begin, Taylor said bluntly, "Pa had some papers piled on his desk and I went though them briefly. The ranch is in deep trouble."

"I know that, but Pa's too stubborn to let me help. He doesn't want any part of me."

"I'd say that's right, except . . ." Taylor took a breath. "I saw his will. The way it presently stands, he's leaving the ranch to the two of us."

"*What?*"

"Celeste isn't even mentioned."

"That can't be. Pa lives and breathes for that woman."

"But he's still leaving the ranch to us."

"That must've been an old will."

"It was. It was dated witnessed and notarized before Ma's death."

"Pa must've made out another one leaving the ranch to Celeste. She wouldn't stand for it any other way."

"Then why was it lying in the middle of past-due invoices and papers that needed tending to? If he had made a new will, the old one would've been destroyed."

"Meaning?"

Taylor shook his head. "I'm not sure what I mean." He asked abruptly, "Did Bill Leeds ever mention that Pa made out a new will? Leeds is still the only lawyer in town, isn't he?"

"Yes, Leeds is still Lowell's only lawyer; and no, we never discussed Pa's will because I figured it wasn't my business anymore."

"It is now. Those letters somebody sent to us both made it our business."

Cal's honey-colored eyes pinned him. Taylor felt the impact of his gaze as Cal said, "Don't beat around the bush. Just say what you mean."

"All right. I'm saying something is wrong at the Texas Star, something that goes beyond the condition of the ranch or Pa's health."

"Pa had a run of bad luck. Cattle disease, rustling, water problems, the ranch hands leaving, and he's starting to show his age, is all."

"I'm telling you, there's something wrong at the Texas Star, Cal, something I can't put my finger on. It didn't take me more than a few minutes in that house to sense it."

"To *sense* it?"

"That's right, and I've had enough experience to know that when the hair on the back of my neck stands up like it did, something's wrong."

"When the hair on the back on your neck stands up . . ."

"Listen to me, Cal!" Exasperation tinting his tone, Taylor said, "You knew I wasn't the drunk I was pretending to be the first time you saw me. Well, pretending to be a drunk got me onto the Texas Star and placed me in the bunkhouse so I could—"

"In the bunkhouse?"

"You didn't think Pa would let me stay in the main house for any length of time, did you?"

"The bastard!"

Taylor's glance was cold as he continued, "You're not familiar with my recent history, but believe me, I know what I'm talking about when I say something's wrong there."

Cal studied Taylor's expression, then asked, "What do you want me to do?"

"Talk to Bill Leeds. Find out if Pa did write a new will."

"He won't tell me."

"Tracking down those rustlers like you did made you a more respectable member of the community than you seem to realize, Cal. Leeds will talk to you if you approach him right." Taylor added with a laugh, "One thing's for sure. He'll talk to you before he'll talk to your no-good, drunken brother."

Cal frowned. "What difference does it make if Pa did write up a new will?"

"It could make a huge difference to Celeste."

"I don't care about Celeste."

"I do."

Cal raised his brow quizzically.

"Find out for me, Cal. It's important."

"Tell me what's going on, Taylor."

"I don't know yet, and that's the truth."

Silent for long seconds, Cal said finally, "All right. I'll talk to Leeds tomorrow—if you'll tell me what you discover the moment you find out anything definite."

"You know I will." Taylor's voice dropped a note softer. "There's nobody who has a better right to know than you."

Taylor saw the difficulty with which Cal swallowed before he extended his hand. His own throat tight, Taylor shook it firmly, knowing the bond between them had never been stronger.

"Hey, there he is!"

Big John's greeting resounded over the festive din of the Last Chance as Taylor walked through the swinging doors and saw Randy, Mitch, and Big John lined up at the crowded bar.

Frowning darkly, Taylor edged up beside them and motioned to the bartender for a drink. The saloon was filled to capacity, the smoke thick, the noise overwhelming, and Taylor's mood was foul. It had been a long ride to the Rocky W and then to town, and he was feeling more exhausted by the moment. If not for Vida, he would probably have turned back to the Texas Star and slipped silently into the bunkhouse for some much-needed sleep after talking to Cal, but peace of mind did not allow it.

Taylor considered that thought briefly. Peace of mind? Vida had demonstrated beyond dispute during their professional association that she was more than capable of taking care of herself. Besides, he hadn't asked her to come to Lowell, had he?

His mood grew darker as he picked up his glass and emptied it the moment it was set down in front of him.

"That don't look good, boy." Big John shook his head, his smile fading. "You keep on emptying your glass like that and it'll be a short evening for you."

"I know what I can handle."

"What's got into you, Taylor? You're as jumpy as a loco steer."

Speaking up from his spot at the bar beside Big John, Mitch queried with a half smile, "It couldn't be seeing your sweetie Ellie all cozied up to that wrangler over there that's put you out of sorts, could it?"

Taylor glanced at Ellie and the cowpoke beside her, then scanned the crowd casually. He did not see the woman he was seeking as he responded, "Ellie was fine for last night, but that doesn't mean the two of us are set for life. I figure there's more fish in the sea than her."

"Oh ho," Big John baited. "Any woman you want is yours for the asking, is that it?"

"Big John . . ."

Ignoring Randy's warning interjection, Taylor looked at the large man beside him and asked solemnly, "Are you looking for trouble, Big John?"

"No, not me." Big John drew back good-humoredly. "I remember what a tough little fella you was growing up and I'm not about to take you on. I was just asking a question."

Deciding to respond to the oversized cowpoke's question with equal cockiness, Taylor said, "I may be out of sorts because I'm tired . . . but I'm not tired enough to spend the night alone."

"Did you hear this young fella?" Big John slapped Taylor heartily on the back, then leaned forward to say conspiratorially, "Who'd you pick out to keep you company tonight? There's Lulu, but she plays hard to get sometimes. Then there's Mitzie, yet I need to warn you, she's damned bowlegged underneath her skirt. Then there's Opal—another Last Chance jewel, if you know what I mean. Of course, there's always Poppy. I should make it clear, though, that those girls aren't in the kind of business you're interested in. You'll have to charm them first before they'll . . ."

Big John's voice faded from Taylor's hearing as the crowd shifted and he saw Vida standing surrounded by admirers. She made a smiling comment that left the fellows laughing, then started winding her way through the crowd in his direction. Taylor took a deep breath as he watched. Vida always had been spectacular in every way, but, damn her, she didn't miss a beat in the saloon-woman attire she was wearing. As a matter of fact, he couldn't think of another woman who'd look as good as she did in that gaudy green satin . . . or any other woman who had as much to spare in brainpower as she did at her neckline.

Taylor's expression darkened at the smiling comments made along the bar as Vida walked by. It occurred to him that maybe she looked *too* good, considering the way most men seemed unable to take their eyes off her. The trouble was, he knew what they were thinking, and he didn't like it. Vida didn't seem to realize—

"You didn't hear a word I said, did you?" Big John's voice was tinged with amusement as he continued, "I hate to say this, boy, but you look hungrier than a starving wolf when you look at that woman. But if you're smart, you'll take a little advice from me. Don't go wasting your time thinking about latching on to Vida Malone for the night. She's not that kind. If I was you, I'd get myself another drink and start looking elsewhere."

But Taylor was hardly listening. His gaze never leaving Vida, he noted the moment when a familiar cowpoke grasped her arm, halting her. Jaw tight, Taylor stopped himself from stepping forward as Big John commented, "You'd think Derek Beecher would be smart enough to realize Vida won't waste her time with a loser like him."

Taylor tensed as Derek's grip on Vida's arm tightened noticeably. He moved into action the moment Vida stroked her upswept hair with a delicate thumb held rigidly upward. It was her signal to him.

"Where you going, Taylor?"

Big John's question trailed behind him, but Taylor was not of a mind to respond.

"I'm busy, Derek."

"Too busy to spend some time with me?"

Vida smiled, fighting down her inclination to rip her arm free of Derek's grip as she said, "I spent some time with you earlier, remember? I said all I had to say then."

"That's all right with me." Derek leered as his grip tightened. "I don't rightly feel like talking anyway."

Vida glanced again toward the bar and frowned. Where was Taylor, anyway? She had given him the signal, but if he had been too deep into his role as a drunk to see it, she'd make sure he—

Vida gasped as a strong arm slipped around her waist from behind, drawing her back against a hard, familiar male body. Tremors of delight moved down her spine as Taylor whispered in her ear, "There you are, darlin'. I was looking for you."

Those tremors. It happened every time Taylor touched her, a phenomenon that occurred with no other man Vida had ever known.

Reacting with a smile, Vida had no time to speak before Taylor clamped his hand onto Derek's where Derek held her arm. He was so good an actor that she could almost believe his anger was real when he said, "We haven't met, fella, but my name's Taylor Star. I figure you didn't know Vida's with me tonight, or you wouldn't be bothering her."

"I ain't bothering her." Derek glowered. "And since when is she with you?"

"Since right now." Taylor looked down at her, his clear gaze intense as he said, "Isn't that right, Vida, honey?"

Her voice emerged huskier than she intended when she responded, "That sounds fine with me."

"Wait a minute!" Derek snarled at her, "That ain't the way you was talking earlier."

"That was before, Derek, and this is now." Vida added with a dismissive glance, "Talk to me again when you get things straightened out between you and your 'friend.' Until then, it's *adios*."

Taylor turned her toward a vacant table in a corner of the room and Vida snuggled tight against him. She felt his tension when he seated her and pulled his chair intimately close as though for a loving whisper. "What was that all about, and what do you want with a derelict like Beecher?"

Annoyed at his tone, Vida leaned forward to whisper seductively against his lips, "I haven't been spending time with Derek without a reason." Unable to resist, she touched Taylor's mouth with the tip of her tongue. The jolt that shuddered through him reverberated within her as well as she continued, "Everybody thinks he's just a blowhard, but I have a feeling there's more to him than there seems."

"Damn it, Vida." Taylor's gaze dropped to her lips. His chest began a slow heaving as he said, "I'm warning you. Don't pour it on too heavy with me tonight. I'm tired, and I'm not up to games."

"You're a professional, Taylor, and everybody's watching us." Cooing the words, she brushed his mouth with hers. "Either we make it look believable or it's all over. You don't want that to happen, especially now, when I have something to report."

"If you keep this up," Taylor warned again, "I can guarantee we won't be doing much talking."

Annoyed, Vida drew back abruptly. "If that's the way you want it."

"That's not what I *want*, and you know it." Pausing, Taylor said, "Oh, hell . . ." Vida saw a flicker of change in Taylor's gaze the moment before he curled his hand around the back of her head, holding her fast as he fitted his mouth fully to hers. Swallowing her surprised gasp, Taylor pressed his kiss deeper, nudging her mouth open to savor her more fully. His tongue stroked hers, and she had no mind to resist as he drew her tighter, as he—

Stunned when Taylor pulled back abruptly, Vida saw the flash of anger in his expression when he said, "That's as much as I can take right now."

Vida struggled to ignore her inner trembling as she whispered, "I think that'll do for a while. Now, do you want to hear what I learned tonight or not?"

Taylor's gaze scorched hers. "Is it important?"

"Maybe."

"So, tell me."

Vida said abruptly, "Maybe now's not the time, after all."

"This is a helluva time to come to that conclusion!"

"Why?"

"If I wasn't sitting down, Vida, the answer would be obvious."

"Oh." Momentarily amused, Vida said, "Well, I need your complete attention if you want me to continue."

"Believe me, you've got it."

"Taylor . . ."

His patience obviously in short supply, Taylor snapped, "Just say what you've got to say."

Vida said softly, "Don't be angry, Taylor."

"I'm not angry."

"You aren't?"

Taylor leaned closer. He stroked the bared flesh of her back as he whispered, "As a matter of fact, what

I'm feeling right now doesn't bear any resemblance to anger."

"Be serious, Taylor. I need to talk to you."

Vida could feel Taylor's heart pounding against her breast as he said hoarsely, "Believe me, I was never more serious."

"Taylor, I—"

A startling musical flourish from the piano in a corner of the room jerked Vida upright in her chair.

"What's the matter?"

"That's my cue."

"Your cue—"

"To sing."

"Vida . . ."

Aware that all eyes had turned toward her at Harvey's musical introduction, Vida stood up. She was intensely conscious of the moment when Taylor's hands slipped back to the table, allowing her to turn toward the piano.

Breathless as Taylor's gaze followed her, Vida maintained her smile with sheer strength of will while her mind chided, *Snap out of it! You're letting Taylor sweep you off your feet, and you know better than that. Taylor loves you like he loves all women.* The voice paused briefly to amend, *No, that's not true. It's different between you and him. Taylor respects you in a way that sets you apart from the others because you've proved that, aside from being a woman, you're his equal in every way.* The voice added firmly, *. . . and because you've also proved you know how to smile when he walks away.*

Vida took a deep breath as she reached the piano. Casting Harvey a flirty wink, she turned around to face the eager crowd, admitting another silent truth: that it wasn't always easy to smile when Taylor walked away.

Taylor watched as Vida made her way across the crowded floor. The fact that grinning cowpokes were beginning to applaud even before she sang her first note sent a hot flush through him.

Either consciously or unconsciously, Vida had set every one of those men to salivating—and the realization that he had inadvertently joined the crowd did not escape him.

Taylor's scowl tightened. What in hell was wrong with him?

His flush heated up another notch when Vida winked at the old man playing the piano, and Taylor sat back scowling. She'd never change. She was all woman, and she knew it. She liked to flirt, to see men respond to the mere flutter of her eyelashes. He was no exception, and he enjoyed watching him squirm.

Taylor eyed Vida intently, his eyes taking in her perfect features and the womanly form that left all other women wanting. She was smart, too, damn it, but tonight she'd been too smart for her own good. If that piano hadn't interrupted them, he had the feeling she might have—

Taylor halted his thoughts abruptly. What *was* the matter with him? Vida had come to Lowell to help because she was worried about him. He should've realized that she would follow him. He knew he would've done the same without a moment's thought because . . . because she was *special* to him.

Special.

Taylor shook his head. But special or not, he couldn't take much more of Vida's well-acted attentions. Somehow, when Vida was in his arms, he lost contact with reason—a dangerous situation since Vida trusted his professionalism.

His professionalism.

Taylor sighed.

Damn.

"You promised me! You said I'd always be first with you! You said you'd never let your sons worm their way back into your affections!"

Celeste had been crying and sulking for hours as Buck tried to console her. Her husband had followed her back to their room after Taylor had stated so arrogantly that he would apologize to her if Buck could tell him, without any doubt on Buck's part, that Celeste had married him only for love. Shocked by Buck's revealing hesitation, Celeste had fled the room. She had not yet recuperated.

The bastard's progeny—Taylor—had proved himself to be an even greater bastard than his father! He had since left the ranch with the rest of the hands, leaving her with Buck's pathetic efforts at reassurance.

Celeste struggled to conceal the hatred smoldering inside her. She had spent *years* submitting to Buck's fumbling lovemaking . . . *years* pretending ecstasy when she felt only revulsion . . . *years* lost in awaiting full fruition of her vengeance. The return of Buck's sons had been an unexpected setback. The appearance of an illegitimate daughter had been stunning. Yet, despite it all, she had been certain she finally had Buck

115

exactly where she wanted him. Buck had already agreed to tackle the stack of past-due bills with her the following morning. She had rehearsed in her mind the surprise she would pretend when his will came to the top of the pile, her brief welling of tears, her claims that she would not discuss the will because she could not bear the thought of being without him, then her reticence as she allowed Buck to convince her of the need for excluding his sons from his will.

She had been able to *taste* victory.

Celeste looked up at Buck as he stood over the chair where she sat. He was so grief-stricken at the sight of her tears. He was so placating, so humbly loving.

Liar!

"Celeste, darlin'—"

"You said you loved me!"

"I do love you. There's no one on this earth that I love more."

On this earth . . . A stipulation Buck would not have made prior to the return of his sons and the renewing of Emma Star's sainted memory.

But Emma was dead, and she, Celeste, was alive and occupying Buck's bed. She would again use that advantage to the fullest if necessary.

With that thought in mind, Celeste replied hoarsely, "No . . . you doubt me."

"I don't! It's just that Taylor took me by surprise."

"Surprise isn't an excuse. If he had asked the same question of me, I wouldn't have hesitated to tell him how much I love you."

"Celeste . . . darlin' . . . I'm not as well or as strong as I pretend to be."

"What are you saying?"

"I'm saying that a few years ago, I would have come back at Taylor more sharply."

"That's just an excuse."

"No, it isn't. I'm tired, darlin', but it's a weariness that couldn't be helped by a good night's sleep. It's a weariness that's settled inside me. I have a feeling I'm not going to rebound from it this time."

Weariness? Celeste silently railed. The damned fool was dying!

Celeste struggled to affect a sincere denial as she said, "It isn't true! You'll get well. I know you will."

"I hope so, Celeste. I . . . I don't want to leave you alone here."

"Don't talk like that!"

"Celeste—"

"All I want to hear you say is that you didn't hesitate to answer Taylor because your feelings for me have changed . . . because you've begun doubting me."

"No. I've never loved you more."

"Do you mean it . . . you've never loved me more than you do at this moment?"

"Of course I mean it."

"Oh, Buck."

Standing abruptly, Celeste thrust herself into Buck's bony embrace. She grimaced as his body swayed weakly from the gentle force of her feigned enthusiasm. She gritted her teeth as his arms closed around her and she pressed herself against his scrawny chest. She swallowed the bile that rose to her throat as Buck raised her face to his for his kiss.

Bastard . . . adulterer . . . lecher.

She slid her arms around him and opened her lips to his.

* * *

The evening was over at last.

Taylor pushed open the swinging doors of the Last Chance and allowed Vida to precede him out onto the street. The last of the straggling customers filed out behind them. It had not missed Taylor's notice that Big John, Mitch, and Randy had left hours earlier. Nor had he missed the wink Big John had aimed in his direction before parting, or the way the other two men had shaken their heads with smiling disbelief at the sight of Vida sitting so intimately close to him.

They envied him. He supposed he would envy himself, too, if he could really collect on the promises in her eyes.

Forcing himself to cast that thought aside, Taylor scrutinized the street around them as Vida and he approached the hotel. It hadn't been easy, but the sight of Vida and him together had finally discouraged Derek Beecher for the evening. Taylor hadn't been able to learn much more about the reason for Vida's alleged interest in Derek because of the attention every damned fellow in the saloon seemed to be paying to their conversation. But he knew Vida. She felt she had something important to tell him, and he knew that if she thought it was important, it probably was.

In the meantime, he had watched and listened and struggled to stay awake during the endless minutes when Vida was not with him.

He was so damned tired.

Vida took that moment to snuggle closer against his side. His exhaustion abruptly ceased when she raised her face toward him. He said firmly, "I have the feeling our conversation should be limited when we reach your room."

Vida raised her brows daintily. "Taylor . . . I don't know what you mean."

"You know, all right." Unable to suppress a smile, Taylor dipped his head toward her for a light kiss. Astounded by the impact of the brief contact, he drew back and stared at her soberly. It was getting more and more difficult for him with Vida. She would despise knowing how possessive he had become of her; how difficult it was for him to see her pretending an interest in other men, even if it was a part of their job; and—an admission he had not previously allowed himself— how hard it had been to leave her in that New Orleans carriage after receiving the letter about Bonnie.

Vida was his partner. The association between them was *professional*.

There was that word again.

"What's wrong, Taylor?" Acknowledging the knowing leer of the hotel clerk with a smile as they turned toward the staircase, Vida continued softly, "You look like something's troubling you."

"Just the usual."

Vida frowned at his mumbled response, and it occurred to Taylor that she was beautiful even then. He watched as she withdrew a key from her bosom when they reached her door. He'd be damned if at that moment he didn't envy that worn piece of metal.

Vida preceded him inside and closed the door behind them. "The usual?" she asked.

"Skip it, Vida." Irritated by her question, he said, "What did you want to tell me?"

"You certainly are tired."

"I'm not that tired, so be careful."

"Be careful?"

Ignoring her question, he pressed, "Did you have something to tell me?"

"Don't you want to make yourself comfortable first?"

"No."

Vida shrugged. "Well, I intend to."

Sitting casually on the bed, she bent down to remove her satin slippers. Taylor took a stabilizing breath as her bosom bulged at the neckline of her dress.

Vida straightened up when she saw the direction of his stare.

"Taylor, I thought we were past that in our relationship."

"Well, you were wrong." His response more harsh than he intended, he demanded, "What did you want to tell me?"

"Taylor!" Her feet bared, Vida took the few steps to his side. She was again frowning as she said, "You *are* angry." She paused. "Are you angry that I followed you?"

"No, but—"

"But what?"

"I'm not angry that you followed me," Taylor responded flatly.

"Well, that's good, because I don't intend to leave Lowell yet."

Taylor looked at Vida's resolved expression. Of course. He hadn't expected her to say anything else.

"Because I found out something very interesting tonight." Vida sat on the side of the bed and pulled Taylor down beside her as she continued, "You probably suspected that Derek Beecher is one of the Last Chance's best customers. What you might not know is that he always seems to have a pocketful of money although he doesn't have a job as far as anyone in Lowell can tell."

Briefly silent, Taylor then said, "That doesn't mean much."

"He considers himself a ladies' man."

"A ladies' man?"

"He tells anybody who'll listen that beautiful women are attracted to him."

"Like you."

Vida smiled. "Like me."

"That's just barroom talk, Vida."

"I don't think so. I had a feeling about him, so I made it my business to get him talking pretty freely before you came in."

Refusing to ask how she had accomplished that, Taylor said, "So?"

"Derek bragged about a beautiful blonde woman he's been 'satisfying' for a while . . . a woman with a sick old man for a husband who wasn't able to do for her what Derek did."

"That doesn't mean—"

Vida interrupted to continue, "He said the old man thinks that butter won't melt in her mouth, but the old man doesn't know her like he does. He said he was useful to this woman in the past—but he got edgy when I asked him how. I got him to admit that the situation changed recently, and now she's starting to think she can do without him."

"That still doesn't mean—"

"Let me finish." Vida added, "Derek said that this blonde young woman came from New Orleans, that she intends to go back to the high life there when the old man dies. The way he was talking, it looked like she wasn't expecting it to take much longer."

"You believe this Beecher fellow. You think he was telling you the truth."

"Yes, I do."

"You think the old man is my father, and the blonde woman he's talking about is Celeste."

"I think that's a reasonable conclusion. Everybody in town describes Celeste as beautiful, blonde, and as nasty and cold as a winter day to everyone but your father."

"You're good, Vida, but all I can say is that my father would take exception to your conclusion. He thinks Celeste loves him. Besides, there's never been any talk of Celeste being unfaithful."

"It seems to me Derek has changed that . . . and as far as your father is concerned, something tells me he wouldn't be the best judge of Celeste's character." Vida hesitated, then asked gently, "Would it bother you, Taylor, if Celeste *is* the woman Derek was talking about?"

Taylor looked down into Vida's dark, empathetic gaze as he considered her question soberly. There were times when she could see right through to his soul with those eyes, and this was one of them. He knew there was no use trying to avoid the truth as he said, "I'm not sure if it would bother me. My father is an arrogant old bastard who deserves anything he gets, but"—Taylor shook his head—"he's an old man, and he believes in Celeste."

"More than he believes in his sons?"

Taylor did not respond.

"I'm sorry, Taylor."

"I'm sorry, too." Taylor added, "And I'm not in the mood to talk anymore."

"That isn't all I've got to tell you. Derek—"

"And I'm too tired to hear anything else about Derek right now, if you don't mind." Suddenly past exhaustion, Taylor said, "All I can think about at this moment is this bed I'm sitting on."

"Taylor—"

Overwhelmed by a need beyond desire, Taylor heard himself say, "I'd like to stay—just to rest for a little while, Vida."

Vida's gaze was unreadable when she responded, "I thought you were anxious to go home."

Taylor smiled wearily. "The truth is, I don't know anywhere else where I feel more at home than when I'm with you."

"Taylor—"

"Just for a little while, darlin'."

Taylor saw the hesitation in Vida's gaze. He noted the exact moment when her hesitation vanished, and he slid his arms around her. Drawing her with him, he lay back on the bed and pulled her close.

Vida was lying beside him, her head on the pillow next to his when Taylor closed his eyes.

Vida in his arms, and a soft bed underneath them.

But their relationship was professional.

Professional.

Damn.

Chapter 5

Taylor opened his eyes to the dim light of sunrise. Momentarily disoriented, he looked at the woman lying asleep on the bed beside him, her head resting on the pillow only inches from his.

Vida.

Her dark, unbound hair lay in glistening disarray in the dim light, the incredible length of her lashes were like dark fans against the rise of her cheekbones, her slender nostrils quivered with each breath, and her full, enticing lips were slightly parted.

Was he dreaming?

How many times had he had this same fantasy?

How many times had cold reality dismissed it?

Taylor turned toward her. He slid his body against her lush warmth and pressed his mouth lightly to hers.

She did not fade into the shadows.

He pressed his kiss deeper, and Vida's lips separated further, allowing his kiss. She felt so good in his arms . . . so right as he drew her closer to caress her fluttering eyelids with his lips, to trace the curve of her cheek, and then to return to her lips with renewed hunger. The rise of her breasts warmed his chest, and he slid his lips over the white, firm flesh. He bathed it with his kiss, then suckled the erect crests lightly.

This was a dream come true, and he did not question the moment as his caresses grew more intimate, as he devoured her with his kiss. Vida was in his arms in a way she had never been before . . . in a way he had not allowed himself to consciously entertain. She was his, totally, as he raised her skirt and slid his hand into the delicate undergarment beneath.

She was warm and moist to his touch. She was ready for him . . . and he was more than ready. In a moment he would—

Loud voices sounded in the hallway, and Taylor's head jerked up. The voices rose sharply, followed by the pounding of heavy fists and the thudding of bodies against the wall as a fight ensued.

Fully awake now and breathing heavily, Taylor looked down at Vida to see her draw back from him with a gasp of dismay. Her expression raised an ache inside him so deep that the pain was almost physical. "Vida, I'm so sorry," he whispered. "I didn't intend . . . I don't know what happened just now, except that it felt so damned good to hold you in my arms."

"I know what happened." Vida drew back further, struggling to regain her composure. As breathless as he, she adjusted her gown as she whispered in reply, "You needed somebody, and I was here. I can understand that . . . but . . . but I don't want to be just a body to you, Taylor. Can you understand that, too?"

Could he?

Maybe.

"Taylor?"

"You'd never be just a body to me, Vida."

Vida's smile trembled as she whispered, "I almost was."

"No."

"Think about it."

Taylor stared at Vida's beautiful, sober face. If she only knew how often he had thought about it.

But Vida was trembling, her feelings clearly visible. She was upset. She felt somehow betrayed, and the ache inside him tightened. He said sincerely, "I don't know what else to say, except I'm sorry."

Vida did not respond.

Giving her an embarrassed smile, Taylor whispered, "The truth is, you're just more than I can handle sometimes."

"I'll remember that."

Would she? He almost wished she wouldn't.

That thought lingered as Taylor pushed himself to the side of the bed and reached for the boots he had managed to shed sometime during the night. Ready, he stood up and turned to see Vida standing behind him, her expression sober and controlled. He was about to leave when she said unexpectedly, "You didn't let me finish what I was saying last night."

His response sharper than he intended, Taylor said, "The last thing I want to talk about right now is Derek Beecher."

"You'll want to hear this." Vida continued insistently, "You didn't ask what made me believe that Derek's talk about this blonde woman was connected to your father."

"I thought you'd explained that."

"There's more. It was Derek's indirect connection to the Texas Star that caught my attention."

Taylor went still. "To the Texas Star?"

"Derek struck up a relationship with a man called Bellamy—the same man who tried to kill Jace Rule on the Texas Star—the same man who kidnapped Honor Gannon, your half-sister, from the Texas Star and used her as a hostage in order to trap Rule."

"What?"

"Bellamy and Derek were strangers when Bellamy came to town. I've accepted that as fact, but they became as close as 'two peas in a pod' as soon as they met . . . drinking together, whoring together." Vida paused again, her gaze intent. "I asked myself why, and the answer was simple. They shared something in common, Taylor . . . something which was definitely underhanded and related to the business Bellamy wanted to accomplish on the Texas Star."

"What're you saying?"

"Think, Taylor! Bellamy was proved to be a professional killer. He had a job to do in Lowell, and he wouldn't hang around any longer than was needed in order to accomplish it. The only reason he would've been interested in an obnoxious fellow like Derek was if he could get information from him."

"Information? Like what?"

Her patience waning, Vida pressed, "Derek drinks too much. He must've said something that caught Bellamy's ear and made Bellamy realize Derek could tell him things about the situation at the Texas Star that would be helpful, things he couldn't learn elsewhere. Where else would Derek get information like that, except from the young, blonde woman he was servicing?"

"That's all supposition."

"Two and two are four, Taylor."

Silent for a moment, Taylor said, "Bellamy was a killer?"

"Right."

"If you're right about everything you're thinking, Derek may be a killer, too."

Vida nodded, and Taylor's expression tightened. "You believe what you're saying is true—that Beecher might be a killer—and you're still baiting him?"

"I can handle him."

"No!"

"What do you mean, no?"

Taylor grasped Vida by the shoulders, a knot of fear twisting in his gut as he demanded, "I don't want you taking any chances by getting close to that man if you think he could be a killer."

"I said, I can handle him."

"I don't care what you said."

"Taylor, this isn't the first time I've handled a situation like this."

"But it's the first time you're doing it for me!" Taylor paused to regain his composure, then tilted Vida's face up to his to say more calmly, "I don't want you putting yourself at risk for my sake, Vida."

"It's for my sake, too, you know." Candid, Vida said without blinking an eye, "You know I could have any man I want . . . especially as a partner at Pinkerton. Allan wouldn't deny me any choice I would make, and you also know that there isn't an agent on Allan's rolls who wouldn't jump at the chance to work with me." Vida paused before continuing, "But the truth is, I want *you*, Taylor. We're a good fit as partners. We work well together because our responses are instinctive, immediate, and in tune with each other. It's safe and comfortable for both of us that way, and that's the way I want it to stay."

"You don't have to get involved in my situation in Lowell in order to keep me as a partner."

"Maybe I do."

"Vida . . . I don't want you getting mixed up with Derek Beecher."

"But you can't stop me, can you?"

Briefly silent, Taylor spoke in a softened tone as he entreated, "Listen to me . . . please. I wouldn't be able to live with myself if something happened to you."

"Then you should understand that I feel the same way," Vida responded just as softly.

Suddenly angry, Taylor snapped, "You have an answer for everything, but the truth is, you're just a hard-headed witch who doesn't have the sense to realize she could be heading for trouble!"

"I suppose I could say almost the same thing about you, couldn't I, Taylor?"

Taylor stared down at Vida's disheveled beauty for long seconds. His small smile was fleeting when he finally surrendered to her relentless logic and said, "What am I going to do with you, Vida?"

Slipping his arms around her with heartfelt concern, Taylor whispered against her hair, "You're right, of course. I can't stop you from doing what you think you should. All I can say is that I want you to be careful. Especially careful . . . for me . . . because I meant what I said. You're special to me."

Taylor brushed Vida's mouth with his, then turned silently to the door without waiting for her reply.

*   *   *

She didn't like it. Not one bit!

Celeste drove her buggy down the familiar trail toward the rendezvous cabin which had become so familiar to her. Her lips tight, she fought to contain her annoyance. Buck had had a difficult night and was still sleeping when she left. She hadn't stopped to consider what excuse she would fabricate for her leaving when he awakened, but whatever she said, he would accept it. She had no concerns there.

Taylor hadn't returned to the ranch from his night on the town yet, but that didn't bother her. Rather, she was irritated to be making this same trek for the second time. She had raised the signal for Derek to meet her, but he hadn't been there when she'd gone to the cabin a day earlier. It wasn't like him not to jump at the chance to see her, and she resented the possibility that he was deliberately making her wait.

Celeste considered that thought with brows knit. Derek had better be there this time or she'd know the reason why.

She rounded the bend in the trail, then smiled stiffly at the sight of Derek's mount tied up at the rear of the cabin. Her good humor restored, she approached the cabin briskly and reined up. Her smile gradually faded when Derek did not immediately appear in the doorway with the salacious expression she had come to expect.

Her irritation increased when the door of the cabin remained closed as she stepped down from the buggy and approached it.

No, she didn't like this at all.

Celeste paused as the door of the cabin slowly opened and Derek was visible at last. She was looking her best in the crisp green cotton she had recently had shipped from New Orleans, and she knew it. She had purposely worn that particular garment because it emphasized her bosom in a way that appeared innocently demure, because it clung to her minute waistline enticingly before sweeping liberally to the floor with a fabric just sheer enough to allow the shadow of her long, slender legs to show through . . . and because the garment was easy to remove.

Celeste paused to allow Derek the full impact of her appearance. Stunned when he walked back into the cabin with scarcely a glance, she followed him inside and closed the door behind her. She asked sharply, "What's wrong, Derek?"

"Nothing's wrong." Derek looked up at her, his mood obviously foul. "What do you want?"

"What do I want?" Taken aback, Celeste replied, "I thought we had established a mutually profitable agreement between us—it's not just what *I* want."

"Yeah . . . well, it ain't been so profitable for me lately."

"For me either," Celeste said haughtily, "but I thought I was providing you with 'special benefits' worth more than money."

"Nothing's worth more than money." Derek surprised her by adding with a snarl, "Besides, maybe I got other prospects that might work out pretty good if I wasn't at your beck and call."

"Other prospects? Is that why you took your time responding to my summons?"

"I got more to do than just sit around and wait for you to 'summon' me."

"Oh, really? Like what?"

"Like . . . wouldn't you like to know?"

"Don't tell me you've got yourself a woman."

"Why?" Derek took an aggressive step. "Is that so hard to believe?"

Stunned at the unexpected stab of jealousy that scorched her, Celeste laughed and said, "Honestly? I'd like to see what this enticing piece of femininity looks like."

"She looks a helluva lot better than you!"

Celeste's smile faded. "I don't believe you."

"No? Well, believe it. And she don't want to share what I got to offer with somebody who just calls me whenever she gets an itch she can't scratch."

Aghast, Celeste snapped, "You told this harlot about me?"

"I ain't that stupid—and she ain't no harlot!"

"You're trying to tell me a beautiful, respectable woman is so hot for your body that she wants you all to herself?"

"That's about it." Derek shot Celeste a dismissive glance. "And I figure she'd be worth the trouble."

Stunned, needing time to recover from her surprise, Celeste said, "Who is this paragon?"

"Nobody you know."

"How can you be sure?"

"Because she's new in town. And there ain't a man who sets eyes on her who ain't glued to her trail . . . including that *stepson* of yours."

"Taylor?"

"Yeah. But she as much as said she'd throw him over the minute I gave her the word that she wouldn't have to share me."

Taylor's tall, tightly muscled image flashed into Celeste's mind. She remembered her own reaction to the impact of his startling blue eyes and the purely masculine heat he exuded. If not for the fact that she despised the blood flowing in Taylor's veins, she knew she would have enjoyed making every male inch of him quiver.

Celeste compared that man mentally with the filthy degenerate standing in front of her. A thought occurred to her abruptly.

"This woman . . . she's not the new saloon girl at the Last Chance that I've been hearing so much about, is she?"

Derek's head snapped up revealingly. "Maybe."

"You fool—"

"I ain't no fool, and I ain't no puppet waiting for you to pull the strings, either!"

"She's a tramp . . . a saloon girl . . . a woman who uses her body as a tool to support herself. You said Taylor was on her trail last evening. Well, he didn't come back to the ranch last night, so whose bed do you think he was sleeping in?"

"As if you're any different."

Celeste walked slowly toward him. Silently smarting at his response, she shrugged her dress off her shoulders and said softly, "But this woman can't do for you what I can, and you know it."

"Yeah?" Derek took a step backward as he continued, "That ain't the way it looks to me."

"Derek . . ." Celeste inched closer. "Do you want me to prove it to you?"

"No." Derek shook his head. "The deal we made ain't put money in my pocket for a long time now. I figure it's time to start looking elsewhere."

"Don't make any quick decisions you might regret,

Derek." Derek's body odor assaulted Celeste's nostrils sharply as she stopped a hairsbreadth from him. Perversely, it increased her heat, as did the sensual flicker of his eyelids as she boldly curled her palm around the swelling bulge between his thighs. Her own heartbeat escalated in time with his shortened breaths as she caressed him and whispered, "I know how to make you ache for me . . . and then how to make all that aching more than worthwhile." She smiled. "You know I can do it, don't you?"

Manipulating him more intimately when he did not reply, she demanded softly, "Don't you?"

"Yeah . . . I guess so."

Celeste heard Derek's low grunt when she abandoned the hardened bulge and slipped her dress down to her waist. She knew she had won when she cupped her perfect breasts in her hands and whispered, "Yours for the taking, Derek . . . and so much more."

He was on her in an instant, and Celeste gasped with the surge of pure animal lust that assaulted her. She dug her nails into his back, groaning, encouraging his primitive ministrations.

Thrust suddenly backwards against the cot behind her, Celeste moaned her satisfaction as Derek's heavy body fell atop her. He tore at her clothes and then at his own, and she allowed his rioting passion. She smiled triumphantly when he jammed himself inside her, then joined him in the savage rutting that brought them both to grunting consummation so hot and fast that it was over almost before it had begun.

Derek rolled back against the cot beside her, and Celeste looked at him coldly. His breathing was still ragged when she climbed on top of him with a determined smile, straddling him as she said, "I'm going to make sure you won't forget this morning so easily, Derek. I'm going to make sure each time that harlot looks at you, you'll think of me." When Derek did not respond, Celeste whispered, "Do you hear me, Derek?"

He nodded.

"Speak to me."

"I hear you."

"Tell me you want what I'm offering."

"I want it, all right."

"Tell me you'll be at my 'beck and call' as long as I need you."

"I ain't—"

Celeste made an attempt to get off him, but Derek held her fast.

She demanded, "Tell me!"

"I'll be here any time you call me."

"That's what I wanted to hear." Celeste slid down Derek's body with the trailing whisper, "Get ready, Derek . . . because I've just begun."

Vida gave her image a last-minute check in the dresser mirror before preparing to leave her room. The sun was shining brightly against her window shade, but her mood was no match for its brilliance as she reviewed the morning's events again in her mind. She had been unable to make herself move when Taylor walked out of her hotel room earlier that morning. The warmth of his arms holding her close had lingered, as had the bittersweet memories that had followed.

She had awakened to his kiss . . . a kiss that was

sweet and searching, and she had indulged it because she had been searching, too. All conscious thought swept from her mind, she had known only the sensation of Taylor's lips against her eyelids, the curve of her cheek, her breasts. Overwhelmed by emotions formerly held strictly in check, she had returned his kiss, wanting . . . needing more. Swept by heady yearning, she'd had no thought beyond the moment, no need greater than the one consuming her—until harsh reality returned with the sound of angry shouts and thudding fists in the hallway beyond.

She remembered Taylor's expression so clearly after the startling interruption that brought them both to their senses. He had appeared as stunned as she by what had transpired between them.

He'd said he was sorry . . . but she knew Taylor would never fully comprehend how sorry she was, too. What she had left unsaid when speaking to him afterwards was that she would not have been able to bear the thought of becoming nothing more to him than another in a long line of temporary liaisons.

He had said she was *special* to him.

She was uncertain if that word amply described her feelings for him.

The bond between them was rare. She needed no one to tell her that it bound them together in a way that was totally intangible, but in a way that was stronger than any alliance either of them had formed with other people. She would not—*could not*—risk damaging it.

Holding that thought, Vida had bathed Taylor's scent from her body and prepared to face the day. She reminded herself that Taylor needed to settle the past before he would be able to face the challenges of the future. That was necessary for him, and for that reason, it was necessary for her, too.

Brightly dressed, with a smile secured on her lips, Vida drew open her door and started down the hallway. Taylor had not said where he was going or what he intended . . . but she felt sure of one comforting fact: He would be there for her if she needed him.

The bond between them would never fail her.

Yet Vida had become certain of another truth, also. She needed to bring this matter of Taylor's past to as swift a conclusion as possible. She needed to get back on familiar footing . . . before she lost her step.

She had stayed longer than she should, but she did not regret it. With a small smile on her lips, Celeste looked back at Derek as she bathed the last of his odor from her naked body, then reached for her clothes. Derek's gaze followed her every movement although she had spent the last hour pleasuring him until he was too exhausted to continue. She had then dispatched him for water so she might bathe away her perspiration and the unmistakable smell of mating. It was a precaution she normally did not feel necessary to take, but this time was different. A knot of annoyance tightened inside her at the realization that there had been moments during their exchange when she had been out of control, when she had slipped to a point of mindless, animalistic passion.

Celeste drew on her dress, then turned toward Derek. Whatever had passed between them during those frenzied moments, she was again in control—a situation which pleased her greatly. And Derek, the poor fool, was again her slave.

Satisfied at last that her guise as a proper rancher's wife had been restored, Celeste addressed Derek directly.

"I think we're both agreed that I've proved what I can do for you, Derek." Celeste added in a more intimate tone, "You also know there's more of it in store for you—so much more—if you continue to please me as much as I please you."

"Please you . . ." Derek snarled unexpectedly, "I asked you before and I'm asking you again. What do you want, Celeste?"

"What do I want?" Unable to resist taunting him a few moments longer, Celeste whispered, "You're asking me that question in spite of the incredibly tender, intimate moments we've just shared?"

"Out with it, dammit!"

"What do you think I want?" All trace of a smile dropped from Celeste's delicate features as she said coldly, "Information! That's all you're able to provide for me at present, isn't it?"

"Information?"

"I want to know what Taylor Star is doing when he goes to Lowell. I want you to report to me every person he sees or attempts to talk to, every move he makes apart from his customary drinking and whoring."

"It seems to me you'd be in a better position than I am to know what he's about, with him working at the Texas Star."

"Taylor won't be working at the Texas Star much longer if I have anything to say about it." Celeste unconsciously nodded as she added, "But I have a feeling that even if he's thrown off the ranch, he won't just disappear. There's something about him. I don't like him, and I don't trust him, either. He's after something—maybe to get back into his father's good graces—but I'll be damned before I'll let that happen!"

"You're so hot . . ." Derek's smile grew briefly mocking, "But you ain't been able to get that old man to change his will like you want, no matter how hard you try."

"That situation is about to change. All I need is a few more days."

"I've heard that before."

"Have you really?" Suddenly angry, Celeste took an aggressive step toward him and snapped, "It seems to me you were considering canceling our association in favor of the promises of a saloon harlot a short time ago—until I proved to you how much more I could offer than she could." She raised her delicate brow with the question, "So, doesn't it make sense to you that I'd be saving the *best* I'm willing to give for the old man who holds the key to my future?"

Satisfied that she had reignited a spark of sensual heat in Derek, Celeste laughed and spat, "That's right, I have more tricks up my sleeve than you know, both in the bed and out of it, so don't underestimate me, Derek. That would be a very great mistake."

When Derek remained silent, Celeste demanded flatly, "I want full reports on Taylor's actions while in town. I want to know anything he does that looks in the least suspicious, do you understand?" And when he did not respond, "Answer me!"

"I understand!"

Softening her voice, Celeste added, "I proved to you that I'll make it all worthwhile for you, even before the old man is safely in his grave and I've settled his assets to our mutual advantage, didn't I?"

"Yeah, you did."

"I thought so."

Sweeping Derek with a lascivious gaze, Celeste then turned toward the door without another word. She climbed back into her buggy—satisfied that she had accomplished her purpose.

His mind far from the deeply rutted trail back to the Texas Star, Taylor rode his mount at a moderate pace. His hat pulled down low on his forehead, his compelling blue-eyed gaze oblivious to the passing landscape, and his broad-shouldered frame held erect. He recalled Big John's amused glances, and Randy's and Mitch's incredulity at his success with Vida. He had no doubt they were all waiting for him at the ranch, ready with a full round of teasing questions.

He also had no doubt his father was waiting for him, but he knew his father's questions would be entirely different. Celeste didn't like him, and his father would do anything to please her. He needed to avoid being thrown off the ranch for as long as possible. He wasn't ready to leave yet. He needed time . . . to think.

Vida returned spontaneously to mind, and Taylor's expression tightened. Refusing to review again those few moments when Vida and he had come so close, he switched his thoughts instead to the conclusions she had forced him to consider. He had heard it all before: the story of Honor Gannon's brief employment on the Texas Star ranch as cook while Madalane recuperated from her injury; Honor's relationship with Jace Rule, Lowell's present sheriff who was now her husband; and the way Bellamy had kidnapped Honor in an attempt to kill Jace Rule. Yet he had never considered the connections Vida had made:

Bellamy and Jace Rule.

Jace Rule and the Texas Star.

The Texas Star and Derek.

Derek and Celeste.

Bellamy and Derek.

Back to: Bellamy and Jace Rule.

Ending with: Jace Rule and Honor Gannon.

Taylor frowned and unconsciously drew his mount to a halt. He looked up at the position of the sun in the cloudless sky. It was mid-morning, and hands on the Texas Star didn't ordinarily attend to full chores on Sunday. He had a few hours before he needed to show up at the ranch to prove to his father that he wasn't lying drunk in a ditch somewhere.

Determined, Taylor turned his mount back toward town. If there was one man who might be able to further clarify the connections Vida had made, it would be Jace Rule. He needed to talk to Rule, and unless his instincts were failing him, there was no time to waste.

Back in town, Taylor rode down Lowell's main street, his eye on the sheriff's office formerly occupied by the aging Sheriff Carter. Carter's image returned to mind as Taylor had last seen the man: gray-haired with a perpetually squint-eyed, assessing gaze, a jowled face, and a slow but reassuring smile. Taylor had heard that Rule had saved Carter's life. He wondered if Rule was half the man or the sheriff that Carter was. He supposed he would soon find out.

As Taylor drew his mount to a halt in front of the sheriff's office, he saw movement inside. He dismounted and crossed the boardwalk in a few long strides, then knocked briefly on the office door before pushing it open. He paused in the doorway as his eyes acclimated to the darkness within, then went stock-still, unable to move when the slender woman standing behind the desk looked up at him.

She had sandy-colored hair, hazel eyes, and even features, but . . .

Taylor remained motionless as the woman spoke. "You're Taylor, aren't you?" A choked sound escaped her throat as she continued haltingly, "My name is Honor . . . Honor Gannon Rule." He saw the tear that trailed down her cheek before she brushed it away and whispered, "I know . . . it's a shock. I look just like Bonnie."

Freed from his immobility by the sound of Bonnie's name, Taylor walked around the desk and stood looking down at Honor. Reacting instinctively, he encircled her slenderness with his arms and hugged her fervently tight. He felt her trembling—or was it his own? Honor looked up at him and stammered, "I'm so sorry about all this, Taylor. I didn't intend to disrupt your lives when I came here. I just wanted to meet Buck Star so I could understand how it all happened, how my mother's life could have been changed from the moment she met him. I expected to leave as soon as I exposed him to the town as an adulterer—but when I arrived, nothing was the way I thought it would be. I met Cal, and my heart went still. Then I met Buck, and everything seemed to take its own course after that. I wish it all could have been different. I wish—"

"Nothing is ever the way we wish it could be. I understand that more than you realize, just like I wish I hadn't been such a damned hardheaded fool about meeting you." Hardly able to believe he was speaking the words, Taylor said thickly, "The trouble was, I didn't know . . ." He paused, then managed a smile as he whispered, "I just never thought I would ever see Bonnie again."

"I'm not Bonnie."

"I know, but—"

"Taylor, please . . . don't be misled! I may look like Bonnie, but I'm nothing like her. Cal told me about Bonnie. She was sweet and loving and forgiving. I'm not. I'm tough. I have a hard, determined streak, and I—"

"And you're my sister. I've never been more sure of anything than I am of that right now."

"Taylor—"

"Aren't you?"

Suddenly surrendering to that ultimate truth, Honor hugged him tightly. She rasped against his chest, "To find two brothers I never knew . . . how could I have been so lucky?"

Later, his emotions under strict control, Taylor sat across from Honor in the office stillness, silently marveling at her expressions as she spoke. Her intensity, the open honesty in her gaze, the unexpected flicker of her smile—they were familiar to him in so many ways. They freed bittersweet memories imprisoned by a painful past.

"I don't know anything about the letters that brought you and Cal home," she said soberly, "and I can't tell you anything more about the situation at the Texas Star than I've already said. Buck threw me off the ranch when he found out who I was, and I haven't been back since."

144

Taylor prodded softly, "That isn't the way I heard it. Buck didn't just throw you off the ranch. He told you to decide between Cal and him, but the choice didn't go his way. That's closer to the truth, isn't it?"

"Maybe . . ." Honor looked at him soberly. "But to choose between a man who coldly declared he didn't love my mother even at the moment when I was conceived, and the brother who had accepted me lovingly, without hesitation—was there really any choice at all?"

"Maybe . . . if you were someone else."

"But I'm not. I told you, I'm tough and determined. I'm sometimes unforgiving, and I'm—"

"And you're more like Bonnie than you think you are."

"Taylor . . ."

Taylor glanced at the window, then frowned at the realization that it was approaching noon. He stood up and said, "I have to go."

"You're working at the Texas Star."

Taylor nodded.

"I suppose you have your reasons."

He nodded again.

Honor searched his gaze, then said, "Anything that Jace or I can do . . . anything . . . just let us know."

More like Bonnie than she realized.

His throat again tight, Taylor responded, "You aren't sure when Jace will be back?"

"No. He had to deliver a prisoner and stay to testify at the trial."

"I'd like to talk to him when he returns."

"I'll tell him.

Taylor turned toward the door. He heard the hint of

hesitation in Honor's voice when she asked, "I'll see you again, won't I, Taylor?"

Taylor turned back to his sister, the young woman who had quietly restored a part of him for which he had grieved. Aware that some of the driving unrest inside him was now at ease, he nodded, then walked wordlessly out onto the street.

The afternoon was hot and humid. Aware that his aristocratic face was unshaven, that his clothing was rank and stained from his inhumane confinement, and that his shirt was sticking to his back in the most common manner, Pierre Maison walked back through the doorway of his New Orleans mansion. He breathed deeply of air scented with a profusion of flowering blooms, recalling vividly the fetid odor of the prison cell from which he had just been released. Waving off his servants, he turned to the nervous lawyer at his side and stated sharply, "I will not accept your failure! Lisette did not . . ." Pierre paused to correct himself. His narrow nostrils flared with suppressed anger as he continued, "*Vida Malone* did not disappear into thin air. She went somewhere, and I want to know where that somewhere is."

"Pierre, listen to me, please." Nervous perspiration beaded his forehead as Gasper Bouchet pleaded, "You make a mistake if you believe you will be able to exact revenge from this woman without paying a heavy penalty."

"I want to know where she is."

"You say she could not have disappeared, but she seems to have done just that. She met with Allan Pinkerton as I reported. I had no difficulty having her path traced until that point, but afterwards she vanished. The woman is untraceable."

"Excuses! I will not accept them! You will find her for me and you will do it without delay. I have had my fill of waiting."

"You must remember that your release is tentative, Pierre. I pulled many strings in order to have it effected. If you make a mistake—"

"I do not make mistakes." Grimacing at his unthinking statement, Pierre again corrected himself by saying, "I made *one* mistake, and that was to trust the beautiful *Lisette Tordeau*. But I have learned from that error in judgment, and I do not intend to make another."

"Then why do you want to—"

His haughty expression transcending his disheveled appearance, Pierre snapped, "*I* am the one who asks the questions here, and you are the person who answers them. Is that understood?"

"Pierre—"

"Is that understood?"

Retreating a significant step backward, Gasper nodded, "Of course I understand."

"Then find her!"

"But—"

"I said . . . find her."

Turning toward the servants who stood in a nearby doorway awaiting his command, Pierre ordered, "Prepare a bath for me so I may wash the prison stench from my body. Then ready my clothes and summon my secretary." Turning back to Gasper, he continued, "I will need my secretary to send out invitations to the 'welcome home' soiree I will be hosting for myself, a soiree larger and more elaborate than any I have ever given. There will be no shortage of guests at my party. No one will dare refuse my invitation, because everyone knows that the charges brought against me will be disproved in the end."

"Pierre, you must be cautious. Your legal difficulties are more serious than you seem to realize."

His expression deadly, Pierre responded with a simple command.

"Find her."

Chapter 6

Buck walked unsteadily toward the bunkhouse as the mid-afternoon sun began a gradual descent in the cloudless sky. He grimaced at his slow progress, remembering a time when he had covered the same distance in long, firm strides. He had taken his health for granted then, just as he had taken many other things for granted in his lifetime.

Buck's frown darkened as his breathing became labored. He didn't enjoy looking back on his life. He had felt so sure about some things that he was now beginning to doubt.

Buck glanced at the kitchen window behind him, uncertain if Madalane was watching his shaky progress across the yard. Strangely, he never felt free of that woman's scrutiny. The truth was, no matter how much Celeste denied it, he had never really believed Madalane liked him—which was unusual. In the days while he was still young and handsome, he had easily won over most women with his charm.

But those days were long gone. They had disappeared, along with his deteriorating health.

Grateful to be nearing the bunkhouse at last, Buck smiled as Celeste's image appeared before his mind's eye. Few had remained true to him through the years of decline—decline that encompassed the Texas Star as well as his health. Celeste was the most prominent of those few, who also included Randy, Big John, and Mitch. She was overly possessive of him—he silently conceded that point—but that was because her first widowhood had hit her hard, making her cherish even more dearly the happiness they shared.

He remembered the first time he saw her . . . so beautiful, so innocent, so needy. Emma had died only a short time before. Emma's death had rocked his world, sending him into a vortex of grief from which he had seemed unable to extract himself. Strangely, he had never realized how much he had depended on Emma's love, how the sound of her voice and the warmth of her smile had made life worthwhile, or how empty the world would seem without her. He had made himself believe he could wash away his grief with alcohol and loose women who were only too happy to console him. He had thoughtlessly amused himself in that way so many times during his marriage. He had been truly uncertain whether Emma knew about his escapades and the many temporary liaisons he had struck with women who were susceptible to his charm—and at the time, he hadn't cared. He had known that the vows Emma and he had spoken and the children they shared would always bind them together.

Always—a time cut painfully short when Emma unexpectedly breathed her last.

Indulging his grief, he had left Cal in charge of the ranch and his younger siblings. Buck knew he would never forget the moment when Margaret Beamer came running toward Cal and him, screaming that Bonnie had fallen into a well.

His dear Bonnie was dead, too, and he had been inconsolable.

He had berated Cal for failing to watch out for her. He had sworn he would never forgive his eldest son for that; and when Cal proved his culpability by disappearing in the middle of the night before Bonnie's poor, broken body could be laid in a grave beside her mother, he had sworn he would never forgive the boy for that, either.

Taylor had been stunned and heartbroken by the double loss. But, too deep into his own grief to console him, Buck had gone his own way.

Celeste had miraculously walked into his life shortly afterwards. She had needed him, he had needed her, and their love had been inevitable.

Buck paused to catch his breath. Admittedly, he began losing Taylor the moment he met Celeste. Taylor resented his fascination with Celeste. He had vigorously protested the new marriage so soon after his mother's death.

Celeste didn't like Taylor, either.

It had not been too difficult to indulge his new young wife by sending Taylor away to school. He'd convinced himself it was the only way, that supporting Taylor and educating him was sufficient at the moment; and as time quickly passed, Celeste more than compensated for the loss of his son from his life.

Still striving to catch his breath, Buck unconsciously

shook his head. He had not envisioned a time when he would be old and sick, when he would be looking back and questioning his actions. Nor had he ever envisioned a time when his older son would return to stir up old griefs, when his younger son would come back to mock him, or when he would discover he had another daughter—only to have *her* turn her back on *him*.

Buck resumed his pace. Celeste had ridden out to take some time for herself, an exercise he encouraged. It was good for her . . . and good for him. It allowed Celeste to expend some of her youthful energy, and it allowed him time to think.

Thinking had driven him out to the bunkhouse when Randy had unexpectedly returned from the day's scheduled work.

The bunkhouse door opened as Buck stepped up onto the landing, startling both men as Randy exclaimed, "What are you doing out here, boss?"

"It's my ranch, isn't it? A better question would be, what are *you* doing back here?"

"I lost my gloves somewhere along the way and I just came back to pick up my spare pair."

"Time was when a man worked with his bare hands, not worrying about a few cuts and bruises when he was stringing wire." At the twitch of Randy's mustache, he added, "But I guess times have changed. I needed to talk to you in private anyways, and I figured this was the best chance we'd get."

"Sure, boss."

"I need to talk to you about Taylor."

Randy's expression tightened revealingly. "Taylor's doing fine. He's working hard."

Buck continued harshly, "Taylor hasn't gone to town

since last weekend, and I want you to tell me the truth. Is he doing his drinking in the bunkhouse at night?"

"Drinking? What makes you think that?"

"You're not answering my question."

"No, he hasn't been drinking in the bunkhouse. Now is that all you wanted to know?"

"No, it isn't. I want to know what you think of him."

"What do you mean?"

"What do you think I mean? I want to know if you have any idea why he came back to the Texas Star."

"He told you why. Somebody sent him a letter telling him it was time to come home."

"If there really was a letter, it wouldn't be enough to make a man come back to a place he wasn't wanted."

Silent for long moments, Randy replied, "Maybe Taylor didn't realize he wasn't wanted."

"He sure as hell gave the impression he felt that way when he decided against returning to the ranch after he finished school back East."

"Maybe he didn't come back because you didn't act like you wanted him to."

"That's what I mean! So why did he decide to come back now?"

"The letter—"

"The letter be damned!"

Randy paused again, then said simply, "The Texas Star is his home. His mother and sister are buried here."

"Which he conveniently forgot during all those years while he was amusing himself drinking and whoring."

"Like father, like son, you mean?"

Buck's face flushed hot at Randy's presumptuous remark. He snapped, "I didn't ask you for your opinion of me. I asked you what you think of Taylor and what in hell you think he's doing here."

"You want my opinion?"

"That's what I said."

"You might not like it."

"I didn't say I needed to like it."

"I think Taylor came *home* because he needed to. I think he came *home* because, like Cal, he has more of his mother in him than he has of his pa. I think he came *home* because he needed to settle the past with an irascible old man who might be dying off soon. I think he came *home* because—whether he knows it or not—he figured if he waited any longer, it would be too late."

Buck's pale eyes narrowed. "That doesn't make any sense, and you know it. Taylor hasn't made any attempt to make peace with me."

"You haven't given either Cal or him a chance."

"I don't want to talk about Cal!"

"That's what I mean."

"I said, I don't want to talk about Cal!"

"All right, but there ain't any difference between the way you treat Taylor or Cal. You let Celeste lead the way with both your sons when she—"

"And I don't want to talk about Celeste! She doesn't have any part in this."

"Doesn't she?"

"No!"

Randy shrugged. "Then I figure I've said all there is to say."

Trembling despite himself, Buck grated, "It's my sons who let me down, not Celeste."

Randy did not reply.

"Do you hear me?"

"I hear you, all right."

Buck turned unsteadily back toward the house. From behind him, he heard Randy say, "Do you want me to walk back to the house with you, boss?"

Buck did not deign to reply.

"What took you so long?" Big John's bellowing question echoed in the sunny pasture as Randy dismounted from his horse, pulled on his gloves, and walked toward the fencing. "Next time you need to go back to the bunkhouse for your gloves, I'll go instead. I'd enjoy a little break from this damned sun, too."

Uncertain whether Big John's comments were just more of his good-natured teasing, Taylor looked up in time to catch the telltale expression on Randy's face. Maybe Big John was fooling, but Randy wasn't.

Randy's silence was more telling than words as he pulled the fence wire with a strength fueled by anger, and Taylor frowned. He had been working the week long with the ranch hands in an attempt to better evaluate the condition of the ranch. It wasn't good, but that wasn't the only conclusion he had reached. He was confused. He hadn't seen Vida in a week. It was the weekend again, and he wanted to get into town to talk to her. There were so many things he needed to discuss.

Celeste—he didn't like the way she was sneaking around. He wondered how his father could trust her so implicitly.

Madalane—he had the feeling she had an agenda that she was concealing.

Both were perceptions, but they became more firmly fixed in his mind with every day that passed.

As for Buck, the old man was watching and waiting. Taylor had the feeling his father wasn't sure how to handle his return, but he knew Celeste wouldn't be satisfied until he was gone. He had no doubt Madalane had reported to Celeste that he had been looking through the bills that day. Yet the whole stack of invoices—with the will still lying in the middle—remained just where it was. Untouched. He could only suppose the reason was that his father hadn't been well enough to tackle them.

The presence of his father's will mixed in with the invoices worried him. Why should it be there except to be reviewed and changed? Did Buck plan to strike Cal's and his names from the document? He sensed, somehow, that more rested on the potential change in that will than he cared to consider.

Randy cursed aloud when the fence wire snapped back on him, and Taylor looked up. He saw Big John's reaction and noted the silence that ensued. It wasn't like Randy to lose his temper.

Waiting only until Mitch and Big John were working out of earshot, Taylor asked, "What happened when you went back to the ranch, Randy?"

Randy's head jerked toward Taylor revealingly as he said, "What are you talking about?"

"Come on. It doesn't take a mind reader to see that something happened to sour your mood."

"My mood ain't sour."

"Isn't it?" Taylor hesitated, then said, "Did you have a run-in with Pa?"

"Your pa and me . . . we got an understanding. He gives the orders and I take them."

"So?"

"So maybe I like it that way, and I don't like him coming to me asking questions that don't have nothing to do with my job here."

"Questions? What kind of questions?"

"Dammit, Taylor!" Randy slapped his hammer down onto the fence post as he continued, "That old man of yours don't want to hear the truth."

"The truth?"

"He wanted to know how you were working out, but he wasn't satisfied when I told him you were toeing the line here on the ranch. He was looking for me to tell him that you was drinking in the bunkhouse at night—probably because that wife of his has been filling his head with that kind of nonsense."

"And?"

"And he didn't like it." Randy frowned, then corrected his statement. "No, that ain't exactly right. He didn't *believe* you wasn't swilling down the liquor while all of us watched. And he doesn't know why you came home."

"I told him why."

"Yeah, well, like I said, he still wants to know why." Randy hesitated, then said, "I think the truth is, down deep he doesn't know why you should care enough to bother coming back."

"Neither do I."

Randy gave a short laugh. "Well, that's tellin' it like it is." He added, "That's what I tried to do, too, but it didn't matter none what I said. Celeste came out on top in the end."

"Celeste—"

"She can't do no wrong in his eyes. Hell, the man has to be blind!"

"Maybe."

"There's no maybe about it! There's nothing that woman can do to turn your pa against her."

"Maybe."

His expression sober, Randy said softly, "It's a hard thing to accept, but you got to put your mind to the truth of it, Taylor. That woman has your pa dancing to her tune, and that's the way it's going to stay. So, if that's the reason you're working yourself so hard here—hoping you can change things—it ain't going to happen."

Randy . . . more a father to him than his own father had ever been.

Taylor replied, "Don't worry about me, Randy. I'm doing what I need to do, and that's right for me now."

His expression sincere, Randy replied softly, "I hope so, boy . . . for both you and Cal."

Taylor turned back to his work, his throat tight. They were where they should be and doing what they needed to do—Cal, himself, and Honor, too. He knew that without any doubt.

But then there was Vida . . .

The applause was deafening as Vida walked away from the piano, leaving Harvey with a wink and a smile. She sauntered toward the card tables, unwilling at the moment to approach the crowded bar and the eager cowpokes already awaiting her despite the early evening hour. If she were truthful, her guise as the local chanteuse and the most sought-after woman at the Last Chance was already growing old.

Or maybe it wasn't only that.

Vida inadvertently glanced up at the swinging doors as she caught movement there out of the corner of her eye. She looked away, disappointment weighing heavily on her heart. Taylor hadn't been back to town since he'd left her room the previous Sunday morning. She remembered the circumstances of his departure, and she wondered what was keeping him away, then chided herself for doubting him. Yet she couldn't count the times that same doubt had arisen when the saloon doors swing open to reveal another anonymous face.

No, Taylor had made it clear to her that working with her meant as much to him as it did to her.

But he'd also said, *the truth is, you're just more than I can handle sometimes.*

Was she really? Had working with her become too heavy a burden for Taylor?

Vida sighed. To make matters worse, she hadn't learned anything new or anything that would prove her suspicions about Derek one way or another since Taylor had left. She had, however, noticed a distinct change in Derek's behavior. Although he had been in the saloon almost every day, his gaze following her, he had hung back from approaching her at the beginning of the week. Yet as the week had worn on, he had become progressively more aggressive, and she—

"Where're you going, Vida?"

Speak of the devil.

Derek's rasping voice turned Vida with a forced smile toward his perpetually oily face. He gripped her arm familiarly as he continued, "I saw you sigh a minute ago, and I figured you was thinking about me again. Was I wrong or was I right?"

Vida did not bother to hide her displeasure as she removed her hand from his arm and said, "If I said you were wrong, you wouldn't believe me. And if I said you were right, I'd be lying."

Surprising her, Derek laughed. "That's what I like about you, darlin'. You've got the quickest mind I ever saw."

"Do I?" Vida took the plunge and stepped closer to the obnoxious fellow as she said, "What about that blonde woman you did so much talking about? Doesn't she have a quick mind?" Answering her own question, she said, "Oh, I forgot. It isn't her mind you're interested in."

Derek's smile changed to a snarl as he said, "I didn't come here to talk about her. I made a mistake talking about her in the first place, and as far as I'm concerned, she's off limits in any conversation we're going to have."

"Is she? Well, maybe we don't have anything to talk about, then."

Derek gripped her arm again, his tone suddenly menacing. "Yes, we do. You've been putting me off this whole week while you've been having a high old time with every cowpoke in this saloon who offers you a drink, and I'm getting tired of it!"

"Are you?" Her gaze hardening, Vida responded, "Well, maybe I'm getting tired of it, too . . . tired of your pretended interest in me while you've got that woman on the side. You don't fool me. You didn't come near me at the beginning of this week because you and your blonde 'lady friend' met up someplace this weekend, and she gave you a good enough time to keep you happy for a while."

At Derek's unexpectedly revealing flush, Vida laughed aloud and said, "I was right, wasn't I?" Without waiting for his reply, she continued, "So you're feeling the itch again and you're looking for me to fill in. Well, it's not going to happen. Unlike you, none of the fellas I've been spending time with this past week have been looking for more than I'm willing to give. They've been as honest with me as a woman here can expect, wanting no more than a good time at the bar." Vida swept Derek with a deprecating glance. "You're looking for a good time, all right, but it wouldn't stop here."

"You're acting like all your good times end at the saloon doors, but I know different. What about that Taylor Star? He left with you Saturday night, and he didn't get back to the Texas Star until near noon the next day. I figure he spent his time in your bed, and he didn't do much sleeping, either."

"How do you know when Taylor got back to the Texas Star?"

"I got my ways."

"Well, maybe your 'ways' can mind her own business!"

"That's fine with me, just as long as we don't talk about nobody else . . . just you and me."

"There isn't any 'you and me'—unless you want to make it *only* you and me. I don't take second place to any woman. Does that make it clear enough?"

Vida noted that a bearded cowpoke at the bar was starting toward them with a frown. Addressing the concerned cowpoke as he neared, she said, "Don't worry, Billy. Derek and I are done talking. I was just telling him I'm going to join you for a drink." She turned toward Derek as the cowpoke stopped beside her. "Isn't that right, Derek?"

A sneer his only reply, Derek walked back to the far end of the bar. Vida cast him a dismissive glance, then turned toward the waiting cowpoke with a smile.

"Did you talk to her?"

Taylor scrutinized Cal's sober expression as they sat their horses, side by side, in the familiar Rocky W glade. His whistled call had brought his brother out for their meeting as it had once before, and it occurred to Taylor that he hadn't doubted for a moment that Cal would respond to his summons. He supposed it should seem strange that their years of bitter separation had disappeared with the first words they spoke to each other, or that the instinctive brotherly trust in each other should return as well, but it didn't. He knew that aside from their similar stature, they didn't look much like brothers, with Cal resembling their ma so much that it sometimes hurt, and with him carrying the dark hair and light eyes of his father's side. Yet he also knew that outward appearance was where the disparity stopped.

Taylor took a breath and continued, "Yes, I spoke to Honor. You were right and I was wrong, Cal. I realized it the moment I saw her."

"Because she looks like Bonnie?"

Taylor was momentarily unable to respond.

"It goes deeper than her looks, Taylor. I sensed there was something special about Honor even before she told me who she was." Cal added hoarsely, "I didn't doubt her for a minute when she said she was my sister, because I could see it in her eyes . . . that she had Bonnie's sympathetic heart."

"She says she's hard and unforgiving."

"Maybe Honor had to be hard while she was growing up, and maybe it was good for her to be unforgiving for a while, because it brought her to Lowell. But that's all in the past, because Jace Rule and she have made a place for themselves here. She's home, no matter what Pa has to say about it."

Not needing to voice his agreement, Taylor nodded. He asked, "Did you get a chance to talk to Bill Leeds yet about Pa's will?"

"I did. He said he couldn't tell me what was in Pa's original will, of course; but I'd say he's not too fond of Celeste, because he added that Pa hasn't made any changes to his will as far as he knows, and he seemed kind of pleased about it."

Taylor responded thoughtfully, "Celeste is losing patience with having me at the ranch, and Pa's will might be one of the reasons. She's making it hard for Pa, and he's looking for an excuse to get rid of me."

"That damned old man!"

"That doesn't change anything as far as I'm concerned, Cal. However Pa tries to get rid of me, I don't intend to leave until I find out who sent those letters, or until we can find some way to . . . to settle things for us all."

To settle things.

Taylor knew that Cal would understand his ambiguity. It had been a part of their lives for so long.

The firm clasp of Cal's hand in his confirmed that silent thought before they parted.

* * *

The evening was stretching tediously long. Guilt briefly surged as Vida looked up into the smiling face of the cowpoke now beside her. His name was Jake. He worked on the Lazy A, he was young, footloose, and happier to have her returning his smile than she deserved.

Because she was using him.

She had carefully shed Billy, her protector from earlier in the evening, when she realized Derek was focusing his obvious resentment on him. She had since cautiously spread her attentions equally among the fellows at the bar. As a result, Derek was presently focusing his enmity on *her*.

As if he had any right at all.

The sheer presumption of the obnoxious fellow almost erased her smile as Vida raised her glass again to her lips. She was only too aware that although the drinks were watered down for her benefit, sheer volume was making its effect known. Uncomfortable with the feeling, she forced a laugh as Jake moved closer. She saw the cowpoke's smile dim the moment before a strong arm slipped around her waist from behind, effectively moving Jake aside as a deep, familiar voice whispered into her ear, "Were you waiting for me, darlin'?"

Was she ever.

Taylor motioned for a bottle and two glasses, as Vida turned toward Jake to whisper, "Excuse me, darlin'. I have a previous commitment."

Vida did not wait to assess Jake's expression as Taylor led her toward an empty table in the rear of the room, his arm gripping her tight against his side. Instead, she looked up lovingly into the incredible blue of his eyes as she whispered, "What in hell kept you, Taylor?"

"Business, darlin'." Taylor dipped his head to brush her lips with his. Was it her imagination, or did his kiss linger a moment longer than necessary?

Seating her, Taylor drew his chair close to hers and kissed her again, this time more deeply than before. She struggled to hide her breathlessness when he drew back and glanced down at her moist lips to say, "You taste like cheap whisky, Vida, but I'll be damned if I ever tasted anything sweeter."

Turning her face away as his mouth again closed in on hers, Vida glanced at the empty glasses on the table and whispered, "Speaking of cheap whisky, maybe you'd better fix us a drink so Bart will be satisfied that I'm earning my keep."

"From the look of things, you've been doing a pretty good job of doing that already tonight."

"By that, I hope you mean my vocalizing." Vida raised her brow warningly. "Because I haven't come near my drinking limit."

"If you say so."

She countered, "I might be inching up on it, but I wouldn't be if it hadn't taken you so damned long to get here."

"I had something to take care of. I didn't figure my delay would be a problem."

"Dodging Derek Beecher all evening was the problem."

Vida was startled by the menace in Taylor's expression when he looked up at Derek's turned back and muttered through clenched teeth, "If that bastard's been bothering you, I'll set him straight once and for all."

"Taylor, please." Vida gripped Taylor's chin and turned him back to face her. "I told you. I can handle Derek."

Taylor repeated, "If he's been bothering you—"

"He's after me like I'm a bitch in heat, if that's what you want to know, but that's the way I want it."

"You're playing with fire."

"Maybe, but I'm not the one who's going to get burned."

"Vida—"

"Listen to me, Taylor. Derek's panting for what he figures I have to offer, and it's loosening his tongue without his even realizing it."

"What are you talking about?"

"He's jealous of you, Taylor. He knows you spent the night in my room last weekend. Do you know what that means?"

"What could it mean? He can't be the only fella who saw me leaving your room that morning."

"But he's the only fella who knows exactly when you arrived back at the Texas Star. How do you suppose he knows that?"

Taylor did not reply.

"Derek all but admitted that he spent time with his blonde mistress last weekend; and when I asked him straight out how he knew what time you got back to the ranch, he said *he had his ways*. His ways? Nobody from the Texas Star has been in town all week to say anything about when you got back to the ranch."

"So you're saying . . . ?"

"Three things should be very obvious. The first is that Celeste is his lover. The second is that she's the one who mentioned what time you got back to the ranch. The third is that she has poor taste in men."

Vida glimpsed the sadness behind Taylor's reply as he said, "I always knew my father gave up the memory of my mother for nothing more than a pretty face and a willing body."

She responded, "You wanted to know the truth, didn't you, Taylor?"

"It may be the truth, but it won't do any good if my father won't accept it."

"Maybe he would if we could prove it to him."

"I don't know if that's the way to go."

Startled by his response, Vida said, "You came here to discover who sent you that letter, didn't you? The only way I know to do that is to find out what's really going on here."

"I had other reasons for coming back, too."

"I know . . . you came to make peace with your brother." She added, "What about your sister? Have you talked to her yet?" At Taylor's surprise, she explained, "Like I said, there isn't much about the Star family that's a secret in Lowell."

"No, I guess not."

"If you've handled those things, I'd say your return has been pretty successful so far."

"Maybe."

Vida's intended response died on her lips when she noted Derek's sudden interest in the intensity of her conversation with Taylor. She responded instinctively by pressing her mouth to Taylor's with a whispered warning. Yet she was unprepared when he responded by separating her lips with his as he pulled her breathlessly close.

The din of the saloon faded from Vida's hearing as a slow lassitude overtook her. When Taylor drew back, Vida's breathing was as ragged as his. "Derek's still watching us," she mumbled.

"Thank you, Derek," Taylor responded hoarsely and kissed her again.

His chest heaving when he separated himself from her at last, Taylor whispered, "It's going to be a long night."

"Celeste, are you sleeping?"

Celeste struggled to hold back a groan. Darkness had closed in over the Texas Star. To Celeste's disgust, it was the signal for her aging husband and her to go to bed. As was her custom, she feigned sleep almost immediately in the hope of escaping his searching hands—a tactic that wasn't always effective. It appeared that tonight was going to be one of those nights.

"Celeste?"

Pretending to be asleep was no longer a possibility, so Celeste responded, "Did you speak to me, darling?"

"Yes, I did. I hope I didn't wake you up." Celeste patted his bony arm, only to be rewarded by Buck clasping her hand tightly. She inwardly grimaced. Madalane had not dispensed any of her potion to Buck for more than a month. The Negress had warned that Buck was presently so weak that even the smallest dose might be fatal. Fortunately for Celeste, Buck's health had deteriorated to the point that full recovery was out of the question. All she needed now was for him to live long enough to change his will, which the bastard still stubbornly avoided doing.

"Celeste?"

"Is something wrong, dear?"

"No, not really. I was just . . . thinking."

Thinking. The bastard had nothing else to do.

"I talked to Randy today—about Taylor."

Immediately alert, Celeste said in a voice she hoped sounded quietly sincere, "You spoke to Randy? If you were concerned about something Taylor did, why didn't you talk to me?"

"I wasn't concerned about something Taylor did. I was worried about something he might be doing."

"Oh, you mean his drinking."

"Randy said Taylor's been working hard, and he hasn't had a drink all week."

"You don't believe him, do you? Taylor probably has bottles hidden somewhere so he can go off by himself and drink himself into a stupor before he falls into bed."

"Randy would know. He said Taylor's been sober."

"What else would you expect him to say? You know how he always stands up for Taylor. The only person he's against on this ranch is me."

"That's not true. Randy doesn't know you the way I do, that's all."

"It *is* true, and you know it." Using a ploy that had never failed her, Celeste allowed a tear to fall as she whispered, "He wants to turn you against me."

"I didn't mean to upset you, darlin'." Buck wrapped his arm around her and Celeste forced herself to cuddle close to his skeletal body as he continued, "It's just that I was thinking maybe sending Taylor away to school so soon after his ma died was a mistake."

"It wasn't a mistake, Buck." Celeste drew back far enough that Buck might glimpse her tear-streaked cheek as she said, "He was unhappy here, and you provided him with an alternative place to stay, and a good education besides."

"But this was his home. I sent him away and didn't give him another thought while he was at school."

"He wasn't a child, Buck. He was fifteen years old, and he was making life miserable for us!"

"I know, but I figure all I did was make him resent me even more. Maybe I should've tried to understand him. Maybe I—"

"Maybe he should have tried to understand *you*, Buck! You were suffering much more than he was. He was young, with a whole life ahead of him, but your whole life was turned upside down. It was only a stroke of fate that brought us together so we could console each other. If Taylor really loved you, he would've understood that."

"But he had lost his mother, his sister, and then his brother."

"And you had lost your wife and your daughter, and had the hardship of knowing that your oldest son's negligence was responsible for his sister's death. Your loss was greater than Taylor's."

"But he was alone. I had you."

"He wouldn't let us enjoy our lives together! He was jealous, mean, spiteful."

"He was young. He didn't understand."

"He was selfish! He didn't love you or anybody else.

He only loved himself, and he hated you even though you did the best you could for him by sending him away to school."

"Celeste . . . was it really the *best* I could do for him? Maybe I should've tried to be more of a father to him by understanding that he was grieving, too."

"What's the matter with you, Buck?" Trembling with barely controlled rage, Celeste rasped, "Is your memory failing you? We loved each other so much, and Taylor did everything he could to ruin our happiness."

"He didn't, he only—"

"He *did!* Look at him now! That should be proof of the boy he once was. Taylor is a drunk, a saddle tramp who doesn't even own a saddle! He came here so drunk that he could hardly stand, he berated you in front of the men, and he hasn't shown an ounce of respect for you since."

"Yes, but—"

"No buts! He's a despicable human being whose only desire is to come between us. That story about his receiving a letter telling him to come home—you don't believe it, do you? He came home because he had nowhere else to go, because he's hoping to make you feel guilty enough that you'll put up with his lazy, drunken ways!"

"But—"

"Cal and Taylor are alike, two persons who are unworthy of the name *men*. They're trading on friendships you and Emma forged for them as children, but they aren't worth a damn, and you know it!"

Silence.

"Buck . . ."

Silence.

Suddenly realizing she might have gone too far, Celeste sobbed, "Oh, Buck, I'm so sorry." She clutched his wasted frame closer. "I didn't mean to be so harsh, but everything I said is true. I just can't bear to see you blaming yourself for your sons' failures. Buck . . . forgive me, please."

"Celeste, don't cry. There's nothing to forgive."

"Yes, there is. I was uncharitable . . . unkind."

"You could never be unkind, Celeste. I was the one who was unkind and thoughtless for even bringing it up."

"Buck . . ." Celeste looked up at him pleadingly. Aware that the limited light allowed him a glimpse of her magnificently contrived distress, she whispered, "I love you. I don't want anything to come in the way of our love."

"Nothing ever will, darlin'."

Aware that her expression was a dramatic masterpiece, Celeste pressed her mouth to Buck's papery lips. She steeled herself as she pressed her kiss deeper and felt Buck's growing response. She pretended a groan, then prepared herself for another of Buck's groping failures as he drew her nearer. She closed her eyes, telling herself the night would prove worthwhile after all, because Buck had provided her with the perfect reason to bring up his will again. And this time she wouldn't accept any excuses.

Vida stumbled over a rut in the unpaved street. Taylor reacted with a raised brow. "I thought you said you hadn't drunk your limit tonight."

Vida shot him a threatening glance, but she did not bother to reply.

Arm in arm, they stepped up onto the boardwalk in front of the hotel as the saloon went dark behind them. They boldly entered the lobby without bothering to acknowledge the sleepy clerk's knowing glance and walked up the staircase to Vida's room.

Vida unlocked the door and pushed it open. Her heart pounded, but she refused to react as Taylor entered automatically behind her. She lit the lamp, conscious that a tense awareness between them had heightened as the evening waned. She turned toward him to say, "I suppose you need to stay for a while. Everybody will be expecting it after the show we put on tonight."

And what a show it had been.

Vida looked up at Taylor, her lips still throbbing from his kisses, her body sensitized to his touch. What she had originally meant to be a mere charade for Derek's benefit, had somehow gotten out of control. Now, looking up at Taylor's suddenly sober expression, she saw a look in his eyes—

"I don't think so." Taylor spoke abruptly. "That might not be such a good idea tonight."

"What?"

Taylor's voice was tight as he said, "Maybe you didn't hit your limit tonight, but I'm thinking I did."

"You didn't drink that much."

"I'm not talking about drinking."

Vida swallowed, but she could not make herself move. It had felt so good to be in Taylor's arms. It had felt so right when his mouth was warm against hers. She knew they had been playacting to accomplish a purpose tonight, as they had done so many times before, but the line had became so blurred that it was difficult for her to determine where acting stopped and reacting began.

"I'm going."

Snapped from her thoughts, Vida searched Taylor's shadowed expression. "Where?"

"Anywhere but here."

The evening had been difficult for him, too, apparently. He had told her once before that she was more than he could handle sometimes—and this, evidently, was one of those times.

Vida responded with more confidence than she felt, "We're professionals, Taylor. We know what we're doing."

"I thought I did."

"Taylor . . ." Vida took a step toward him.

"Stay where you are. Because the truth is, if you take another step toward me, it may be one step too far."

"Taylor . . ."

"Hell, I'm not made of stone, Vida." Taylor's voice was ragged. His handsome face was tensely drawn and his light eyes singed her as he continued, "Right now, I don't have a thought in my head about the Texas Star, the damned letter that brought me here, or anything we were trying to prove tonight. All I can think about is how it felt to hold you in my arms, and how it would feel to carry you the few steps to that bed behind you."

"Taylor, I—"

"No, don't say anything. I know you came here to protect our professional relationship. I know how you feel about me, because I feel the same way about you. We're friends."

A knot clenched in Vida's innards.

"But I need to tell you that friendship won't be

enough for me tonight if I stay. I know you don't want it that way, and the fact is, neither do I, really."

The knot twisted painfully tight.

"You're so damned special to me, Vida. I don't want to mess things up." He turned abruptly toward the door. "I'm going."

Vida managed, "Tell me where."

"I don't know."

"To Miss Ida's fancy house?"

Taylor's glance was deprecating. "I didn't pick up that trait from my father."

"There's always Ellie."

"And I don't settle for second best."

Vida gasped as Taylor turned suddenly back toward her and snatched her up into his arms. His mouth on hers, he kissed her long and deep. His tongue caressed hers as his palms smoothed her back searchingly, as he pressed the hard bulge of his passion hot and tight against her.

Pulling back just as abruptly, Taylor was breathless as he rasped, "If anybody asks, make whatever excuse you want for the reason I left so soon . . . that I got rough—"

"No, I won't say that!"

"Then we had a lover's spat."

Able to manage no more than a nod as Taylor turned again toward the door, Vida said, "I need to know where you're going."

Taylor replied harshly, "Always the professional, needing to know where your partner is headed." His smile cold, he said, "I'm going back to the ranch, but before I do, I'm going to pick up a bottle to bring back with me. I figure that's the only way I'll get to sleep tonight."

"Don't do that, Taylor. Don't prove your father right."

Vida knew she'd never forget the way Taylor's gaze raked her before he jerked open the door, then pulled it closed behind him. Vida turned toward her bed, her throat tight. What was wrong with her?

Foolish question . . . because the answer was becoming painfully clear.

She couldn't accept second best, either.

Chapter 7

Pierre Maison stood rigidly erect as he stared at his perspiring attorney across the carved mahogany desk in his study. Elegantly dressed in clothes tailored to his lean physique, perfectly groomed and in complete control of his ire, Pierre was aware that he bore no resemblance to the disheveled, rank, odious creature that had departed the New Orleans prison. "I will not accept excuses," he said. "I want you to find her."

"I *will* find her. You have my word, but in the meantime I must insist that we discuss your defense against the crimes with which you have been charged."

"Insist all you want, but I will not be bothered with unnecessary details." Pierre waved his hand dismissively. "Make whatever payments are necessary to have the charges dismissed."

"That isn't possible this time. Too much evidence has been accumulated against you."

"Have the evidence destroyed."

"Pierre, that solution is not an option."

"It is *always* an option."

"Pierre . . ."

Rounding the desk in a few, lengthy strides, Pierre stared hotly into his solicitor's twitching expression as he rasped, "I told you, I will not discuss my *case*. I want you to handle it so I will *never* have to discuss it. I don't care what it costs. Neither do I care what it will cost for you to find out where Lisette has gone."

"I have already informed you that her name is Vida Malone."

"I prefer to think of her as Lisette."

Gasper nodded warily. "My most experienced men are on her trail. I'm doing my best."

"Your best isn't good enough."

"You must have patience."

"My patience wears thin."

"Pierre . . ."

Pierre's sudden cold smile sent a chill down Gasper's spine as Pierre said, "I have a surprise for my dear Lisette, Gasper, and I am anxious to see that she receives it. She always appreciated surprises."

"I warn you, Pierre—"

"Don't warn me! Just do what I tell you to do." Turning away from him, Pierre said unexpectedly, "You may go."

"But I—"

Pierre was no longer listening.

The sun radiated brilliantly on the yard beyond the kitchen door, but Celeste and Madalane were oblivious to its golden glow. Conversing in hushed tones, they both watched the progress of the ranch hands as they walked toward the barn after their Sunday morning breakfast. Their conversation briefly lagged as Taylor broke away from the group to walk toward the pasture beyond.

"There he goes . . . not satisfied to stay with the other *hired hands*." Celeste's expression was tight. "He pretends to work as one of the men, but he acts as if he still *belongs* here."

Madalane nodded as Celeste continued malevolently, "Taylor hopes to earn back his father's approval—I'm sure of it. Before I talked to Buck last night, Taylor had already begun making Buck doubt the way he handled the situation after Taylor's mother died."

"He could not make your husband doubt himself."

"No?" Celeste stared at her servant belligerently, then glanced back in the direction of the bedroom, where Buck still lay abed. "I told you what Buck said to me. If it had not been for my supreme strength of will in allowing Buck to try to make love to me—a failure that I knew would supersede everything else in his mind—Buck might still be questioning his treatment of Taylor all those years ago."

Madalane turned back to follow Taylor's tall figure. She whispered, "Taylor Star is a devil—like his father."

"Taylor hates me. He'll do anything to turn his father against me."

"Blood proves true."

"His claim that a mysterious letter brought him back here is nothing more than a story he concocted— I'm sure of it. Taylor came home hoping to make his father feel guilty enough to take him in. The drunken sot! How he could possibly stir Buck's regret is a mystery to me."

"Blood is thicker than water."

Her patience expiring, Celeste snapped, "All this talk of blood! My husband never cared about anyone's blood but his own!"

"Your husband is old and sick now. He has time to think. For this reason, Taylor has become a danger to you."

"He will no longer be a threat when Buck changes the beneficiary in his will today."

Hope lit Madalane's dark eyes. "He has agreed?"

"No, but he will. He—"

Celeste's words stilled at the sight of Taylor striding back from the pasture, his expression dark with anger. Her delicate jaw tightened as Taylor approached the house, took the few risers up onto the porch in a single leap, then entered the kitchen.

"What happened to the chestnut mare that was in the pasture yesterday?" he demanded.

"What business is it of yours?"

"She was ready to foal. What happened to her?"

"She was a bother. I sold her."

"Sold her?" Taylor advanced an ominous step. "Does my father know what you did?"

"Does it matter? The horse is gone. I had her picked up just before dark last night."

"While the ranch hands and I were gone."

"Not that it mattered."

"Does my father know you sold her?"

"I told you, I—"

"Answer me, dammit!"

"No, he doesn't! Nor will he care. Buck is unwell. He has turned decisions of that sort over to me."

"I don't believe you. Randy said Pa was counting on that mare's foal. She was valuable . . . probably the most valuable animal on this ranch. Her foal would be worth—"

"You waste your breath! Both the mare and her potential foal are gone, and I'm glad."

"Who did you sell her to?"

"That doesn't concern you."

"My father will—"

"Your father will do nothing. He respects my actions because he does not wish to upset me."

Towering over her, his expression going suddenly cold, Taylor responded, "We'll see about that, won't we?"

Taylor turned toward the bedroom hallway only to have Celeste halt him as she said, "My husband does not feel well. He had a difficult night and is still sleeping. He should not be disturbed."

"He'll want to hear what I have to say."

"I doubt that, especially if you wake him up to inform him of something as inconsequential as the sale of a horse. If you are so determined to speak to him, I suggest you try later when he might be in a mood to listen."

"He'll listen, all right."

Parroting Taylor's reply of moments earlier, Celeste said, "We'll see about that, won't we?"

Celeste stood firm as Taylor turned abruptly and left the house. She watched him until he disappeared into the barn, then faced Madalane, who had remained silent through the volatile exchange. "That bastard will try to turn Buck against me—but he won't succeed. I will not allow it!"

Madalane stood motionless as Celeste stomped away. The Negress stared at the bedroom doorway as it closed behind Celeste. The click of the door latch reverberated in the silence as Madalane's lips moved with a whispered promise: "Neither will I."

"What's wrong, Taylor?"

Big John halted Taylor as he entered the barn. Nearby, Randy and Mitch looked up as Taylor hesitated to reply. Taylor had awakened in a sour mood, a holdover from the previous night and his ambiguous departure from Vida. He hadn't been in any shape to talk before he left her. He had been only too acutely aware that if he didn't leave Vida's room at once, the situation would slip totally beyond his control.

Damn it all, Vida didn't have any idea what she did to him! Vida and he had pretended passion many times during the course of their professional intrigues; yet each sultry glance from Vida's black velvet eyes, each kiss, each caress now eroded his restraint to a precarious degree. After a full evening of Vida's loving attentions, the last thing he had wanted to do in the solitude of her room was talk.

The truth was, the detachment that had served him so well in the past now failed him. He needed to tell Vida how he felt, and that it was getting dangerous to pretend to want her when he wasn't sure if he was pretending or not.

What was worse, Vida was probably angry with him—which she had a right to be. He had kissed her, indulging the depth of his passion, and had then left without an explanation. He needed to go back to town to explain that he wasn't playing games, that whatever he was feeling, it was real. He had already decided that he couldn't let another day pass without straightening things out between them. He had been expecting to leave right after he checked on the mare, but Celeste had changed all that.

"Taylor, you didn't answer me. What's wrong?"

Brought back abruptly to the present by Randy's question, Taylor responded flatly, "Celeste sold the mare."

"The chestnut mare in the back pasture?" Randy shook his head, incredulous. "That can't be. Your pa was counting on that mare's foal to give a boost to the Texas Star's future. That crafty little critter is probably just hiding somewhere out of sight."

"The mare's gone. Celeste had the buyer pick it up last night after we left."

"Why would she do that? It doesn't make any sense."

"To her it probably does." Taylor glanced back at the house. "I wanted to talk to my father about it, but Celeste said he was still sleeping. I'm not sure if I should've believed her."

"Well, maybe your pa is sleeping and maybe he ain't," Big John interjected, "but the boss didn't get up for breakfast. You know that ain't like him."

"She's taking advantage of his sickness."

"That's not news to us, Taylor." Randy's tone was grim. "But the fact is, there ain't nothing we can do about it."

"There's something I can do about it!"

"Like what? You and your pa aren't on the best of terms, and your pa is so weak right now that he probably don't much care what's going on, either."

"Maybe Pa doesn't care about much, Randy, but he *does* care about the ranch."

"And Celeste." Mitch added, "And if there's one

thing we can depend on, Celeste will take full advantage of the way he feels in the bedroom."

"She can't change the fact that she's the one who sold the mare."

"Taylor, listen to me. Wait until your pa gets up. When he's on his feet, he'll feel more independent and he'll be more likely to listen when you try to talk some sense into him." Randy cautioned, "But if you're expecting him to go against Celeste, you're in for a rude awakening."

Big John laid a heavy hand on Taylor's shoulder as he said, "You'd best listen to Randy, Taylor. I'm thinking the boss ain't got the stamina for a face-off right now."

Momentarily silent, Taylor shrugged. "All right. I'll wait awhile for my father to get up." Frowning as the image of Vida's stunned expression returned to haunt him, he continued, "But I've got things to do in town, and if he doesn't get up by this afternoon, it'll have to wait a little longer."

"Buck, darling, don't upset yourself. You're tired. You should rest. The ranch can get along without you for one day."

"That's not the point, Celeste." Buck was pale and perspiring. He had attempted to stand a few times during the morning hours, but he had been too lightheaded to stay on his feet.

Celeste's expression reflected a concern she did not feel as she insisted, "The ranch hands will take care of the necessary chores. If you rest today, you can get up early tomorrow when the men start out for a full day's work."

"I should be out there now."

"No, you shouldn't. You should rest."

"Celeste . . . the ranch is *my* responsibility."

Barely concealing her annoyance, Celeste studied Buck's expression for a silent moment. He was so stubborn! Taylor was waiting to confront him with the sale of the mare the moment he reached the kitchen. She had gotten rid of the animal because it was a point of hope for the Texas Star's future—a future she was determined would not come to pass. She had expected to break the news to Buck gently, with the excuse that she felt the mare needed more care than they could afford at the present time. She knew she'd be able to convince Buck her intentions were genuine if she were allowed ample time—but Taylor was determined to cut that time short.

However, Taylor would not risk disturbing his father in the sanctity of the bedroom Buck and she shared— she was sure of that. She had no choice about what she must do.

Celeste offered gently, "Yes, the ranch is your responsibility, Buck, but *you* are *my* responsibility, and I won't allow you to harm yourself." Celeste snuggled closer to Buck on the bed they shared. "I'll stay with you. We'll make the day a special treat that only the two of us will share. I'll have Madalane serve us our meal in bed this afternoon." She smiled lovingly. "How does that sound?"

"Good . . . real good, but—"

"No buts." Celeste stroked Buck's emaciated cheek. "Just the two of us."

Celeste saw the momentary hesitation in Buck's gaze. She sensed victory when his mouth twitched in a half smile before he said, "If that's what you want, darlin'."

Celeste pressed her mouth to Buck's pale, dry lips. Barely restraining a grimace, she said, "Alone together all day . . . so we can talk. Yes, that is what I want."

Taylor sat at the kitchen table with the other hands, consuming the second meal of the day while keeping one eye on the bedroom hallway. Morning had faded into afternoon and Buck had still not emerged from his room. Somehow, Taylor had expected as much. Celeste was a sly witch. She was depending on Taylor's concern for Buck's health to delay him long enough for her to devise a satisfactory excuse for the sale of the mare.

As if there could be one.

Despite what Randy and the others might be thinking, Taylor had no illusions. He knew Buck would believe Celeste over him simply because he *wanted* to believe her. Yet Taylor was determined to say what he thought, whether Buck wanted to hear it or not.

It appeared, however, that the discussion he had hoped for was not going to happen that afternoon.

Taylor moved his arm as Madalane placed a bowl of gravy in an open spot on the table near him. Waiting until she moved back, he liberally moistened the dry beef on his plate and continued eating. How Madalane could manage to cook good Texas Star beef into dry slabs of boot leather was a mystery he expected never to solve. But it was either eat or go hungry. Taylor poured more gravy on the beef and chewed more vigorously.

"Pass the gravy, will you, Taylor?"

His plate almost emptied, Taylor picked up the gravy bowl with a knowing glance in Randy's direction, only to have Madalane knock it from his hand as she swept a platter from the table. Jumping back, Taylor managed to avoid the hot gravy that splashed onto his chair. Teeth gritted, he glanced up to see that Madalane's gaze was cold.

Too bad. She'd missed.

His patience expired, Taylor snapped, "Out with it, Madalane. Is Buck getting up today or not?"

Madalane did not bother to look his way as she cleaned up the spill and replied, "Celeste has informed me that her husband is tired. He has decided to spend the day in bed. I have already served them their meal in their room."

"Celeste is making sure my father is taking his rest, I suppose."

"Celeste takes very good care of her husband."

"I'm sure."

Taylor turned toward Randy as the mustached wrangler said, "Whatever you got to say can wait, can't it, Taylor? Buck wouldn't stay in bed if he had a choice."

Yes, it could wait, but Vida couldn't.

Not bothering to reply, Taylor walked out the door and headed for his horse.

Vida glanced up wearily at the cloudless sky as she strolled toward Lowell's only restaurant. She wasn't really hungry, but she knew that if she missed her only full meal of the day, she wouldn't get a chance to eat later. She was well aware that the situation could prove dangerous during the long evening of drinking in the saloon.

Her smile forced, Vida reviewed again in her mind the exchange between Taylor and herself in her room the previous night. Things were getting too complicated. Taylor had reacted as passionately as she to their pretense in the saloon, but his mind was at war with the spontaneous emotions that flared between them.

For that matter, so was hers.

Taylor and she were friends. Good friends. Close friends. *Loving* friends. But, dammit, what she had felt last night in his arms had had nothing to do with friendship!

Taylor wanted them to *remain* friends.

So did she.

He didn't want to risk their working relationship.

Neither did she.

Oh, hell . . . or did she?

"Howdy, Vida! I got to say you look as good in the daytime as you do at night—and that's gospel."

Vida looked at the smiling cowboy as he straightened up from where he had been leaning against a storefront. She replied with a wink, "Milton, darlin', you set my heart aflutter with your flattery."

Flushing, Milton responded, "If you've a mind for company, I'd be pleased to walk with you for a while on this fine Sunday . . . that is, if you don't have other plans."

Vida's heart went out to the shy cowpoke. Not wishing to encourage his attentions, she replied lightly, "It just so happens that I do have plans right now, but make sure you come to see me at the Last Chance tonight, you hear? Or you will break my heart."

"Yes, ma'am." Milton tipped his hat. "You can count on it."

Her gaze fixed on the restaurant a few stores away, Vida continued on down the boardwalk, only to be startled when a young woman stepped out from a doorway and said with a tentative smile, "You're Vida Malone, aren't you?"

Vida went still. The other woman had tawny hair, hazel eyes that held a peculiar intensity, and a look that seemed to pin her down.

"My name is Honor Rule. My husband is Lowell's sheriff."

"Sheriff Jace Rule—I know the name. And you're Taylor Star's sister."

"Taylor's and Cal's . . . yes. I'm their half-sister."

Strangely breathless, Vida responded, "You don't look much like Taylor."

"I know."

"I understand that you look like his sister, Bonnie."

"Taylor told you that?"

"Word gets around."

"Yes, it does," Honor agreed, her determination strangely in conflict with her hesitation as she said, "I heard so much about you that I wanted to meet you. Taylor and you seem to have become friends."

Friends. Vida almost smiled. "Yes, I suppose we have."

Honor stared at her a moment longer, then said, "Taylor's been through a lot. He needs a friend right now. I can see he hasn't made a mistake in choosing you."

Her throat tight, Vida said, "You can see that, huh?"

"Yes, I can. I can hear it in the way you say Taylor's name. And I want to thank you."

"To thank me?"

"For being there for him." Honor continued haltingly, "It was hard for him, a real shock to come home and find the proof of his father's infidelity living here

189

in Lowell. Then with me looking so much like Bonnie . . ." Honor's lips twitched revealingly before she continued, "I wish it could've been different—in so many ways—but the truth is, we hardly know each other even though the same blood runs in our veins. I know Taylor's struggling with this homecoming. Just living at the Texas Star has to be hard, but I can't be any help to him, because even though he's been kind to me, I'm part of the problem for him here. That's just the way things are right now; but if *you* ever need anybody to turn to, besides Taylor, I mean, I hope you'll think of me."

"Honor—"

"Thanks again."

Uncertain what to say, Vida watched as Honor nodded good-bye and turned back into the office behind her.

He didn't feel so good.

Taylor raised his hat from his head and wiped his sweaty forehead with the back of his sleeve. He had been on the trail to town for a while, and it seemed to him that the sun was getting hotter by the minute. It burned through his hat and shirt, scorching him.

He felt shaky . . . queasy.

Drawing back on his horse's reins, Taylor dismounted and rushed to the bushes, where he heaved up the contents of his stomach. But the purging afforded him little relief. He glanced around him as the terrain seemed to waver before his eyes. Another stomach spasm, and he turned to retch more painfully than before. His guts were ablaze.

His thoughts muddled, Taylor fought to clear his mind. He needed to talk to Vida so he could tell her how he felt about her. Pa was sick and getting worse. Cal should be told. Celeste and Pa . . . alone.

Where was Vida?

Taylor stumbled as he attempted to remount. Finally pulling himself up, he nudged his horse forward. He swayed in the saddle, clinging tight when he realized he was losing his balance. It couldn't be much farther to Lowell.

Vida was in Lowell.

Vida. He had to talk to her. He had to see her and explain. He had to tell her . . . to tell her . . .

An eternity later, Taylor rode down Lowell's main thoroughfare, bent low in the saddle. With blurred vision, he noted disapproving glances aimed in his direction all along the street. Over the roar in his ears, he heard caustic comments as he rode past.

"Drunk as a skunk."

"Taking a page out of his pa's book."

"If his ma could see him now."

"If Cal knew."

Cal . . . his ma . . . Vida . . .

Squinting, his stomach on fire, his body soaked with sweat, Taylor slipped to his knees as he dismounted. He pulled himself to his feet, then staggered onto the boardwalk and entered the hotel lobby. He stumbled toward the stairs, making the long climb up as the echo of voices from below whirled in his mind.

Where's he headed?

Vida Malone.

She ain't going to like it.

He don't stand a chance.

They were wrong. They didn't know about Vida and

him. They didn't know that she would never turn him away, that he and she . . .

Reeling, hardly holding himself erect, Taylor pounded on Vida's door. Her door jerked open, and he saw her eyes widen at the sight of him.

She was beautiful.

He needed to tell her. He needed to say—

But everything went dark.

Taylor was lying in her bed, thrashing in the throes of a fever that appeared to escalate by the moment. Inwardly trembling, Vida stood beside Doc Maggie as the older woman examined Taylor. Doc Maggie frowned and snatched up the basin as Taylor retched again. She glanced at Vida when she uttered a distressed sound.

"Don't worry. Taylor's purging his stomach. If we're lucky, he's getting rid of whatever's making him sick."

"What's wrong with him, Doc? Do you think it's something he ate?"

"I can't really say as yet. I'm hoping it's as simple as that."

A chill ran down Vida's spine. She knew she'd never forget the moment when she opened her hotel room door and saw Taylor standing there. *Barely* standing. His face was a strange shade she could not describe, as if it were drained of color underneath his fevered flush. Incredibly, he somehow smiled when he saw her—before he toppled forward.

Fortunately, she'd been able to rouse him and get him to her bed before he lapsed into unconsciousness. She recalled looking down at him, momentarily frozen with the numbing fear that he was dying.

Then she had snapped into action . . . running to the head of the staircase to shout into the lobby below for someone to fetch Doc Maggie. She recalled the moment when she realized no one had moved, when one of the men there called back, "He'll sleep it off."

Her feet barely touching the stairs, she was down in the lobby within seconds, where she said with ominous clarity, "Taylor's sick. He may be dying. Somebody had better get the doc now, dammit, or I'll make sure each and every one of you wish you'd never been born!"

Nor would she ever forget the look on Doc Maggie's face when the older woman first saw Taylor. Her expression had said it all.

"What do you mean, you hope it's as simple as something he ate?" Vida pressed, "Food poisoning is dangerous, isn't it? I mean, it could be fatal."

"Yes, it could." Doc glanced back at her, then lifted a glass of medicine to Taylor's lips as she continued, "But if he did eat something that was tainted, he's strong and can probably weather it."

"What do you mean, 'if'?"

Taylor coughed and sputtered as he drained the glass, and Doc laid him back against the pillow. She then turned, concern written in the tight lines of her face as she said, "Have you sent for Cal? He should know about this."

"Someone rode out to tell him a little while ago. Somebody rode out to the Texas Star, too."

"It's Cal I'm concerned about."

"Cal is Taylor's brother, but . . ."

Doc glanced back at Taylor, seeming satisfied that his thrashing was gradually slowing and his physical distress appeared to be lessening. She said, "That medicine might relieve him. I hope so."

"You hope so?"

Doc Maggie's eyes filled unexpectedly. Appearing to be embarrassed by her momentary unprofessionalism, she muttered, "Sometimes I'm more woman than doctor, but that's neither here nor there. Taylor could've gone to Cal, to me, or to any number of folks who would've helped him, but he came to you when he was sick, so I figure you've got a right to have your questions answered." She took a breath. "Yes, I hope the medicine relieves him, but I can't be sure . . . like I can't be sure if his sickness is coming from tainted food."

"What are you saying?"

"This sickness . . . it seems familiar."

"Familiar?"

"This is the way Buck Star's sickness started . . . stomach purging, fever, hallucinations, extraordinary and debilitating weakness. It reduced a strong, healthy man to physical ruin after almost killing him on the spot. But the similarity goes deeper than that. It's Taylor's color. Look at him." Doc shook her head as she turned back toward him briefly. "The unusual tint of his skin, that almost purple color. His father turned that color the first time he was stricken. For a long time it looked like Buck's skin was going to be permanently discolored in that way, but as his physical deterioration progressed, he lost all his color."

The significance of Doc Maggie's statement shook Vida. "You're thinking Taylor's sickness may be hereditary?" she whispered.

Doc's eyes brimmed.

"Is there a chance Taylor may die?"

"I don't really know. If he's like his father, this is only the first of many attacks. All I can say is, he's very sick. The next few hours should tell the tale."

No. That couldn't be.

Numbed by the thought, Vida stared down at Taylor. She moved closer to his bedside as his incoherent mumbling began again; then she turned back to Doc abruptly and said, "I won't let him die."

"I don't think it's up to either you or me. All either of us can do right now is try to keep his fever down, and wait and see."

"I won't accept that."

Doc did not respond as Vida grasped Taylor's hand and clutched it tightly. Vida's knees gave way and she sat down abruptly on the chair beside the bed. She leaned toward him. Taylor was vulnerable in a way she had never seen him before. He had realized it himself when he came to her today. She couldn't be sure what it meant to Taylor, but the impact of the moment when he appeared at her door had swept all her confusion aside, leaving her with a clear-cut realization she had steadfastly avoided acknowledging.

She loved Taylor.

Dammit all, she did! She loved his sometimes mocking gaze, his occasionally chiding tone, and the smiling arrogance that concealed the intensity of emotion between them—emotion they had both attempted to deny. The thought of being without Taylor, of spending even a moment of her life with him not in it, was more than she could bear.

Why had she waited so long to tell him?

Had she waited *too long?*

Leaning closer as Taylor's lips moved in incoherent speech, Vida stroked his cheek. Her throat tightened when he turned at her touch; his eyes briefly opened into narrow slits before falling closed again.

"Taylor . . ." Vida swallowed, then whispered again, "Taylor, I have something to tell you. Can you hear me?"

Taylor stirred. His eyelids flickered. Hardly aware that Doc Maggie had left the room, Vida rasped, "I don't know if you can hear me. I hope you can, because I want you to know . . . I love you, Taylor. We've been friends—good, true, honest friends—and we'll always be friends even though I love you. I'm going to stay right here beside you until you're well again. I won't let anything happen to you. You know I say what I mean, and I mean what I say. *I won't leave you.*"

Was it her imagination, or did Taylor seem to relax?

"Taylor, can you hear me?"

Taylor's lips moved again, but no sound emerged.

Vida heard Doc come back into the room, but she did not stir from Taylor's side.

The next few hours should tell.

Why had it been so hard to say she loved him before now?

Celeste did not look at the ranch hands gathered within hearing distance as the rider from town turned his horse and galloped back down the trail. She opened the porch door and walked into the house. She paused only to stop at her bedroom to listen for the sound of steady breathing that indicated her husband was asleep, before she turned toward Madalane's room. She did not pause to knock before pushing the door open.

Madalane turned toward her as Celeste carefully

pressed the door closed behind her and whispered, "You did it, didn't you?" Madalane did not immediately respond.

"You heard what the rider from town said—I know you did! Taylor barely made it there. He's sick, so sick that Doc Maggie sent word back here that she isn't sure he's going to survive."

Madalane returned her stare coldly.

"He's vomiting. The purging won't stop. He's weak . . . fevered . . . delirious," Celeste said.

"With any luck, he will *not* survive."

"Fool! Don't you see what you've done? Taylor was drunk, but he was fit and healthy when he came here. Now he has been suddenly stricken with the same malady that struck his father. It's too great a coincidence not to cause suspicion!"

"The same blood runs in their veins. It is a believable coincidence."

"It is not! You have raised questions in the minds of many, questions that will hinder me. Now I cannot press Buck to change his will today for fear of appearing unsympathetic. Nor can I be sure how Buck will react if Taylor dies!" Celeste paused, then snapped, "Will he die?"

"Perhaps."

"What do you mean, *perhaps?*"

"I cannot be certain how much of the gravy Taylor consumed."

"You put your potion in the gravy you served at the table this afternoon? What if one of the other men had taken some?"

"I made sure none of them did. I am not a fool!"

"Yes, you are!"

197

"If you are wise, you can turn Taylor's death to your own advantage."

"Can I?" Celeste's gaze grew scathing. "I *told* you my husband is experiencing doubts for the first time about his treatment of Taylor. If Taylor dies, his insecurities may turn into guilt!"

"Taylor is a devil! He does not deserve to live."

"That was not your choice to make."

"Yes . . . it was."

"Because of you, I must now tread even more lightly than before with my husband. More wasted time . . . more waiting, when victory was so close."

"You fool yourself! Your husband would never have rewritten his will while Taylor resided in the bunkhouse . . . while Taylor worked with the hired hands . . . while memories of what his life might have been were stirred more vividly by Taylor every day."

"I have spent the day with my husband. I have cooed my love to him, catered to his whims, used my body to assure him of my undying devotion. I also made sure to speak my fears of what would happen to the Texas Star ranch if it remained unprotected from his sons, and from the claims of his illegitimate daughter. I had him convinced!"

"For the moment."

"Damn you!"

"Damn me if you wish, but Taylor's fate has already been sealed, one way or another."

"If he dies—"

"If he dies, you will whisper to your husband that you fear for the future of the ranch when he is not there. You may press him to prepare for that eventuality by reconsidering his will."

"As if his sons never existed."

"*Because* his sons existed."

Celeste gave a harsh laugh. "It is always so easy to see a clear path when you are not the person who will be forced to tread it."

Her venomous gaze suddenly blazing hot, Madalane hissed, "Do not speak to me of the difficult path you must take! It is not you who has suffered most at the hands of Buck Star! Your mother, my darling Jeanette, suffered the most crushing blow at his hands—a blow so lethal that it stole her life!"

"My mother suffered, but she made her choice."

"A choice forced on her by the vile, heartless man whose bed you share each night. He is cursed by his deed. He is deserving of each day of suffering he experiences—no matter how deep—before he receives the final punishment he has earned."

Livid, Celeste rasped, "You do not make the decisions here! It is I who will decide how Buck Star's punishment shall be meted out—is that understood?"

Madalane did not respond.

"Answer me!"

Madalane nodded.

"You will not, ever, use your potions again without my knowledge—is that also understood?" At the silence that ensued, "Answer me, dammit!" she cried.

"I understand."

Trembling, Celeste took a backward step. "I will reverse this debacle you have created. I will make sure that final vengeance is reached *without your help*. Is that clear?"

"Yes."

"Remember, you are my servant. You follow my orders. I do not follow yours!"

Waiting only until Madalane again nodded, Celeste stamped from the room, hardly managing to close the door quietly behind her. She did not see the stubborn set of Madalane's jaw, or the black look of determination that followed her.

Cal stood beside the bed where Taylor lay. He looked at his brother, hardly able to believe that the frighteningly still man lying there was the same virile fellow he had conversed with so easily in the wooded glade. He remembered the casual manner of their parting, as if the thought had never entered either of their minds that they could possibly be meeting for the last time.

Cal's throat choked tight. Young Elmer Harden had ridden out to the Rocky W to tell him Taylor was in town, deathly sick. Cal recalled that Elmer had hardly had time to turn his horse around before he was mounted and pounding down the trail behind him. He had expected to find his brother in Doc Maggie's office. Instead, he had followed the young man to the hotel room of the new saloon woman in town.

Cal glanced at Vida Malone. She was still dressed in her saloon clothes, a bright red dress with gaudy spangles, but her expression did not match her gay attire as she sat beside the bed. She was holding Taylor's hand, although she had not spoken a word. He wondered why Taylor had gone to her when he was ill. As Cal understood their relationship, they were only recent acquaintances. It didn't make sense. He knew his brother. Taylor would not have come to this woman in such a sorry condition if he didn't trust her.

Inwardly shaken, Cal approached the bed and said, "Taylor . . . it's me, Cal. Can you hear me?"

No answer.

"Taylor, can you open your eyes?"

No movement at all.

Cal looked at Vida Malone. Her beautiful face was impassive, unrevealing. Only a slight twitch of her full lips indicated the emotion she restrained.

His own emotions too close to the surface for comfort, Cal turned back to Doc and said, "What's wrong with him, Doc? Can't he hear me?"

"I don't know . . . what's wrong with him or if he can hear you."

Cal shook his head, incredulous at her reply. In response, Doc Maggie came to stand beside him. Her eyes were worried as she whispered, "I thought at first it might be food poisoning, but his condition looks more severe than that. Cal, I don't know how to say this. I mean, it's hard for me to tell you—"

"Doc Maggie thinks Taylor may be suffering from the same malady that's ailing your father." Vida Malone stood up abruptly. Her jaw tight, she continued, "Doc thinks it may be a hereditary disease—but I don't believe it."

Doc interjected, "Vida, I know what you want to believe, but his condition is too familiar to me for comfort."

Vida released Taylor's hand and approached them. She addressed Cal, saying, "There are too many coincidences to make that conclusion plausible. Taylor came here to find out who sent the letters you both received, and he—"

"How did you know about the letters?" Cal demanded.

"Those letters and the intimate details of your family history are no secret in this town; but even if they were, Taylor would have told me."

"Why would he have told you?" Cal stared at Vida more intently. The determination in her expression, her clipped, measured recitation of the details . . . "You only met him recently. Taylor isn't the kind to spill secrets to strangers."

"We're not strangers."

"That isn't what I heard."

"You heard what Taylor and I wanted to be heard."

"What are you saying?"

"I've said all I'm going to say. It's up to Taylor if he wants to disclose anything else."

"Taylor can't speak for himself right now."

"That's only temporary."

Cal glanced at Doc Maggie. The old woman looked less than certain of that fact. He swallowed hard before continuing, "I want to know what's going on."

Vida moved closer. Cal saw the subtle change in her expression, a softening that touched her dark eyes before she whispered, "Taylor's your brother, Cal. I know you love him, and he loves you. You want to see him well again. So do I. Taylor came to me because he knew he could trust me, whatever happened."

"He could've trusted me, or Doc."

"But he came here."

"Look," Cal said softly, "I appreciate all you've done for Taylor, but he needs more care than you can give him. You just don't have the necessary experience. He should be with Doc until he's well enough to be moved. Then I'll take him back to the Rocky W."

"No. He's staying here."

"I need to know my brother's getting the best care possible."

"He'll get it here."

"With you?"

"With me . . . and Doc." Vida turned to the silent older woman. "Isn't that right, Doc?"

"You know I'll do all I can for him."

Turning back to Cal, Vida whispered, "That should be enough to satisfy you for now."

"It isn't. None of this sounds right to me. I need to know Taylor will be safe."

"He'll be safe." Without a trace of embarrassment, Vida lifted the corner of her skirt to her thigh, exposing a derringer contained in a jeweled holster secured there. She said flatly, "This gun looks pretty, but it's also deadly, and I'm a good shot."

Interrupted by a sudden mumbling from the bed, Cal noted the speed with which Vida moved to Taylor's side to say reassuringly, "I'm here, Taylor, with Doc and Cal. I'll be here as long as you need me."

Taylor mumbled, "Vida . . . need to tell . . . need to say . . ."

Cal watched the play of emotions across Vida's face as Taylor's voice faded. She struggled for control, then whispered, "You can tell me later, Taylor. We'll have plenty of time to talk."

Vida looked up at Cal. She said softly, "I'll make sure you know as soon as Taylor is able to talk coherently. Don't worry. I'll take care of him. I promise."

Feeling a sudden thickness in his throat, Cal turned to the door. When Doc stepped out into the hallway behind him, he said, "Taylor trusted her, Doc. I can't exactly say why, but I trust her, too." He added, "Just make sure I hear the moment there's a change in Taylor's condition."

"All right." Doc smiled, then reached up unexpectedly on tiptoe to kiss his cheek. She whispered, "You and Taylor are my darlin' boys, you know. Now that you've both come home, I don't want to lose either of you again, so you can set your mind at rest that I'll take care of Taylor." She added, "And I have a feeling that woman in there will guard him with her life."

Cal nodded. "Me, too."

That thought lingered as Cal mounted up and rode slowly back down the street. He knew what he needed to do.

What seemed an eternity later, Cal approached the Texas Star ranch house. This time, he did not pause when Celeste appeared on the porch with a venomous tirade meant to halt him in his tracks. Ignoring the ranch hands who gathered watchfully nearby, he strode past her and the glaring Negress in the kitchen. He knocked, but did not wait for a response before entering his father's room.

Cal stopped still at first sight of Buck. Pale, skeletal, his physical deterioration shocking, Buck appeared almost bloodless as he snapped in a voice charged with anger, "What are you doing here?"

"Hello to you, too, Pa."

"I ain't your pa. You changed all that years ago."

"Maybe, but that isn't the reason I came."

"Whatever it is, you can get out!"

Cal took a strengthening breath, then continued, "I'll leave as soon as I say what I came to say."

"What's that . . . that you turned out to be the good

son, after all, because you became the town hero and your brother turned out to be the town drunk?"

"Taylor's in town. He's sick."

"He's too drunk to make it back to the ranch, you mean. Celeste told me about the rider who came out to tell me Taylor wouldn't be back tonight because Doc has him holed up in a hotel room somewhere until he sleeps it off."

"Taylor's not drunk, Pa. He's sick . . . so sick that Doc isn't sure what's going to happen."

"I don't believe you."

"Taylor got sick the same way you did . . . fever, stomach spasms, weakness. He's unconscious."

"I don't believe—"

"Listen to me, will you?" Cal took an angry step forward. "Taylor wasn't drunk, and Doc thinks his condition is too severe for food poisoning. His sickness looks familiar to her. She thinks . . . she thinks what's wrong with him might be hereditary."

"Hereditary."

"Taylor could be dying, Pa."

Buck's breathing became labored. "No, I don't believe it."

"It's true!"

"That's enough!" Her expression livid, Celeste stood in the doorway behind Cal as she ordered, "Get out! You've told your father enough of your lies."

"They're not lies, and you know it."

"Lies, lies, lies! You even sent a rider out from town to spread them, but neither Buck nor I believed him. Taylor is lying in town drunk, because he *is* a drunk, and neither your father nor I will accept excuses for him!"

Cal stared at Celeste's venomous expression, then turned back to his father and said, "Do you believe her . . . that the whole town is in cahoots to lie to you about Taylor's condition?"

Trembling but unyielding, Buck responded, "I believe what I saw, that your brother is a drunk. Once a drunk, always a drunk."

"Then we have nothing else to talk about." Standing squarely, facing his father with broad shoulders erect and honey-colored eyes cold, Cal said flatly, "You don't have to worry that I'll be back. Like you said, you're not my father anymore—but make no mistake about it, it's not because *you* disowned *me*. Rather, it's because you were satisfied to forget the daughter you lost, then to sacrifice the daughter you never knew you had when she was miraculously restored to you; and because you're willing to give up the only son you still claim to have—*all for the sake of a woman who isn't worth a damn!* As far as I'm concerned, you're welcome to the life you chose with Celeste—because *you deserve her.*"

Turning away without waiting for a response, Cal walked out of the house—past Celeste, past the ranch hands who remained silent and unmoving. He mounted up, his heart silently aching at the knowledge that he would never return.

The room had darkened as night fell. It was lit only by the lamp at the bedside as Vida studied Taylor's motionless figure. The purging had stopped, but he was intermittently delirious, mumbling incoherently, calling her name; then silent and frighteningly still. Doc had stayed until it was obvious she could do no more. She had left several powders to be given to Taylor during the night if his fever worsened, promising to return at daybreak.

Vida recalled responding to a knock on the door before Doc left, to see Honor standing there with a tray in her hands. Food for Doc and her, with clear broth for Taylor—all of which remained untouched where the dear girl had left it.

Honor hadn't said much. She hadn't needed to. A multitude of regrets for time irretrievably lost between Taylor and herself could be easily read in her clear, hazel eyes—eyes where tears were carefully restrained. A few moments at Taylor's bedside, a light kiss on his cheek, and she was gone with the promise to return with breakfast. Honor had said all that needed to be said in their short, almost prophetic meeting earlier in the day, and Vida knew instinctively that Honor had meant every word.

Her throat tight, Vida perused Taylor's agonized expression. He grimaced as if in pain, then mumbled again. She leaned closer in an attempt to understand what he was saying, but his words were no more than disjointed phrases. She stroked back a strand of heavy dark hair that had fallen forward on his heated forehead, noting the tormented fluttering of his stubby, dark lashes. She longed to see his light eyes open wide with clarity and recognition, to see his pale lips stretch into the smile she had always found irresistible. She wondered how she had ever convinced herself that her feelings for him did not go beyond friendship, when all she wanted now was to feel his arms around her, to hold him close, to share his love forever.

Vida's head jerked up at a shout of laughter from the street below. It was late, but the din from the saloon echoed along the otherwise quiet street. She had changed from her saloon finery into a modest sleeping garment and robe that were more comfortable, although modesty had never been a problem between Taylor and her. They had always done what was professionally necessary at the moment, without looking back.

The sound of footsteps in the hallway turned Vida's head. She reached for the revolver on the nightstand, then released it when the footsteps continued on past. That gun was a more suitable weapon than the concealed derringer she normally wore, and she kept it close at hand. The door was locked, but she wasn't taking any chances. No one would get in the room without her permission. If anyone tried, he would pay with his life.

She didn't believe in coincidences, especially since the situation in Lowell was riddled with them. If someone had indeed caused Taylor's illness, that person would not get a second chance to end his life.

She would protect Taylor at all costs.

Vida glanced at the clock that ticked on endlessly upon the dresser. She was tired, and the chair on which she sat had become uncomfortable. She needed her rest if she was to remain alert.

Her throat tight, Vida shed her robe and slippers, then drew back the coverlet on Taylor's bed. She slipped in beside him without hesitation and pressed herself lightly against his side. It was where she needed to be . . . where she *wanted* to be.

Yes, she loved him.

"He seems to be breathing more easily. But he's not asleep." Doc Maggie looked up at Vida where she stood near Taylor's bed, then clarified, "He's unconscious. That worries me."

"He doesn't have a fever anymore. I can tell by touching him."

Dressed simply in a blue cotton gown that complemented her coloring despite the shadows of sleeplessness underneath her eyes, Vida did not bother to explain that she had lain close to Taylor's side through the night, wakeful until the moment she realized he was no longer feverish. She had been dressed and ready to receive Doc when she walked through the doorway at dawn. It was now a few hours later. True to her word, Honor had arrived with a breakfast tray and had departed, obviously distressed at Taylor's condition; Cal had visited and had left looking more concerned than before; and through it all, Vida had sensed Doc was holding something back.

Doc said levelly, "I'm worried because I'm afraid Taylor might have damage from his high fever. His temperature is normal. He should have awakened or at least said a few coherent words by now."

"What do you mean, you're worried about damage?"

"Sometimes the brain gets scorched by a fever."

Firmly denying the knot of fear that clenched tight inside her, Vida insisted, "No, not Taylor. He'll be fine."

Doc shrugged. "I wish I could be as certain of that as you seem to be, but I—"

A knock on the door turned both women in its direction. Vida reached instinctively for her gun as Doc walked toward the door and said, "Who is it?"

"It's me, ma'am. Randy Butler from the Texas Star."

Vida maintained her grip on the revolver until Doc

drew the door open and the mustached cowhand walked into the room. She noted Randy's stricken expression when he looked at Taylor lying so still.

"Damn it all," he said. "I was almost hoping Celeste was right and everybody was covering up for Taylor while he was sleeping off a drunk."

"Is that what that woman said?" Doc's round face flushed with heat. Not waiting for Randy's response, she went on, "I guess I should've expected it. Did she send you here to check up on him?"

"No, ma'am. She has the boss convinced that Taylor will come crawling back to the ranch when he runs out of money, but I knew that wasn't true. I went out to work with the men this morning and came here to see how Taylor was as soon as I was sure Celeste wouldn't find out. I figured there'd be hell to pay if she did, and I decided a long time ago that I wasn't going to do nothing to make her fire me and the boys so she'd have the boss and the Texas Star to herself."

Randy's shoulders slumped as he walked closer to the bed. He acknowledged Vida politely and said, "I guess Taylor knew what he was doing when he came here, sick like he was, but I got to admit I was surprised when the rider from town said he was here instead of at Doc's office. Cal came to the ranch to talk to his pa, but he was so fit to be tied when he was done that he left the ranch without stopping to tell us anything."

Doc Maggie remarked, "I didn't know Cal went to the Texas Star. He didn't say anything about it when he came back to see Taylor this morning."

"Well, he sure enough did. Cal stormed into the

house and had it out with the boss. I figure he won't be back—his choice, not the boss's."

"That sounds like Cal."

That rasping comment from the bed snapped all heads in Taylor's direction. Stunned, they saw that Taylor's eyes were open as he concluded hoarsely, "But he should've known what Pa would say."

Despite herself, Vida burst into tears.

"What do you mean, Vida ain't going to be coming in to work for a while?" Derek stared at Bart, who was standing behind the bar. "You're not telling me them rumors are true, that she's taking care of that drunk, Taylor Star?"

"I'd say that's a case of the pot calling the kettle black."

"You trying to say I'm a drunk?" Derek sneered, "I'd be careful if I was you. You might just lose one of your best customers."

"That's what I'm saying."

"I ain't no drunk, and you ain't answered my question!"

"Is Vida taking care of Taylor because he's sick, you mean?" Bart shrugged. "I don't much care why she ain't coming in for a while. I figure whenever she comes back, she'll be welcome."

"Yeah . . . like she's something special."

"You seem to think so."

"What's supposed to be wrong with Star, anyway?"

"I don't know. Talk is he came stumbling into town real sick—couldn't keep nothing down and could hardly walk. Everybody at first thought he was drunk, but it turned out different. Some of the fellas who saw him said he must've had a fever, because his face was a funny color like none of them ever seen before."

Taylor Star's color had looked strange? Derek prompted, "What do you mean?"

"The fellas said his face was real red—so red it almost looked purple."

A chill crawled up Derek's spine. Celeste had remarked to him about Buck Star's peculiar coloring each time he had a "spell"—until he got so bad that he didn't have any color left at all. He questioned, "He was sick . . . like his pa?"

"I guess so."

Derek went silent. The cold-blooded witch.

Derek pressed, "What did Doc have to say about it?"

"I don't know."

"What do you mean, you don't know?"

"Look." Bart's expression darkened. "I don't know nothing else except Vida can come back whenever she's ready."

Derek unconsciously nodded, then ordered, "Give me a whisky."

Derek downed the contents of the glass the moment it was placed in front of him, then took a gulping breath. He sure as hell needed that.

"You can't eat too soon. Doc said to take it easy."

Taylor looked at Vida as she held a plate of clear broth in one hand and a spoon poised in the other. He felt terrible . . . washed out . . . as weak as a kitten, but he was finally lucid, and she looked a helluva lot better to him than what was on that spoon.

His voice still hoarse, Taylor said, "I'm hungry. I need to build up my strength."

"Taylor, only two days ago you were sick—sicker than you realize. Doc actually said . . ." Vida hesitated. Her dark eyes clouded as she forced herself to say, "Doc said she thought you might not survive."

"What?"

"Don't you remember how sick you were?"

How could he forget it? Whirling thoughts; nightmares that crowded in, one after another; nausea, weakness, and pain in his gut so debilitating and constant that only unconsciousness saved him from it.

Taylor looked at Vida. But through it all, soothing him, had been the sound of Vida's voice and the sensation that she was near him.

He said, "It was pretty serious, huh?"

"Yes."

"Were you worried about me?"

"Of course I was!"

"How worried?"

Vida looked at him, her gaze scrutinizing. "You don't remember much about it all, do you?"

"I don't even remember how I got here. All I recall is the sound of your voice and the feeling that you and Doc were close by, no matter how damned sick I felt."

"You remember nothing else?"

Taylor looked at her more closely. "Should I?"

Vida shook her head. She supposed not. Doc had felt sorry for her, thinking she was sleeping in the chair, and had arranged to have a cot delivered to the room for her to sleep on after the first night. She had used it when she became more certain Taylor was recovering,

213

because she had wanted to make sure he was resting comfortably—a sacrifice for her, when all she had wanted to do was crawl in bed beside Taylor so she could be close to him.

Vida stirred the contents of the bowl before raising another spoonful of broth to his lips. She responded, "Should you remember more? No, I suppose not."

"Vida—"

"Swallow, Taylor."

Taylor dutifully swallowed, than commented as if in afterthought, "Doc was worried I wouldn't make it, huh?"

"She was concerned."

"Why? I figure that water I drank from the water hole on the way to town probably did it." He shook his head. "That water didn't look right to me, but I'd left the ranch without filling my canteen, and I was so damned thirsty."

Vida's face paled noticeably. "Doc thought it might be more than that."

Vida's hesitation, the tone of her voice, gave him pause. He pressed, "How much more?"

"Doc said the symptoms were the same as your father's. . . . and what struck her was that your skin turned the same unusual color your father's did the first time he got sick."

Taylor went momentarily numb.

"Taylor—"

"You're saying she thinks whatever it is, it might be the same sickness my father has?"

Vida did not respond.

"She thinks I may have inherited it from my pa?"

Still no response.

"But I'm getting better. Pa's getting worse."

"Doc said your father had remissions at first, too."

Taylor could not speak.

"Doc's wrong, Taylor!" Her face suddenly hot with emotion, Vida continued, "I told you how I feel about coincidences, and there are too many here to sit right with me. I've been doing a lot of thinking: Your mother died unexpectedly from a heart attack when she never had a sign of heart problems before. Celeste showed up shortly afterwards, *coincidentally* a young, beautiful widow, when everybody knew your father had a weakness for young, beautiful women. Your brother was riddled with guilt and was already gone, and then you were banished from your home so the lovebirds could be alone. *Coincidentally*, Celeste and your father were alone when your father's unexpected sickness hit him for the first time shortly afterwards— a sickness *coincidentally* coinciding with the gradual downward spiraling of Texas Star affairs."

"You're saying Celeste has something to do with my father's sickness? Why would Celeste want to harm my pa? He gave her everything she wanted, and as far as the ranch is concerned, its downward spiral hurt her, too."

"Maybe not."

"What are you saying?"

"I don't know for sure, but somebody sent you a letter telling you and Cal both to come home. Maybe it was a warning of some kind."

"No, I don't think so. If the letters were meant as a warning, they wouldn't have been phrased the way they were . . . almost mocking Cal and me."

"What's your explanation, then, Taylor?" Vida

shoved another spoonful of broth between Taylor's lips as she continued, "Is what Derek said *coincidental*, too, about his young, blonde lover with the old, sick husband? Is it *coincidence* that he said things had recently changed just as Cal put an end to the rustling that had devastated the Texas Star? Your brother put an end to the rustlers, too—except for *one* who escaped. Is it a *coincidence* that Derek, with his young, blonde mistress, always had a pocketful of money although nobody ever saw him work?"

"That's all guesswork."

Ignoring his comment, Vida continued, "Is it another *coincidence* that when you came back and managed to get yourself situated on the Texas Star, Derek's young, blonde mistress had use for him again?"

"And that's a stretch, Vida."

"Really? Tell me something. Did you do or say something recently that Celeste could construe as a threat to her . . . something she might be afraid would change the way your father feels about her?"

"No. Wait . . ." Correcting himself, Taylor said gruffly, "I told her I was going to talk to my pa about her selling his prize mare, which she'd find hard to explain. She said I couldn't because my pa was too sick to discuss it, so I put the discussion off for a day because I wanted to come into town to talk to you. That's when I got sick—on the way here—before I could talk to him."

Her expression grim, Vida thrust another spoonful of broth into his mouth. Taylor swallowed, then grated, "I don't want any more of that stuff, dammit!"

"I thought you said you were hungry."

"I'm not hungry anymore."

"Lost your appetite?"

"Vida, this isn't funny."

"Believe me, I don't think it is. You could've died, Taylor."

Taylor held Vida's gaze. She was so damned beautiful. She was looking at him like . . . like . . . Taylor inwardly groaned. As weak as he was, he wanted her, but common sense told him that even thinking about it would be a disaster.

Besides, the possibility of a hereditary disease . . .

Taylor said stiffly, "I'd say this whole thing hinges on who sent Cal and me those letters." Allowing a moment for that thought to settle, Taylor said, "Get me some real food, Vida."

"I thought you weren't hungry."

"I'm not, but I have to get myself out of this bed and back on my feet, and I need real food in order to do it." He continued more softly, "I'm not saying I agree with anything you said, but I do need to settle things, one way or another."

"Doc said you shouldn't be eating yet."

"Food, Vida!"

Vida shot him a fulminating look, then slapped the plate down on the nightstand and started toward the door.

Chapter 8

Celeste waited impatiently inside the dark rendezvous cabin she had used so many times before. It was filthy and rank, and her flesh crawled as she stood in its dank confines. She glanced at the cot liberally spotted by the marks of passionate meetings past. Bile rose in her throat at the thought of the wild sexual fervor these surroundings had formerly induced.

Perverted, that's what it was, and she had been a willing, enthusiastic participant with her degenerate partner! It was increasingly clear to her that it was time she brought an end to a charade that had already gone on too long—before she became a victim of her own conspiracy.

More impatient with each second that ticked past, Celeste glanced out the mottled window toward the heavily foliated trail. Where was Derek? She had raised the signal for a meeting with him several times during the past week, and he had not responded to any of them. Were it not for the comments of the ranch hands, rumors repeated around the kitchen table about the drunken spectacle Derek was making of himself at the Last Chance of late, she might have thought he had left the area without telling her. She had formerly prided herself that she was indispensable to him in the most intimate of ways, but his most recent actions now cast doubt on that conviction.

It had not missed Celeste's notice that the same ranch hands who freely discussed every other aspect of their lives at mealtimes cautiously avoided any reference to Taylor Star's absence. More than a week had passed. She hadn't heard a word about his condition, and ignorance of the situation was driving her mad.

Doc Maggie had visited Buck on several occasions in the time since. Buck had stubbornly refused to inquire about Taylor, as had she, and Doc Maggie had not offered any information.

Damn the old hag! And damn Derek, her errant ally and degenerate lover!

Movement on the trail abruptly caught her eye, and Celeste went still. A hard smile curved her lips when Derek rode slowly into view. She waited as he approached the cabin, as he dismounted and walked just as slowly toward the door.

Unwilling to wait a moment longer, Celeste jerked the door open and snapped, "Get in here!" She waited until Derek complied. Then she slammed the door closed behind him and said, "What happened? What kept you?"

"What do you mean?"

"You know what I mean. You know you were supposed to keep me informed about what's going on in Lowell, but you ignored my signals for a meeting."

"I ain't your lackey, you know."

"Oh? It seems to me you never hesitated to do my bidding if I paid you well enough."

"That was before."

"Before what?"

"I've been doing a lot of thinking."

"A lot of *drinking*, you mean."

"I've been *thinking*—about what happened to Taylor Star."

"What are you talking about?"

Derek's oily face drew into a sneer. "I ain't no fool, you know. Taylor Star hardly made it into Lowell before he collapsed. Talk is, he almost died."

"So?"

"You did it, didn't you?" Derek gave a harsh laugh. "First the old man, and now the son."

"I don't know what you're talking about."

"Don't you? Taylor Star was getting too close to his pa. He was in your way, and you fixed him real good."

Celeste snapped, "You're imagining things, but even if I did, what difference would that make to you? You were only too willing to see to it that Cal Star got a bullet in the back. What's so special about his brother?"

"A bullet's one thing. It's quick and hard, and it's over with."

"So?"

Derek's gaze narrowed. "I don't like poison. A man don't die like a man that way. That is what you did, isn't it—poison him?"

Celeste did not reply.

He said slowly, "When's it going to be my turn?"

"Don't be a fool, Derek!"

"I don't expect to be, so I'm telling you now, things gotta change or I'm calling it quits with you."

"What?"

"We was on even terms before, but I got the feeling now that I'd be taking a chance turning my back."

"Your *back* isn't the part of your body where I do my best work."

"Yeah, well, a roll in the hay ain't worth my life."

"Derek . . ." Celeste took a spontaneous step toward him.

"Stay where you are."

"You're being ridiculous, Derek. You're my ally. I need the information only you can bring me. I'd be cutting off my nose to spite my face if I did anything to change our association. Besides"—she chanced another step—"being with you is the only thing keeping me sane until my husband is in the ground where he belongs."

"That's what I mean!"

"Are you telling me you're surprised to hear that? You always knew where our association was headed. You never complained about the big payday that's almost within our reach. Buck is disgusted with his sons. He's already disowned Cal, and he believes Taylor is nothing more than a worthless drunk."

"That ain't what the townsfolk are thinking."

Celeste tensed. "What do you mean?"

"Taylor rode into town swaying in the saddle. He went straight to Vida Malone's room, staggering every step of the way. Everybody figured he was drunk. They ignored him, and they ignored Vida when she called for a doctor—but Vida set them all straight. She got him a doctor, all right."

Bristling at the hint of admiration in Derek's tone,

Celeste said, "You're salivating for her, for a saloon tramp."

"She ain't no tramp! She's a helluva lot of woman. She says what she means . . . and she's loyal."

"How would you know?"

"She's been taking care of Taylor Star, and the talk is, it ain't been pleasant. She hasn't even come to work because she don't want to leave him."

"Why isn't Taylor with Doc Maggie?"

"How do I know? Maybe because he's doing fine where he is. Talk is, he'll be on his feet soon."

"I don't believe it."

"No? Well, then you're fooling yourself." Derek laughed. "That fella might end up right at your door again."

"What did Doc Maggie say caused his sickness?"

"She said Taylor ate something he had stored in his saddlebag on the way to town—because he was hungry—because that servant of yours can't cook to save her life. Doc figured whatever he ate was spoiled."

Celeste nodded.

"But it wasn't the food in his saddlebag that almost done him in, was it?"

Celeste did not reply.

"That's what I thought."

Celeste took another step toward him. She said softly, "I need your help, Derek. I'll make the payoff worthwhile, I promise."

"Stay away from me."

Her face flaming, Celeste went rigidly still. "You have other plans, is that it, Derek?"

"Yeah, I do." Derek's small eyes narrowed as he said,

"I figure I earned a part of that big payoff you talk about when that old man of yours is finally out of the way. Maybe I'll help you out as best I can until then, but I ain't taking payment on that cot behind you no more."

"You have your eye on that saloon woman."

"That's right! She's tied up with that Taylor Star right now, but she already as much as said she's got a yen for me. When I tell her I ain't bothering with any other women and I have enough greenbacks to show her I mean what I say, I figure she'll come my way."

"You're dreaming."

"No, I ain't!"

"What about Taylor?"

"I'll take care of him if I have to, but I'll do it right and fast."

Celeste scrutinized Derek more closely. He was serious. He actually believed that saloon woman would prefer him over Taylor. She said abruptly, "That's fine with me, but if you expect to collect, you'll have to do what I say. You'll have to be ready to move when I tell you."

"That's fine with me."

"I'll need you to keep an eye on things in town, too . . . to tell me what's going on with Taylor so I can be ready for him."

Derek sneered.

Celeste stared at him in silence. He was nothing but a slovenly, odoriferous saddle tramp. And that saloon woman had a yen for him? Celeste almost laughed aloud. She said, "Are we agreed?"

"That's fine with me." Derek added unexpectedly,

"But I'm warning you. Don't try nothin', because I got my eyes open."

"I'm glad to hear it."

Perversely, Celeste held out her hand. "Shake on it?"

"No, thanks."

Her smile faded. "If that's the way you want it."

Celeste jerked the door open and strode toward the buggy hidden behind the cabin.

Bastard . . . ignoramus . . . but she needed him, dammit!

Her only consolation was that she wouldn't need him very much longer.

"I don't want you to go back there!" Vida said adamantly. "It . . . it's too dangerous."

Dawn had barely touched the morning sky as Taylor stood beside Vida. He was thinner than he had been by several pounds, he was sure; but his clothes were clean and freshly pressed thanks to Vida's diligence, his strength had returned, and he was ready to go. In a little more than a week since he was stricken so violently, he was almost restored to the man he had been.

Vida was so close that Taylor took a backward step. He needed to. She had remained by his side, responding to his every need while he was needy, challenging him to survive.

Paradoxically, the purpose that had driven him to her when he was sick, his intention to explain his muddled feelings about their previous parting, was no longer an issue. His feelings were no longer muddled.

He loved her.

Considering the intensity of the emotions presently

raging inside him, he now wondered how he could have been so blind.

Yet he kept his silence in the face of an uncertain future. If Doc Maggie was right, if his heredity doomed him to the same sort of deterioration his father had experienced—a deterioration that had wrung a formerly vigorous man dry of masculinity—he had little to offer her. And he wanted to offer Vida so much . . . his love, his fidelity, and a life that was rich and full.

Vida insisted Doc was mistaken; yet if she was right and his father was paying so high a price for his own selfish lust, that truth would be almost as difficult to bear.

He was silent a moment longer as Vida looked up at him, her beautiful countenance drawn into lines of concern. Then he said, "Don't worry about me, Vida. I need to go back to the ranch. If you're right and Celeste is behind my pa's sickness, I need to be close by to watch things."

"If she tried once to poison you, she'll try again."

"No, she won't. Once is explainable. Twice would be a dead giveaway."

"*Dead* . . . you said it yourself, Taylor."

"I'm almost certain Celeste wouldn't try that again."

"Almost certain?"

"One thing I can be sure of is that I won't put anything into my mouth from a plate that the other ranch hands haven't helped themselves from first."

"You're still taking a chance."

"That cover story Doc made up about my eating something that went bad on the way to town should take care of any suspicions Celeste might have when I go back to the ranch."

"You're doing what you need to do, is that it?"

Taylor did not respond.

"All right. Go."

"Vida—"

"Go."

"I don't want you to be angry."

"Too late."

"Vida . . ."

Vida did not respond.

Aware that there was nothing else he could presently say, Taylor tipped his hat and walked out the doorway.

Damn him!

As the door closed behind Taylor, tears of frustration trailed down Vida's cheeks. Taylor was walking right back into the same situation he had barely escaped from a week earlier!

Vida angrily wiped away her tears with the knowledge that the desperation she felt was partially her own fault. Drumming through her mind during their conversation a few minutes earlier had been the thought that if Taylor stubbornly refused to listen to reason, she might never get the chance to tell him she loved him.

The thought was devastating. She had whispered those words to Taylor when he was semiconscious, but they had become lost in a frenzy of delirium and violent purging. He had been so ill, and when he was finally lucid enough to comprehend what she was saying, she had been forced to answer questions about his illness.

A hereditary illness. She needed to prove Doc Maggie wrong, for Taylor's peace of mind, *and* to see justice served to a woman who had escaped its wrath far too long.

Vida reviewed the situation as she saw it.

Taylor discounted her assertion about the suspicious coincidences involved. She could not.

Taylor had returned to the Texas Star. He was doing what he needed to do.

She could remain close by and sit back, hoping Taylor would discover she was right before things changed for the worse, or she could take the necessary steps to prove she was right.

There was only one possible conclusion. Yes, Taylor was doing what he needed to do. It was his way.

Well, it was her way, too.

Incredulous, Celeste stared at the approach to the Texas Star ranch house. The sound of hoofbeats had stirred her from her seat beside Buck at the parlor desk where unpaid bills had remained in a towering stack for more time than she cared to recall. Buck had been back on his feet for two days, and she had finally felt relatively certain that the stress of broaching the subject of the unpaid bills would not do him in. She didn't want that—not yet.

Buck had resisted, of course. She had expected he would, because he knew that the balance of his account in Lowell's bank would be grossly inadequate to cover the amount needed for the bills. Strangely, that reality allowed her great satisfaction. She knew Buck. He would feel an expanding sense of personal guilt with each invoice that must go unpaid. He would feel he had failed the Texas Star and had failed to adequately provide for her. His guilt would be so great that when his will finally surfaced, he would believe the only way he could provide for her future would be to change the document so she would be the sole beneficiary of anything he had left. He would consider that poor recompense for all she had done for him. She knew better. The thought had consoled her until the present moment.

Celeste fought to control her rage as the rider came into full view. It couldn't be he! Not again! Was there no way to discourage Taylor Star from returning to the Texas Star?

"Who is it, Celeste?"

Buck's hoarse inquiry from the desk behind her increased Celeste's agitation. A few more invoices and a few more appropriate comments and she would've had Buck and his will in the palm of her hand.

"Celeste?"

"It's Taylor."

Celeste noted the expression on Buck's colorless face. His look of relief quickly changed to a familiar agitation. Hoping to fan that spark of agitation, she said, "Your son is coming directly to the house. I suppose Doc Maggie managed to keep him away from the bottle long enough for him to come back here to apologize."

"Apologize?"

"For the endless embarrassment he is causing you."

Heavy footsteps on the porch turned Buck and Celeste expectantly toward the parlor doorway as Taylor stepped into view. Celeste noted the lines of concern Buck could not seem to conceal at the sight of his son, who looked paler than she had ever seen him, and pounds lighter. She remained silent as Buck said, "So, you came back."

Taylor's intense blue-eyed gaze assessed his father, then the stack of bills in front of him before he looked at her. He said, "That's right, I'm back, Pa. I'd say I was sorry I worried you, but I can tell it would be a waste of time."

"Why should I worry about a son who spends a week sleeping off a drunk, then comes back home to beg for his job back."

"I was sick, but it had nothing to do with drinking. Doc Maggie figures it was something I ate."

"Something you ate? Here? Nobody else got sick on this ranch."

"Maybe they've all got stronger stomachs than I have."

Ignoring Taylor's explanation, Buck pressed, "So, you came to beg for your job back."

"I came back to my job as soon as I was able, and I came here to tell you I was back."

"Too proud to beg, are you?"

"I have no need to beg, Pa. I didn't ask you for anything I wasn't ready to earn when I came here. You needed help. I did my job, and I've worked as hard as any wrangler on this ranch. Now I'm back, and that's exactly what I expect to continue doing."

"What if I don't want to take you back?"

"Well . . ." Taylor stared hard at his father. "That would be *your* mistake, not mine."

Celeste waited breathlessly for Buck's reply. She saw his face draw into stern lines, and her heart leaped hopefully.

230

"I don't believe a word you said." Buck paused, then continued tightly, "But you look like hell, and I figure whether it was drink that caused it or not, you really were sick—so I'm going to give you another chance."

What?

"But if you step out of line again, extenuating circumstances won't matter . . . the fact that you look like you're too down at the heels to make it anywhere else, or the fact that you're my son. Is that understood?"

His mouth a hard line, Taylor replied softly, "That's understood, as long as it's understood that you're an old bastard who doesn't have the sense to see what's right in front of him."

"What's that supposed to mean?"

"You figure it out, Pa. Meanwhile, I'm going to catch up with the rest of the men—so I can put in a full day's work and earn my keep."

Incredulous at the unexpected turn of events, Celeste ventured, "Are you sure you're making the right decision, Buck? You know what Taylor's like. You can't depend on him."

"He knows what he has to do to keep his place here. If he doesn't do it, he's out."

"But—"

Looking back at Taylor, Buck ordered, "Get moving."

Taylor looked directly at Celeste for a long second before striding out into the yard.

Celeste's face flamed. The damned old man had gone against her again!

She whispered, "Buck . . . how could you?"

"He's my son, Celeste. I have to give him another chance. I failed him once. I don't want to do it again."

231

"Failed him?"

Buck stood up slowly. "I don't want to discuss it any more. I'm tired. I'm going to rest for a bit."

"But . . . but the bills that need to be paid—"

"You were only fooling yourself if you thought we could pay all of them this month. They've waited this long. They can wait a little longer."

Buck turned away from the desk and walked unsteadily toward the bedroom. Celeste watched him, unable to move.

How could it be? How could it have happened . . . *again*?

She was nearing the end of her tether.

The pungent intermingling scents of a city of diverse interests and cultures struck her sharply as Vida stepped out into the New Orleans sunlight. The hustle and bustle of long, narrow streets; well-dressed pedestrians walking briskly; Negro nannies strolling with children running happily ahead—all were familiar to her. All stirred memories of times when Taylor and she had enjoyed the myriad offerings of that magnificent city while pursuing their profession; all were memories she could not presently afford to indulge as she walked briskly toward her hotel.

Vida did not react to the gentleman who tipped his hat as she left the offices of New Orleans's most prestigious newspaper. Dressed in suitable finery, she had put her New Orleans persona, Lisette Tordeau, to good use and had charmed and sweet-talked her way into the archives of that publication.

She had left Lowell a few days earlier, aware she

needed more than coincidences to make Taylor believe her suspicions were correct. Accustomed to traveling alone, she had situated herself in the respectable Hotel Royale before beginning her research into Celeste's background. Fortuitously, she had learned more from the talkative clerk in charge of the archives than from the yellowed newspapers. It hadn't been difficult. She had set the man to talking with a demure smile, a flutter of her fan, and by speaking the name of Celeste's former husband, Henri DuClair.

"Oh, yes," the fellow had declared, "everyone knows that shocking tale. It was the whispered topic of conversation in the most elite circles. Henri DuClair was a wealthy merchant who was left totally alone after the death of his wife. He fell in love with a courtesan from Miss Ruby's house of pleasure. The fact that the woman was younger than Henri by as much as thirty years was almost as great a surprise to his acquaintances as the young woman's former profession. Yet no one was especially surprised when Henri and Celeste's marriage was of short duration, or when he died unexpectedly." The clerk had snickered as he commented, "Marrying a woman as young and experienced as the vivacious Celeste was probably the mistake that cost the old gentleman his life. Celeste disappeared from New Orleans shortly afterwards. No one knows where she went, but the story is, none of Henri's friends were sorry to see her go."

Frowning, Vida approached her hotel. Celeste DuClair a former courtesan from Miss Ruby's infamous bordello? Could it be true? Celeste was obviously educated and smart enough to fool Buck Star into believing she had been a desolate widow searching for a place to start a new life. As for the rest, Vida needed to know more.

When Vida reached her hotel, she turned impetuously to the cab at the curb. There was only one place where she would be able to find out the truth. Waiting only until the hotel doorman drew open the carriage door, she climbed in and gave the driver her destination.

Alighting from the cab a short time later, Vida walked boldly up the staircase of the unpretentious mansion and rang the doorbell. Within minutes she was ushered into an elaborate room beside the staircase where a striking, red-haired, middle-aged woman met her with a smile.

Her own smile disarming, Vida inquired, "You are Miss Ruby, I presume?"

"And you are . . . ?" the woman replied politely.

"My name is . . . Vida Malone. If I may have a few minutes of your time, I have something to discuss with you."

The flickering of hundreds of candles danced against the silk-clad walls of the elaborately furnished ballroom. The music swelled as stylishly dressed couples whirled to the lilting waltz. Conversation and laughter filled every quarter as servants passed between animated groups with trays of miniature delicacies and imported champagne, assuring the success of the evening. Pierre Maison's goal of maintaining an appearance of normalcy despite the criminal charges pending against him had been achieved, yet the success of the soiree did little to dispel his inner anxiety.

His smile stiff, his patience almost at an end, Pierre

did not immediately respond to the plump young woman at his side when she said insistently, "You didn't answer me, Pierre. I inquired why you didn't invite Lisette Tordeau this evening." Her eyes bright with the spirit of retaliation, she continued, "Surely you don't hold that dear girl's peccadillo against her. She was young and inexperienced, just as I am. She was flattered by Taylor Star's attentions. She lost her head. I'm afraid I might have been similarly affected if Taylor had been attentive to *me* on that evening when champagne was flowing so freely."

"Marie . . . dear." Pierre struggled to maintain a pleasant facade. He didn't like Marie Closeau despite her family's political connections. She was overweight and plain; yet she had never forgiven him for choosing Lisette over her. Her inquiry now was a way of burning the humiliation of that evening deeper. Aware that he dared not respond with a sharp retort as he would like, Pierre replied, "You know as well as I that Lisette has left New Orleans. Even were I of a mind to invite her, I have no idea where she is presently residing."

"Pierre—" Marie smiled up at him. "You know as well as I that Lisette has returned to New Orleans. It is the talk of the town."

Immediately alert, Pierre said, "I've heard no such talk."

"I myself saw her."

"Impossible. You were mistaken."

"It's not impossible, and I am not mistaken." Her lips drawn into a pout, Marie continued, "I saw her on the street today, near the Hotel Royale. I tried to get her attention, but her carriage drew away too fast for me to signal her."

"No." Pierre shook his head. "If Lisette had returned to New Orleans, I would know."

"Whatever sources you expected to inform you, they have obviously failed. But you may discredit what I'm telling you if you wish. It isn't my concern, after all."

Pierre halted Marie as she attempted to move away. Despite the pleasure his agitation obviously gave her, he said harshly, "You're certain of this?"

"You know as well as I that it would be difficult to mistake anyone for Lisette. That luxurious black hair, those stunning dark eyes and that perfect profile, her splendid figure . . . she is far too beautiful—"

"The Hotel Royale, you say?"

"Pierre, must I repeat every word I speak?" Marie shrugged her freckled shoulder. "Go and see for yourself. And when you do, tell her Marie was asking for her. I'm sure she'd appreciate knowing that."

His expression dark, Pierre watched as Marie disappeared into the crowded room. He then turned sharply toward his study.

Lisette had returned to New Orleans?

No—she could not be so great a fool.

"She's gone. She has disappeared again."

"What?" At Gasper Bauchet's softly spoken declaration, Pierre said incredulously, "You are telling me that Lisette did indeed return to New Orleans, that a witless female like Marie Closeau knew about her stay at the Hotel Royale—that, indeed, the whole city of New Orleans knew about it—while you did not?"

"Pierre, the whereabouts of Vida Malone is not my first priority."

"I told you that I prefer to refer to her as Lisette Tordeau!"

"Still—"

"Excuses . . . one after another! I will accept them no longer!"

"I warn you, Pierre, I am doing my best to keep you from the clutches of the law, but if you persist in taking vengeance on this woman, she will be your downfall."

"That is my concern."

"No, it is not. As your lawyer—"

"As my lawyer, you are paid well to follow my orders. I remind you that should I turn my affairs over to another attorney, even at this phase of my present difficulties, it would be . . . shall we say, disastrous for you?"

"I know." Beads of perspiration surfaced on Gasper's forehead as he nodded and said, "I am well aware that I am obligated to you in many ways, Pierre, and you may be assured that I will use all the resources at my command to your benefit as I always have, Pierre. It is my duty, however—"

"It is your duty to follow my orders! I need results."

"Yes . . . of course."

"I warn you, Gasper—don't let Lisette slip through your fingers again. If you do, the penalty for your failure may be more than you are willing to pay."

Pierre watched as Gasper left the room.

His small smile was tight. He had just made sure that this time, his very dear Lisette would not get away.

"Where in hell is he?" Randy turned toward the narrow trail that wound through the pasture where the men were working. He looked back at the listless herd they had rounded up that morning and stared at the sorry condition of their hooves. "We need that medicine, dammit! I don't expect to spend all day waiting for Mitch to come back."

Taylor looked up from the fencing they were repairing. He said softly, "Don't get yourself in an uproar, Randy. Mitch probably ran into a problem. He'll be back as soon as he can."

Randy stared at Taylor for a few silent moments, then turned away, still mumbling under his breath. Not that Taylor could blame the conscientious wrangler for his agitation. The situation at the Texas Star ranch house was growing more grim every day. Buck was on his feet, but only barely. Buck accepted Celeste's cloying ways while remaining oblivious to the frustration she caused the men with her purposely irritating and foolish demands. Taylor had come to expect that kind of treatment from her, but he resented it when she harassed the men.

He had tried to talk to Buck about it, but it had been a waste of time. His only consolation was that his father's health had not appeared to worsen. He believed that if Vida was indeed correct in her theory, there would be no change in his father's health until his will came to the top of that invoice pile. Sometimes he wondered whether his pa had the same thought ... whether that was the reason he ignored the stack of invoices so determinedly.

"There he is." Randy looked at the rider coming toward them on the trail. He shouted out as Mitch neared, "It's about time. What took you so long?"

"What are you talking about, Randy?" Mitch dismounted. Taking the sack from his saddle, he handled it to the frowning foreman and said, "It's a long ride to town. I didn't do no more than stop to quench my thirst before I started back."

"Quench your thirst . . ." Randy withdrew the tins of salve from the sack and distributed them as he said, "You should be ready to get to work, then, so let's go."

Taylor was about to follow the men as they headed for the herd when Mitch took his arm. He turned with an inquiring glance. He was surprised by Mitch's frown when the cowpoke asked, "What did you do to Vida, Taylor?"

"What did I do to her? Nothing. Why?"

"I stopped off at the Last Chance to see her—just to say hello—but Bart told me she left town right after you came back to the ranch."

"Left town? Where did she go?"

"Bart don't know."

"What do you mean? She left town without telling anybody where she went? Vida wouldn't do that. She—"

Taylor halted, silently correcting that thought. Yes, she would. Leaving town without telling anybody where she was going was *exactly* what Vida might do, but he'd be damned if he'd let her get away with it this time.

"Here, take this." Taylor handed Mitch the container of salve and turned toward his mount.

"Where are you going?"

Randy looked back toward them when he heard Mitch's question. He echoed, "Where are you going, Taylor?"

"To town."

"We got work to do here."

"I've got something to do in town. I'll be back as soon as I get it done."

Taylor was mounted and on his way before Randy could respond.

"I don't know where Vida went, Taylor." Doc shrugged her shoulders. "You should know even better than me how Vida is when she gets something in her head. She wasn't going to let anybody take you out of her room when you were sick, and she wasn't going to give anybody explanations about where she was going when she left town. All she said was that she had something to do and she'd be back when she got it done."

The grim line of Taylor's lips tightened. He had said almost the same thing to Randy a short time earlier. Vida didn't tell anyone where she was going, because she didn't want anyone to know, but he knew where she had gone. She'd gone to New Orleans to see what she could find out about Celeste.

Taylor felt a hot flush of anger heat his face. She was so damned hardheaded! She was taking a chance in returning to New Orleans so soon after the conclusion of their investigation, and she knew it. Pierre Maison was an influential man, and the charges against him were damning. There was no doubt that he realized the who and how of the way evidence against him had been obtained. There was no telling what Maison's reaction might be if he saw her.

And Vida had left a week earlier. It was too late to do anything but wait.

Departing Doc's office abruptly, Taylor stepped out onto the street. He unconsciously straightened his broad shoulders as he stood momentarily motionless, staring out at the leisurely traffic as the noon sun beat mercilessly down on his head. Whatever his thoughts about Vida's theory, Vida obviously believed in it enough to risk returning prematurely to New Orleans. She deserved to have her suspicions treated more seriously than he had previously been willing to do. He owed her that.

Taylor strode through the doorway of the sheriff's office a few hours later. His expression tightened when Honor looked up from behind the sheriff's desk.

Not bothering with a greeting, he asked tersely, "What are you doing here?"

Honor's lips twitched in a way that was somehow familiar as she replied, "I could ask you the same thing, Taylor."

Not in a mood for courtesy, Taylor replied, "Where's the sheriff?"

"Jace hasn't come home yet. I got a wire from him yesterday. He's going to be gone for another week at least, so I'm putting things together for him."

"I need some information."

"Information?"

"I need help, Honor."

Honor responded without hesitation, "You know I'll do anything I can to help you, Taylor."

Pausing, Taylor stared at Honor for a few silent moments. The bond between them was there as if it had always existed. Honor would help him instinctively, just as she had when he was sick. Somehow he knew that without doubt. He could see it in her eyes.

Regretting his terse manner, Taylor began hesitantly, "I need to know more about . . . about the day Bonnie died."

"Oh."

"I've spent the past few hours talking to everybody who was in town when it happened. It's surprising how many people remember that day clearly. Everybody had something to say about it, but I didn't learn anything new . . . with one exception." Taylor's voice went hoarse as he said, "Millie Ackerman was the only one who had something new to add."

"Millie Ackerman?"

"Millie is the person who found Bonnie at the bottom of the well."

Honor did not respond.

"Millie remembered the day vividly, but she mentioned only in passing that there was a medicine wagon in town that day with a man and an old squaw in it. I didn't remember anybody mentioning that before, so I went back and checked. The wagon couldn't have been in town long, because nobody else remembered seeing it. I wanted to check Sheriff Carter's report on Bonnie's death to see if anybody else mentioned it at the time. I was hoping Jace hadn't gotten rid of Sheriff Carter's old files."

"Jace left Sheriff Carter's files just as they were. They're in the back room. I'm sure the report is there somewhere." Honor added, "I'll find it for you, Taylor."

"I'd appreciate it, Honor. Bonnie . . ." Taylor was unable to continue.

Momentarily silent, Honor said, "I'll let you know as soon as I find it."

"Thanks. Thanks for everything, Honor."

His throat still tight, Taylor left without waiting for a reply.

"What do you mean, Taylor was in town asking a lot of questions about the day Bonnie died? He hasn't left the ranch since he came back."

Celeste sat in her buggy on the deserted trail. She had been annoyed when Derek had ridden out onto the trail in front of her as she had been making her way to the meeting he had signaled at the cabin. She had begun berating him for taking a chance that they would be seen together, until his statement abruptly thrust all other thoughts from her mind.

Derek responded, "Taylor hasn't left the ranch since he came back, huh? It looks like you need me more than you think you do, because Taylor was in town yesterday talking to just about everybody who was there the day his sister was killed."

Celeste mumbled, "It's Randy . . . covering up for him again." She pressed, "What kind of questions has Taylor been asking?"

"He asked everybody to tell him whatever they could remember about that day—who was around, what everybody did, where everybody went."

"What do you mean, who was around that day and where they went?"

"I can't say it no plainer than that." Derek's expression grew sullen. "I don't know what that fella's thinking, but knowing you, I figured you would, so I came right out to tell you. Whatever he's thinking, I don't figure on missing out on the payment that's coming to me because of it. I got plans for that money . . . big plans."

Celeste sneered, "You ought to stop wasting your time on that saloon whore. We've got more important things to do right now."

"You don't have to worry about that. She left town a few days ago, and I don't stand a chance with her if I don't have enough in my pocket when she comes back to show her it'll be worthwhile."

"What makes you think she's coming back?"

"She told Bart she was . . . and I'm telling you now, I'll be waiting."

"It's come down to just a matter of business between us at present, is that it, Derek?"

"You don't fool me. It was *always* a matter of business for you."

"Maybe." Noting that Derek could not have cared less that her response indicated uncertainty on her part, Celeste smarted as she continued harshly, "But right now we need to take care of business if either of us is going to get the big payoff." Celeste did not wait for a reply as she instructed, "Keep your eyes and ears open, Derek. Don't let anything get past you. We don't want to lose out when we've waited so long."

"Don't worry about that. Like I said, I got plans."

Celeste nodded as Derek turned his horse and rode off without the courtesy of a farewell. As her buggy started forward, Celeste was inwardly fuming. That was like him. He was an ignoramus and an ingrate, but the information he had just brought her proved he was essential to her plans.

Celeste drew into the ranch yard a short time later. She rode directly to the house and stepped down from the buggy without bothering to tie it up at the rail.

244

Facing Madalane in the kitchen moments later, she asked in a harsh whisper, "Where's my husband?"

"He is still sleeping."

Moving a step closer so she was face to face with Madalane, Celeste glowered as she said, "You told me you took care of everything that day."

"What day?"

"The day Bonnie was killed."

Madalane took a backward step. "I did take care of everything."

"*Everything?* You're certain?"

"I'm certain."

"You had better be." Celeste hissed, "Because our lives may depend on it."

Chapter 9

Honor's heart pounded like a drum as she stood inside the sheriff's office awaiting Taylor's arrival. The sun was shining brightly—it was another perfect, cloudless morning—but she had no mind for the weather of the day.

Honor glanced at Cal, who stood beside the desk a few feet away. She had felt an affinity for Cal the first moment she had seen him. He had been angry and had not even noticed her as he strode past, but she remembered her reaction to his distinctive honey-colored eyes, and the controlled power in his long, steady strides. She had almost convinced herself not to tell him the truth about who she was; but when she did, Cal had accepted her as his sister with genuine warmth. The spontaneous affection between them had remained steadfast.

It had not been the same between her and Taylor. Cal and Taylor were as dissimilar in looks and temperament as it seemed two brothers could be. Cal's appearance, with his sun-streaked hair and tawny eyes, was in direct contrast to Taylor's thick dark hair and mesmerizing blue eyes; and where Cal was said to resemble his mother, Taylor was undoubtedly the image of his father in younger years. Unlike Cal, Taylor had been the antithesis of the town hero when she first met him. He had arrived in town drunk and with a chip on his shoulder. He had resented her from the moment he learned of her existence and had refused to meet her. When they met face-to-face unexpectedly, however, the ice in Taylor's gaze had melted at the sight of her. Yet, although he had then accepted her warmly, he had still maintained his distance. Despite that distance, she had felt no hesitation about stepping up to help at the time of his sickness. Nor had there been any hesitation on his part in accepting her presence.

But something about Taylor still remained a mystery, leaving her uncertain.

Honor had found and read Sheriff Carter's file. Again, there had been no hesitation on her part, this time in sending for both Cal and Taylor to make of it what they chose—together.

Honor took a breath as Taylor's footsteps approached the door. She pushed back a strand of tawny hair from her forehead, unsure what his reaction would be. She missed Jace's stalwart presence beside her.

Taylor knocked, then entered. He stood stock-still at the sight of Cal. Honor released a tense breath when Taylor said, "I'm glad to see you here, Cal. Honor was right to call you in on this." He turned to Honor and said, "You found Sheriff Carter's file?"

"Yes. I didn't mean to alarm you by having you and Cal both come in to read it. It really doesn't say much more than you both already know." She frowned when she added, "But it does mention a medicine wagon being in town, just as you suspected it would, Taylor. It seems an Indian squaw was with the wagon. The squaw was seen near the well around the time that Bonnie fell in. Sheriff Carter made a notation that the wagon was gone the next day, but he never looked into the reason for its hasty departure because of the commotion about Bonnie's accident."

Cal interjected gruffly, "I need to know what this is all about, Taylor."

Cal listened solemnly, the broad line of his shoulders growing increasingly tense as Taylor outlined the suspicious coincidences that had come to light.

"You're right. There are too many coincidences to be easily dismissed, yet I can't believe that Bonnie's death could have been anything more than a terrible accident."

Taylor turned to Honor as if in afterthought, "You took over the kitchen chores at the Texas Star for a while. Did Pa have any bouts of his sickness while you were there?"

"No, as a matter of fact, he didn't. He . . ." Honor took a backward step. "Taylor, you don't think . . . ? No, that couldn't be true!"

Honor closed her eyes, momentarily weakened by the harsh suspicion that entered her mind. She leaned into the support of the strong arms that enfolded her, then looked up at Taylor as he whispered, "I'm sorry, Honor. I wasn't trying to shock you, or scare you, either. It's just that the deeper I look, the worse all this seems."

Obviously deeply affected, Cal said, "Say what you're thinking, Taylor."

"I don't know what to think yet." Releasing Honor, Taylor continued, "All I am sure of is that things aren't entirely what they seem. The truth is, I don't want to believe the direction my thoughts are heading."

"What about this Indian squaw? What can she possibly have to do with this?"

"I don't know—but I mean to find out."

"You're taking a big risk if your suspicions are correct." Cal's brow knitted with concern. "You barely survived an unnamed sickness hardly more than a week ago. You might not be so lucky a second time."

"You sound like Vida."

Confused, Honor said, "But Vida left town."

"She'll be back." Taylor's expression darkened. "And then she's going to hear what I have to say about her leaving without letting me know."

His gaze direct, Cal said, "It's time you set things straight with us about you and Vida. It's obvious you two aren't strangers."

"That's right, we aren't."

Cal waited.

Taylor glanced at the wall clock and said, "I'll have to save that explanation for another time. I have to get back to the ranch before anyone at the house realizes I'm gone. Randy's a good old boy. He's been covering for my absences during the day, but even his patience has its limits."

"What can Honor and I do to help?"

"Nothing right now, Cal. Everything is uncertain. I'll let you know the minute I find out something definite, but for the time being, it's important that I continue appearing to be your wayward brother. That way no one takes me too seriously."

Cal nodded as he accepted the hand Taylor extended. He said hesitantly, "Taylor, about the letters— did you find out anything?"

"I'm sorry, Cal. I still have no idea who sent them."

Taylor turned back to Honor. She was startled to hear him say, "I'm not sure if I ever thanked you for everything you've done, Honor." She saw the sincerity that flashed in his light eyes when he said, "At least one good thing has come out of this mess. It's good to have a sister again."

Honor's throat choked tight with emotion as Taylor walked out onto the street.

A warm breeze blew briskly, whipping strands of Celeste's upswept hair free as she reached down into the laundry basket for another piece of wet clothing. Livid, she struggled to secure the garment to the line stretched behind the house. She was keenly aware that such a menial task was beneath her, but circumstances had forced her to undertake it. Buck had seemed to be behind her at each turn since early morning, tottering on unsteady legs as she sought the opportunity to speak to Madalane alone. He had since retired to his bed, but she could not be sure that he would not overhear her, no matter how softly Madalane and she spoke. She'd had no recourse but to follow Madalane out into the yard with the pretense of helping her with the laundry.

The wet garments snapped and crackled, flapping as the gusts lifted and twisted them around the line. Celeste struggled to fasten the pins. Grunting when she finally managed to secure a garment, she turned again to Madalane, continuing, "I asked Randy directly this morning. I said I wanted to know if Taylor was putting in a full day's work with the rest of the men. He looked me straight in the face and said Taylor was working right beside them, that he was working hard—maybe harder than he should, considering his recent illness. I was tempted to call him a liar straight out, but I couldn't, dammit! If I had my way—"

"Randy is not your true enemy here, Celeste." Madalane's dark eyes sparked with hatred. "Your enemies are the man who shares your bed and those who share his blood. But of them all, your husband is the one who deserves your vengeance most."

"I'm worried, Madalane. Everything is beginning to slip away from me. I'm becoming uncertain for the first time that things will work out as we planned. I'm losing control of the ranch hands, when I previously had them so afraid to oppose me that they didn't dare move without my approval. I'm even losing control of Derek. Right now, Derek is more interested in that saloon whore, Vida Malone, than he is in me. Most importantly, I'm losing control of Buck. He's beginning to challenge my advice because of Taylor. Taylor's presence is causing him to rethink all manner of past decisions, despite the animosity between them. Buck actually said he thinks he may have *failed* his son."

Celeste's delicate brow furrowed as she said, "Perhaps it's a warning, Madalane. Perhaps we should put an end to things, here and now, without waiting for Buck to change his will. This ranch isn't worth much at present, anyway. We could—"

Celeste's words drew to a halt at the sight of Madalane's sudden rage. She retreated a step as

Madalane rasped, "Never! Never, do you hear me? I will not allow you to renege on your vow . . . on the promise you made to your mother on her deathbed! Neither you nor I will leave this ranch until Jeanette's vengeance is complete, until everything Buck Star achieved is stolen from him, just as he stole my dear Jeanette's life from her!"

"You are obsessed with revenge, Madalane, so much so that you fail to recognize our present danger. We risk losing everything if we stay."

"We do not! Everything was progressing according to plan, despite the setbacks Cal Star and Honor Gannon each brought with them. It is Taylor Star's return and the problems he has caused which now appear insurmountable. If not for him, we would be only days from total retribution."

"If not for him," Celeste mocked. "But Taylor *is* here, and he is growing stronger on this ranch by the moment."

"If he had consumed a few more mouthfuls of my potion, he would be out of our way."

"But he didn't, did he?" Celeste's tone grew shrill. "He is here, affecting our every move . . . making Buck worry about his treatment of his sons and illegitimate daughter . . . and making him doubt *me*!"

"We need to be rid of Taylor Star."

"No!" Celeste drew herself rigidly upright. "You tried once and failed. I will not risk another attempt."

"We need to be rid of Taylor Star, Celeste," Madalane persisted.

"I will not allow you to do it!"

"I did not say *I* would take his life." Madalane's smile

253

was malevolent. "The degenerate, Derek, has been doing very little to earn the 'payoff' he seeks. He is proficient in delivering a bullet in the back, is he not?"

Celeste went still.

"Isn't he?"

Celeste shook her head. "It would be too obvious."

"Why would it be obvious? Taylor Star is a drunk. A drunk makes many enemies. And you, my dear Celeste, are such an excellent actress that no one will doubt your shock or your despair at your husband's grief."

Her breast beginning to heave with excitement, Celeste whispered, "Dare I take the chance?"

"My darling Celeste, who would dare challenge you?" Madalane added, "And you do look so beautiful in black."

A harsh burst of laughter escaped Celeste's throat. The sound was swept away by the warm breeze as Celeste gave a last disdainful look at the wet laundry and said, "I must return to the house now . . . in the event my husband should need me. I will be very careful not to wake him, of course. He will need his sleep."

Celeste's smile broadened as she said, "Poor Buck . . . he has such dark days ahead of him."

"What do you want?"

"What do I want?"

Celeste barely controlled her ire as she faced Derek coldly in the dilapidated cabin that had become so nauseatingly familiar. She had come to the foul structure after an extremely careful toilette. Her blonde, upswept curls gleamed, her fair complexion was blushed lightly with color, and the blue gown that matched the exact shade of her eyes was tantalizingly demure—just revealing enough to tempt the imagination of a man as crude and degenerate as Derek. Yet his only reaction was a blunt question delivered in an insulting tone.

The fool! He didn't know what he was missing.

Celeste ignored her inner rage as she said sweetly, "I have a job for you, Derek. Something simple. Something you will undoubtedly enjoy."

Derek eyed Celeste cautiously, then ventured, "You do? What is it?"

"I want you to kill Taylor Star."

Derek's surprised expression was priceless.

Celeste confirmed with concealed amusement, "Yes, you heard me correctly. I want you to kill Taylor Star. You were previously very explicit about your preference for a bullet as opposed to . . . a more obscure solution. I've decided that I agree. A bullet in the back will do well."

"Wait a minute! What's going on here?"

"It's simple, Derek. Taylor Star is becoming too great a danger to our plans. My husband won't admit it, but Taylor's diligence is beginning to win him over. I can't let that happen."

"Yes, but—"

"Are you hesitating? You amaze me, Derek. I thought you would be anxious to follow through on this. Isn't Taylor the man your precious Vida is amusing herself with while you sit and pant with desire? Isn't he the man you'll have to face down once you have the fistful of money you're certain will make her turn to you instead of him? Who knows? Maybe with Taylor out of the way, the tramp will turn to you even without the money. She may *fall* into your arms."

"Wait a minute," Derek repeated. He paused to study Celeste's expression more closely. "You're not doing this for my benefit."

"I didn't say I was." Her patience waning, Celeste continued, "Actually, it would be the answer to both our problems."

Celeste waited.

No response.

Her smile faded. "Well, what do you say?"

"I'm thinking."

She snapped, "Don't think too hard, Derek. You'll worry a simple solution into something that it isn't. You won't find the task difficult to accomplish. You'll have countless opportunities. Taylor works on the range with the other hands every day. All you need do is wait until he's clearly in your sights. He won't be expecting an attack. He'll be a sitting duck."

"It won't be as easy as you think. The other hands will take off after me the second they hear the shot. Once they get on my trail, I'll never shake them."

"However you choose to do it, then."

No response.

"You've handled this kind of thing before, haven't you?"

"Sure."

"Well?"

"I'll have to wait my chance to get him alone."

"I said, *however you choose to do it*."

Derek's small eyes drilled into hers. "When do you want it to happen?"

"As soon as possible. The sooner, the better."

"You're a cold-blooded bitch, ain't you?"

"A cold-blooded bitch—with the face of an angel.

And you may rest assured that my distress will be impressive to behold when I learn of Taylor's demise."

Derek squinted at her a moment longer. He then turned his back and started toward the door. He said over his shoulder as he drew it open, "It's as good as done."

The brilliant sunshine of midday barely penetrated the clouds of dust raised by the wild stock as Taylor and the ranch hands rounded up the unruly herd. He was as aware as the other men were that every head of stock, even those wily few who routinely escaped their vigilance, was now important to the Texas Star; yet the rider approaching their group at a rapid pace drew his attention from the rebellious animals.

Taylor nudged his mount out of the dust as the rider drew nearer. He recognized young Elmer Harden, and his heart jumped a beat. Elmer had become the unofficial messenger from town to the Texas Star . . . and Elmer was heading directly toward him.

Taylor waited tensely until Elmer drew up and said breathlessly, "I got a message for you from Honor, Taylor. She sent me out to let you know that Vida came back on the morning stage."

Vida . . .

"Honor said she wanted you to know right away, because she thought you had something you needed to clear up with her."

Right.

Elmer inquired, "You got any message for me to take back to Honor?"

"No, she won't be expecting an answer."

"I don't mind, you know. Honor already paid me, and I gotta ride back anyway."

"No message."

"Suit yourself."

Taylor watched as Elmer started back at the same breakneck pace with which he had approached. He turned when Randy commented beside him, "I'm wondering if that young fella will make it back to town without breaking his neck."

Taylor said, "I was thinking the same thing."

"Was you?"

Taylor noted the mustached wrangler's tone. He said, "Is something wrong, Randy?"

"That's what I was about to ask you."

"What are you talking about?"

Randy squinted up at him with an uncertain expression. "Look, Taylor, I don't know what's going on, but I'm starting to get worried. I don't mind covering for you when you say you've got to go to town on business even though you're supposed to be working with the rest of the hands. I figure a man who's been away from home as long as you have might have some pretty important business to take care of—business he maybe don't want to talk about. But I got to tell you, it's getting downright hard for me to cover for you."

"Meaning?"

"Meaning Celeste is getting suspicious. I don't know how she's been finding out things, but she knows you've been in town a couple of times when you should be working here. She's looking for the chance to tell your pa so she can get you fired off this ranch."

"That sounds like her."

"What I'm saying is, whether Honor thinks it's important for you to know your lady friend is back in town or not, I'm thinking it would be a bad idea for you to ride off now when you should be working."

"I didn't intend to do that."

"You didn't?"

"No. It would cause too much talk if I came riding into town right after Elmer brought me the news—and the last thing I need is more talk. But you can damned well bet I'll be going there tonight, right after supper."

"The lady can wait, huh?"

"She'll have to."

Randy eyed him speculatively, then said, "Whatever's going on, I need to say my piece, and it comes down to this. I've been here with your pa through the thick and thin of this illness of his. I've seen him get sick, get better, and then get sicker than before. It's my feeling . . ." Randy's voice grew hoarse. He stopped to clear his throat, took a breath, and continued, "It's my feeling that your pa ain't going to get better this time. He's on his last legs, Taylor, and he knows it. He's starting to look at his life from that viewpoint now, and I've got a feeling he don't much like what he sees. He won't say it, but I think he's glad you're back. I'm telling you this because . . . well, because I don't want you to do anything that'll change that feeling he's starting to get inside him. The fact is, I figure your pa don't have time for any more mistakes."

Taylor could not immediately reply.

"I don't have to tell you," Randy continued, "if Celeste can possibly turn your pa against you, she will. So be careful. There's the devil in that woman."

"I know."

"Just as long as you remember it."

Taylor watched as Randy rode back to the herd. Silent, he followed him.

Pa was dying.

He didn't want to think about that.

Vida was back.

It was a damned good thing she was.

The applause was deafening. It rose like a wave over the saloon, and Vida's flawless skin flushed with pleasure. It amazed her how these weary, lonesome cowhands responded to her.

Vida waved at her appreciative audience, winked her thanks at Harvey, and started toward the bar. She had sung several songs—some of them twice. It was time to let the customers do a little more drinking so Bart would be happy. She—

Vida turned abruptly and walked toward the card tables. Derek was at the bar, and that was one man she would happily forget if she were able. Yet if she were to believe the way the hair on the back of her neck was rising, Derek wasn't going to let her.

A clammy hand closed on Vida's shoulder.

"Did you miss me, Vida? Because I sure as hell missed you."

Vida allowed Derek to turn her toward him. Tired of the game she was forced to play, she said coldly, "Did you?"

She glanced toward the door. Where was Taylor, anyway? Honor had come to her room earlier to tell her she had sent a rider to inform Taylor she had returned. She wondered how much Taylor had told his perceptive half-sister about them. She suspected she knew what Honor was thinking . . . and she reluctantly wished it were true. But she was already several hours into the evening and Taylor hadn't yet arrived.

Damn the man! He was probably trying to teach her a lesson about leaving Lowell without telling him where she was going or when she would return. Actually, she had known that Taylor would realize where she had gone the moment he discovered she had left town—a fact which had probably made him angrier.

As if he had the right to tell her what to do! She had a mind of her own, and a life of her own. She wasn't bound to his approval.

Right.

So, where was he? She was anxious to see him—more than anxious. She had worried about him while she was away. She had missed him, too, and she had important information to convey.

But Derek's grip on her shoulder was unrelenting, and Taylor hadn't arrived.

Vida asked impatiently, "What do you want, Derek?"

Derek responded bluntly, "You know what I want."

The boor was nothing if not tactless.

Vida forced a smile and said, "Well, you're not going to get it. You know my feelings about that. I'm a one-man woman, and I expect my man to be a one-woman man."

"I ain't having nothing to do with that other woman no more, and I told her so."

Sensing that Derek was telling the truth, Vida raised an inquisitive brow. "You did? What did she say?"

"She didn't like it much. As a matter of fact, she didn't like it at all."

"She was real heartbroken, huh?"

"Until she finds somebody else to take my place."

"I thought you said she was married."

"Yeah . . . married . . . to an old man who can't follow through on what he starts. Besides, she don't even like him."

"Doesn't like him? Why did she marry him, then? Strictly for the money?"

Obviously aware he had already said too much, Derek said, "I don't want to talk about her no more. It's you and me I'm interested in now."

"You're a little late. I've got me a man."

"Yeah?" Derek glanced around the saloon. "So where is he? I don't see nobody special showing up to welcome you back like I am. Maybe he don't care as much about you as you think."

"He cares."

"If I was you, I'd want him to prove it."

Vida laughed. "He proves it, all right."

His expression turning dark, Derek said, "We both know you're talking about Taylor Star, so I'm telling you you're making a mistake with that fella. He's a drunk and a waster . . . and he ain't got no future."

Her smile coy, Vida responded, "It isn't his future I'm interested in, Derek. The present will do just fine."

"Well, he ain't got much of a present left, neither!"

Vida's smile froze. "What are you talking about?"

Having again revealed more than he intended, Derek countered with, "He's a drunk and a loser. Everybody knows that. Even his pa can't stand him. When the old man dies, he won't get a cent of whatever's left."

"You seem to know a lot about Taylor's business for an outsider."

"The whole town knows about him. And the whole town is wondering why you're sticking to him like you are."

"I suppose because he has what I want right now."

"What's that?"

Vida answered with a smile.

Infuriated, Derek pulled her a step closer and said, "I can do more for you than he can. And I got me a big payoff coming real soon. You and me can get out of this town and find ourselves a right fine place in New Orleans then, and we can have ourselves a real good time."

"A big payoff? When's that supposed to happen?"

"Soon. Very soon."

"Like . . . tomorrow soon?"

"Soon enough."

Vida pulled her arm free and said, "Talk to me when you have that payoff in your hand, Derek. In the meantime—"

Vida's heart leaped as the swinging doors pushed open and Taylor walked in. He paused just inside the doors to scan the room with an astute gaze all the more potent for the astonishing blue of his eyes and the intensely masculine aura he radiated with no effort at all. It occurred to Vida that even as thin as he was, Taylor dwarfed the average cowpoke with his powerful stature—a stature that reminded her only too vividly of the way she felt when she was wrapped in his arms.

Taylor's gaze halted. He scowled at the sight of Derek standing beside her.

Turning back to Derek, Vida said, "Talk to me again when you've got more than promises in your pocket, Derek. That might make me change my mind about what Taylor has to offer."

Leaving Derek where he stood, Vida wound her way through the tables toward Taylor. The weight of his gaze was almost palpable as she approached him—so intense that she was breathless when she reached his side at last—when she slid her arms around his neck and whispered, "Damn you, Taylor, you're late again."

She then kissed him with every ounce of love in her.

Vida's softly spoken reprimand faded from Taylor's mind as her mouth touched his. Aware of nothing more at that moment than the womanly heat she pressed so tightly against him, and the pounding heart that echoed his own, he wrapped his arms around her and indulged himself in her kiss. Lost to the moment, he drew her closer, his hunger growing, only to be stunned when Vida ended their kiss and whispered lovingly against his lips, "That ought to do it for now. We have a long evening ahead of us."

The cold slap of reality restored the frown to Taylor's face. It was business as usual.

Taylor followed silently as Vida led him toward the rear of the room. A table emptied at her approach, and he saw her wink at the grinning fellows who vacated the spot for them. An emotion he chose not to name clenched tight inside him, causing him to comment with a cold smile as he pulled her chair closer, "It seems like you've made a lot of friends in this place."

Leaning so near that her mouth was only inches from his, Vida responded, "They like me here, Taylor. They want me to be happy so I won't leave again."

"Oh, is that it?"

Vida's smile faltered. "I don't think I care to ask what you meant by that comment."

"Just like you didn't care to ask what I thought about your leaving Lowell."

"It shouldn't have made any difference to you. You made it pretty plain that you didn't want me to come here in the first place."

"That was then. This is now."

"Oh, so your attitude has changed, is that it?"

"I told you. I feel responsible for you. Besides, I owe you."

"No, you don't—and I told you, I can take care of myself."

"Is that why you went back to New Orleans, to prove you didn't need me to get things done?"

"You know why I went there."

"And I know how dangerous it was for you there. Pierre Maison isn't a fool, Vida. He has to know who smuggled that evidence out of his house. He may be in a jail cell, but he's still—"

"Pierre isn't in jail. His lawyer got him out."

Taylor swore under his breath.

"Money talks, Taylor. So does prestige. Pierre has both."

"Did you see him?"

"He didn't even know I was in the city."

"How can you be sure?"

"Because I stayed at the Hotel Royale, and Pierre is bold enough to have been at my door if he knew."

"You stayed at the Hotel Royale? Don't tell me you used the name Lisette Tordeau."

"You know I did. I needed all the charm and influence I could muster to get the information I wanted. Lisette is known well enough in certain circles to accomplish that more quickly than Vida Malone could."

Vida paused as Bart appeared at the table with a bottle and two glasses. Taylor shot him a threatening glance as he placed them down. Annoyed at Taylor's attitude, Vida offered sweetly, "You'll have to forgive my friend, Bart. He's out of sorts because he missed me."

Barely maintaining her smile as Bart departed, Vida said, "I don't know what's wrong with you tonight, Taylor, but everybody in this place is watching us—including Derek. In case you didn't notice, Derek is ready to bust with wanting me. He's trying to impress me with hints about a big payoff he's expecting. He figures when he gets it, he'll be sitting where you're sitting right now, so if you want me to worm any more information out of him, you'd better do a better job of playing your part."

Taylor looked at Derek, his gaze so vicious that Vida was momentarily stunned. She cautioned, "Take it easy. You don't want to scare Derek off. He's important to us."

"Is he?"

Vida assessed Taylor more closely. He was annoyed, angry. She had seen him this way before, but this time it was different. She asked abruptly, "What's the matter, Taylor?"

"Nothing."

"I know better than that."

Ignoring her response, Taylor said, "If everybody is expecting us to give them a show, we'd better give it to them."

Taylor kissed her then—a kiss as angry as his demeanor. His hand stole into her hair to hold her fast as he separated her lips with his, as he plundered her mouth with a searching kiss that Vida struggled inwardly to resist. Shaken when he drew back from her at last, she was startled to see that he looked as unnerved as she.

Unable to speak, she filled the glasses in front of her with a trembling hand, then downed her own drink in a single gulp.

Yes, it was going to be a very long evening.

The saloon was emptying for the night, and Taylor released a silent sigh of relief. The hours had dragged along excruciatingly as Vida alternately teased and tormented him with her attentions. It had been harder than he had ever realized it could be to play the lover when he had to remind himself Vida was acting the whole time.

Vida was returning from talking to Bart at the bar. Despite himself, Taylor could not tear his gaze from the way the lamplight glittered on the raven sheen of her hair as she walked across the room, from the smile she flashed so generously, or from the ample sway of her hips that attracted every male eye. He had always taken for granted the fact that Vida was beautiful; but somehow that term no longer seemed to adequately describe her. He did not recall how many times she had left him to sing for the boisterous crowd, but he did know he wouldn't be able to take much more of Derek Beecher's undisguised lust, or the watchful gazes of the cowpokes at the bar. The knowledge that each and every one of them wished himself in Taylor's shoes gnawed at him almost as much as his certainty that each and every one of them wondered when it could possibly be his turn.

Vida and he had been so carefully watched that they

had not been able to talk privately. Perhaps it was just as well. He couldn't seem to concentrate on anything but Vida's nearness—the way she looked at him, the way she touched him. She was driving him crazy.

Taylor stood up, grateful the night had come to an end. He slid his arm around Vida and turned her toward the door without speaking a word. It had always been like that with them—the silent communication that now seemed to halt when he held her in his arms.

Vida leaned warmly against his side as they reached the street. She rested her head against his shoulder, and they turned toward the hotel. They had walked together with the same easy, wordless familiarity countless times, but this time the spontaneity of Vida's actions choked his throat tight.

Damn . . . how long had he loved her without realizing it?

The tension inside Taylor mounted as Vida and he entered the hotel and walked up the staircase toward her room. He watched as she withdrew her key from the pocket of her gown and opened the door, expecting him to follow her in. When he stood rigidly still, she looked back at him questioningly.

"What's the matter, Taylor? Don't you feel well?"

"I'm fine."

"Then why are you standing there? Aren't you coming in?"

"No."

"Why? And don't tell me I'm too much for you sometimes."

"I wouldn't say that, because it isn't completely true."

"What do you mean?"

Footsteps on the stairs turned them both toward the cowpoke who reached the landing, then started unsteadily down the hallway toward them. The fellow leered at them as he slurred, "Don't let me get in your way. I can see you've got business to take care of in there."

Taylor turned toward the man with sudden anger, only to have Vida jerk him into her room and slam the door closed behind them. She stared at him in semi-darkness relieved by the light of the single lamp she had left burning on her nightstand. The shadows played against her faultless features as she scrutinized his expression. He wondered what she saw. He hoped—

"You're sure you feel all right?"

"I told you, I'm fine."

"What's wrong, then? You know we need to talk. I have things to tell you."

"You can tell me tomorrow."

"Why tomorrow?"

Why?

The answer was painfully clear. He wanted her. He wanted to feel every inch of Vida's sweet flesh beneath him—yielding, warm, and giving. He wanted to feel her arms slide around his neck as she moaned with the joy of wanting him in return. He wanted to taste her, to consume her, to hear her call out his name as he plunged himself hard and deep inside her. He wanted to feel her body close around him as he claimed her so completely that he would never feel uncertain again.

"Taylor . . . ?"

"It's not like it was before between us, Vida." Her lips parted with an indiscernible word as her gaze locked with his. He heard himself say, "It's not all fun and games anymore for me."

"Fun and games?"

"If I stay here tonight, we won't be doing very much talking. I don't want to push you into something you don't want, something you might feel obligated to do. I don't want—"

"I don't want you to tell me what you *don't* want, Taylor." Vida's voice dropped to a husky whisper. "I want you to tell me what you *do* want."

"That's easy," Taylor said, "I want *you*."

Vida's expression flickered at his declaration. A second later, she raised herself on tiptoe and slid her hands onto his shoulders to whisper against his lips, "Like you said, Taylor . . . that's easy."

Vida was suddenly in his arms, and the world rocked around him.

The joy of her. The wonder.

Taylor clutched Vida close as her body cleaved to his, as he savored their kiss. Resenting the few steps it took to reach the bed behind them, Taylor covered Vida's body with his at last. The midnight silk of her hair was cool to his touch as he wound his hands tightly in the luxuriant mass. Her mouth was soft and giving as he caressed its intimate hollows with his tongue. Her flesh was sweet and fragrant as he bathed her warm breasts with his kisses, as he suckled the burgeoning crests. Her body quivered with an anticipation he shared as his caresses traveled a steady downward trail, as trembling hands and fumbling fingers stripped away her gaudy gown.

Vida was naked underneath him at last, and the impact of the moment held him momentarily still. *This* was what he had wanted; *this* was the driving desire he had sought to deny.

Long, languorous kisses . . . intoxicating intimate exploration, all to the muffled gasps of undisguised passion that escaped Vida's perfect lips.

Taylor was breathless, almost mad with the delirium of wanting her as he poised himself, firm and hard, at the moist delta between Vida's thighs. Holding himself diligently in check, needing confirmation of her feelings, he watched the play of emotions on Vida's face as he slowly slid himself inside her. He saw a hunger that he shared. He saw wonder as he met her moist warmth. He saw anticipation building as he stroked her; and as his intimate thrusts gradually accelerated, he saw a need reflecting his own.

Conscious thought slipped away as Vida accommodated him, joining him with loving fervor as her moment neared. He heard her mumble softly. He felt the gradual shuddering that assumed control. He felt her body clench tight around him as she gasped with pleasure. He held himself fast and kissed her long and deep until she stilled, needing to burn the moment firmly into memory, to erase any lingering doubt.

His own passion erupting abruptly, Taylor clutched Vida tight as the moment exploded in a hot, fiery burst that carried her with him, shuddering to breathless culmination.

Sober and motionless minutes later, still joined to Vida, Taylor raised himself to look down into her motionless face. Her thickly fringed lids twitched, then lifted with the languor of complete satisfaction.

Taylor heard himself say, "Did you always know I loved you, Vida?"

271

Her voice ragged in response, Vida whispered, "No, but somehow I always knew I loved you."

Vida's heavy eyelids fluttered as she drew his mouth down again to hers.

In the shadows of the street beyond Vida's window, a male figure stirred, then cursed as Vida's room went suddenly dark.

He had watched as Vida and Taylor entered the hotel, as silhouettes appeared against the blind in a street window minutes later. He had seen the silhouettes blend with mounting passion, then suddenly drop from view.

Seething, he waited, watching the dark window a moment longer.

Silent and unseen, he disappeared into the shadows.

Chapter 10

"Taylor . . ."

Taylor stirred slowly from his intoxicating dream. He dreamed Vida was lying beside him, her naked flesh pressed to his. He—

"Taylor . . ." The voice grew insistent. "It's almost morning. You have to get up and go back to the ranch."

Taylor opened his eyes to the gray light of approaching dawn. Vida was leaning over him. He reached up spontaneously to capture the dream.

"No, Taylor." Vida resisted, insisting, "You have to get up. Buck will be expecting you to start work with the other men this morning."

Harsh reality returned at the sound of his father's name, and Taylor drew himself upright. He watched wordlessly as Vida stood up and reached for her wrapper, her fair, naked skin aglow in the dim light until it was hidden from his view. She sat back on the bed beside him. Her luxurious hair lay in disarray on her narrow shoulders, her saloon makeup was smudged, and her lips had the swollen look of having been thoroughly kissed.

Kissed by him.

Kissed until they were both past thinking.

She had never looked more beautiful.

Taylor touched her cheek gently, and Vida's insistence visibly wavered before she took a breath and said, "We need to talk before you go back to the ranch, Taylor. I have to tell you what I learned in New Orleans—about Celeste."

Celeste.

Warm emotions froze as Taylor asked, "What about her?"

He listened as Vida related the high points of Celeste's past. Silent for long moments, Taylor said, "A courtesan . . . a professional from Miss Ruby's House of Pleasure, then a grieving widow. You're sure about this?"

Vida responded, "I went to Miss Ruby's place of business to speak to her personally." She continued determinedly despite Taylor's grunt of disapproval, "Miss Ruby remembered Celeste well. She said Celeste came to her young, experienced, and ready for any way of life that would raise her up from the streets. She said Celeste quickly became a favorite with her patrons, but she soon learned that Celeste was not what she appeared to be. She said she did not realize until Celeste left to marry Henri, however, that Celeste was adept at using her youth to extract money from her suitors, even claiming to some that she was being kept a virtual prisoner at the bordello. She said Celeste's dalliances after her marriage were the talk of their social set, that everyone knew about them—everyone but Henri. She said Celeste appeared devastated at her husband's funeral, only to recuperate the moment he was interred, when she sold off his estate and then disappeared from New Orleans."

"When she came to Lowell?"

Vida nodded. "The timing matches up exactly."

"But why Lowell, and why Pa?"

Vida hesitated for the first time, then responded, "You'll have to ask your father about that."

Vida's hesitation set off a warning bell, and Taylor demanded, "Tell me what you know, Vida."

She shook her head. "I don't *know* anything. That's the problem. Everything else I heard was rumor that I couldn't corroborate. Ask your father if he remembers a woman named Jeanette Borneau. She was Celeste's mother."

"Was?"

"She's dead. She killed herself."

Momentarily silent, Taylor said, "My father knew a lot of women after his marriage. Honor is living proof of that."

"Ask him about Jeanette."

"Tell me what you heard," he repeated.

Vida stepped away from the bed. "The only way you'll find out anything for sure is to ask your father."

His jaw tight, Taylor stood up and reached for his clothes. He had seen that obstinate look on Vida's face before. She had said all she was going to say.

Fully dressed at last, Taylor turned to look at Vida, who was standing silent beside the door. Her expression was stoic as she waited for him to leave, when a few hours earlier she had lain in his arms with a flush of passion coloring her beautiful face as she whispered his name. But that had been then. They had both been able to close themselves off from the world around them then, until morning had brought back all the harsh realities that had faded with the light.

Vida deserved more than the harsh realities and uncertainties he presently had to offer.

As if reading his mind, she whispered, "It's all right, Taylor. You need to settle this, once and for all."

Reaching out to grip Vida's shoulders, Taylor felt the tremor that shook her at his touch. That tremor reverberated inside him a hundredfold as he said, "I want to know one thing. Will anything you learned in New Orleans about my father affect what we had together last night?"

"No. Never."

He responded with a truth difficult to express, "I'm not sure about how all this will turn out, Vida . . . about how much of a future I really have to offer you."

Vida stepped closer and whispered, "If last night was a sample, I'd say you have plenty."

"Vida . . ." A transitory smile flickered across Taylor's lips, "You never were one to mince words." Grateful for that truth, he drew her close against the heat building in his groin.

Taylor's mouth was descending toward hers when Vida said, "Taylor . . . please . . . go." Looking up at him, her eyes so great and dark that he felt he could drown in them, she whispered, "You've come this far. You need to talk with your father."

Taylor replied softly, "Did it ever occur to you that he might not want to talk to me?"

"Do it . . . before it's too late."

Too late.

Pausing only a moment longer, Taylor kissed her, then determinedly put her at arm's length. "I'll be back."

There he was, the bastard!

From his position across the street in the bank doorway, Derek watched Taylor walk out of the hotel. Derek had spent the night concealed in the dark discomfort there, waiting for Taylor to emerge. He had watched the light in Vida's room go dark, and had then dozed intermittently until dawn stretched fingers of light across the sky.

You're a little late, Derek. I've got me a man.

He proved he cares, all right.

Derek's irritation flared up as Vida's comments rang through his mind. If he wasn't so damned determined to have that saloon witch stretched out naked underneath him, he would've turned his back on the whole situation the moment Celeste began looking at him like he was raw meat; but he was hot for Vida, and there was no turning back.

Anyway, he'd be killing two birds with one stone.

Derek smiled at that thought. Getting Celeste off his back would be a plus, but not half the pleasure he'd take in seeing every jaw in that saloon drop when he walked out with Vida on his arm.

Derek drew himself up straight and watched Taylor Star walk down the boardwalk. Derek almost hooted out loud when he saw Star turn toward the livery stable at the end of the street.

Good fella! Obviously, Star had taken the time to stable his horse the previous night, figuring he wouldn't be picking it up until morning. That would give Derek the head start he needed so he could find the perfect spot to lie in wait until his quarry rode by.

Derek turned toward the alleyway behind him and headed for the horse he had tied to the hitching post behind the bank. He mounted up and smiled at the thought that within the hour, Taylor Star would be out of his way forever.

"He'll do it. You'll see."

Celeste stood beside Madalane, speaking softly. She had left Buck asleep in bed as the morning sky lightened. Grateful to leave the room where the scent of approaching death grew stronger each day, she had joined Madalane in the kitchen. The Negress worked at the stove preparing the ranch breakfast as Celeste continued softly, "Derek won't wait long to get the job done. He's besotted by that saloon whore, and Taylor is in his way."

Madalane looked up at her questioningly, to which Celeste responded with subdued anger, "Taylor won't last out the week, I tell you."

Madalane pressed, "Did you specify that the deed needs to be done quickly? Time is important. Your husband fails more each day."

"I told him to do it as soon as possible."

"You were not more specific?"

"Derek doesn't respond to my orders as he did in the past, Madalane. I told you that! He's gotten independent since he became infatuated with that whore. It's just fortunate that his infatuation influences him in our favor."

Madalane remained silent, but Celeste was aware that she disapproved. She snapped, "Don't look at me like that! This was your idea in the first place. Anyway, I have a final card to play should Derek hesitate. I'm going to tell Buck I can't bear Taylor's presence any longer, that he must tell Taylor to leave . . . or *I* will be forced to leave."

Madalane's head jerked up at Celeste's statement. She said incredulously, "You could not be entertaining such a foolish notion!"

"How many times do I have to tell you that I am tired of this situation? Are you incapable of understanding me? Hear me now, Madalane. I will not allow your fixation on total vengeance to place me in a situation that might put my future in peril. If Derek should weaken and decide that removing Taylor from the scene isn't worth the risk, I *will* give Buck my ultimatum. Buck will either do what I ask—and I will emerge triumphant— or he won't agree, in which case you will see to it that his death follows more quickly than planned. As you said, Buck is my true enemy. Partial vengeance is better than a vengeance that would ruin our plans of returning to New Orleans free of suspicion."

Halting Madalane's spontaneous attempt to protest, Celeste snapped, "I've made up my mind, Madalane!"

Refusing to allow another word to be spoken on the subject, Celeste turned her back on her servant and returned to her room.

His brow furrowed in thought, Taylor rode back toward the ranch at a steady pace. The sky was rapidly lightening. If he was lucky, he'd get back just in time to join the men for breakfast—ready to start a normal day's work as if it were a day like any other.

Nothing could be farther from the truth.

Vida's image flashed before his mind, and a sensuous shudder rolled down Taylor's spine, ending somewhere in the area of his groin where all thoughts of Vida now seemed to settle. His insistence that Vida and he were just friends . . . all the times he had evaded the truth by telling himself his feelings for her did not exceed concern for the welfare of a partner, had been nothing more than wasted time.

Strangely enough, Taylor had never considered the possibility that time might become his enemy.

Vida had told him he needed to ask Buck about Jeanette Borneau. Vida seemed to believe that woman was the key. She'd intimated that whether Buck realized it or not, he had the answers to all Taylor's questions. The problem was, knowing his father as he did, Taylor also knew there was a distinct possibility that Buck might not even remember the woman's name.

Taylor's mount jerked and snorted uneasily, drawing him from his thoughts with a frown. He was tightening his grip on the reins when in a flash of action too quick for him to fully comprehend, his horse reared at the same moment a shot rang out and a hot, searing pain struck his shoulder. Almost knocked from the saddle by the impact, Taylor struggled to retain control of his horse. He was still breathing deeply to keep himself from passing out when a second shot rang out, narrowly missing him. It had come from a rise of ground to his left. Leaning low over the saddle, he reacted spontaneously despite his wound, and began riding full tilt directly toward the mound.

When the shooter emerged into sight and began fleeing at breakneck speed, Taylor spurred his mount to a faster pace, oblivious to his pain. He was committed to the chase. He was aware that he was gaining on the rider, that he would soon be close enough to identify him clearly.

But he was weakening. His grip on the reins was loosening. . . .

Derek cursed under his breath as his mount sped across the uneven terrain. He looked back and cursed again at the sight of Star riding steadily behind him. It was just his luck that Star's horse had reared as he got off his shot. The second shot hadn't stood a chance of connecting, with Star's horse dancing around the way it was, and with Star crumpled down over his saddle.

Derek looked back again. Fear choked his throat at the realization that Star was actually gaining on him! How could that be? The bastard had been hit—he was sure of it. Anybody else would've fallen off his horse, a perfect target for his second shot, but not Star. Instead, the bastard was hot on his heels.

Well, he'd fix him!

Derek turned his mount up a steep rise, forcing the animal to climb the sandy terrain. The ground was rough there, too rough for a wounded man to follow. Star would falter, maybe even fall from his horse. If he did, it would be easy for Derek to turn back and take another shot, and this time he wouldn't miss.

Derek ignored his mount's nervous whinny as he spurred it to a frenzied pace. He inwardly smiled. There was no way Star would be able to follow in his condition. It was just a matter of time.

Derek was still smiling when the sandy soil began crumbling under his mount's hooves. He gasped when his horse started to stumble. He jerked at the reins in an attempt to steady it. His eyes widened when the horse lurched suddenly forward onto its knees, and Derek was catapulted high into the air.

A reflexive curse.

Terrain flashing past in a spiraling blur.

Both registered briefly in Derek's incredulous mind before he struck the ground with a harsh, deadly, final crack of sound.

The dust had not yet settled when Taylor approached the thrown rider. The shooter was lying face down and motionless on the sandy terrain. Taylor slid down from his horse, his gun hanging limply in his hand as he walked closer. Wincing with pain, he rolled the man over with his foot, then stood motionless at the sight of Derek Beecher's battered, lifeless face.

A wave of weakness staggered him, and he looked at his wound, strangely bemused at the sight of his blood dripping onto the ground. Beecher had tried to kill him. Beecher, who wanted Vida. Beecher, whose unnamed blonde lover was married to a dying old man.

Taylor turned back to his horse. Struggling, he mounted. He had to see his pa. He had to talk to him. He had to find out, once and for all.

Celeste heard the commotion in the yard as she started toward the kitchen. Behind her, Buck stepped unsteadily into the doorway of their room as he said, "What in hell's going out there?"

They had both reached the kitchen when Big John, Mitch, and Randy entered the house, staggering under Taylor's unconscious weight.

"It's Taylor, boss!" Randy's lined face was white. "Somebody shot him!"

Celeste saw Buck's pale face turn ashen as he instructed, "Put him on the settee in the parlor."

Buck walked closer as Randy ripped open Taylor's shirt, wadded up the garment, and pressed it tight against a bloody wound in his shoulder. Buck demanded, "How did this happen?"

Big John replied in Randy's stead, "We don't know, boss. Taylor spent the night in town. We was expecting him back any minute when he came riding up on his horse, bleeding and bent over the saddle. All he said before he fell was that the fella who did it was dead."

Randy reported over his shoulder, "It looks like Taylor's lost a lot of blood."

Buck ordered, "Get Doc Maggie, Mitch."

"She ain't in town, boss. We saw her late yesterday. She said she was riding out to the Collins cabin because Mrs. Collins's baby was due. She said she was staying there until the baby came."

"Get yourself out to the Collins cabin, then!" Buck was visibly shaking. "And make it fast!"

Hardly able to believe her eyes, Celeste stood in the doorway as the scene unfolded. Taylor was shot, but he was alive, and Derek was dead!

Celeste turned around to find Madalane staring at her with a stony expression. She jumped as Buck looked up at them and ordered, "Get some clean cloths . . . some water. Damn it, you two, get moving!"

Celeste turned toward the kitchen, too stunned to reply.

* * *

"It's just a scratch, Doc. The other fella got the worst of it."

Doc Maggie looked at Taylor where he lay on the ranch-house settee. She had arrived an hour earlier at Mitch's urgent summons. Sarah Collins's baby had not yet been born. Doc had promised Sarah's nervous husband that she would return as quickly as she could, and she had come immediately to Taylor's side.

Shaken by the news that Taylor had been shot and was unconscious, she had pushed her old mare to the limit getting there, but she had still trailed behind Mitch, who had left her in his dust. It had already been past noon when she arrived.

Taylor had been conscious when she got there. His wound had stopped bleeding and appeared to be relatively clean, thanks to Randy's quick efforts. Doc hadn't even needed to dig out a bullet, since it apparently had ricocheted off a bone.

But it wasn't "just a scratch." Aware that Buck was seated in a chair nearby, where he had been ever since she'd arrived, she said soberly, "You're a lucky fella, Taylor, whether you realize it or not. If that bullet had hit you a little lower, you might not be talking to me right now. What's this all about, anyway?"

Taylor struggled to draw himself to a seated position. Succeeding despite Doc's protests, he said soberly, "I don't know. Derek Beecher fired the shots. I rode out after him, and the damned fool took off so fast that he got thrown from his horse and broke his neck before I could question him."

"Broke his neck?"

"Well, he didn't get up and he wasn't breathing, so I'd say it's a good guess he broke his neck."

Taylor was not smiling. Despite his attempt to minimize the damage the bullet had done, he was weak from loss of blood, and Doc knew his shoulder had to be throbbing like hell. But she realized his wound was the last thing on Taylor's mind as he said, "The boys went back to find Beecher's body before the vultures get to it. They're going to bring it to town and leave it with the undertaker first thing tomorrow. Then they're going to give Honor my report, so she can have it for her husband when he comes back."

Taylor stood up unexpectedly and Doc said, "Where do you think you're going?"

"To the bunkhouse."

"I don't think that's a good idea. I think you should stay right where you are until you're more steady on your feet and we're sure that wound has stopped bleeding."

Doc looked at Buck for confirmation. Instead, Celeste stepped into the doorway to respond, "Let him go to the bunkhouse. That's where he belongs."

"He'll stay right where he is." Speaking up for the first time, Buck frowned at his wife before continuing, "Taylor should be where he can be looked after until he's steady on his feet again."

"Where he can be looked after?" Celeste's face flamed as she faced her husband with undisguised anger. "And who will look after him here? You? Because neither Madalane nor I will play nursemaid to someone who openly despises us!"

Doc saw the tight twist of Buck's lips the moment before Taylor interjected flatly, "I don't need anybody to look after me. A few hours' sleep in the bunkhouse is all I need."

Doc withheld comment. To his credit, Taylor had obviously seen Buck's reaction to Celeste's statement and had known the old man was in no condition to argue.

Taylor started toward the door. Noting that he was shakier than he cared to acknowledge, Doc followed close behind him. She heard the clipped conversation between Buck and Celeste behind her, and she was glad she was out of it.

Waiting only until Taylor reached the bunkhouse and had collapsed on his bunk, Doc said, "Maybe that was a good thing you did, after all. Celeste would have made Buck pay if you had stayed in the house."

His eyes drooping with a fatigue he could no longer deny, Taylor responded, "I didn't want to stay in the house, Doc . . . for more reasons than I can explain right now."

Doc frowned worriedly. "I'll tell the boys to watch out for you."

"Don't worry about me, Doc. I'll be fine here. Like I said, a few hours' sleep is all I need."

"You lost a lot of blood, Taylor. Do yourself a favor. Stay in bed for a day or two, at least."

Taylor gave her a hard-eyed stare, and Doc said, "All right, do what you want. Be your own doctor. I don't care."

"Doc . . ."

She was silent for long seconds as she brought her emotions under control. "Just remember, you're like a son to me, Taylor. I'll be damned angry if you do anything that might make your condition worse."

Taylor smiled. "This isn't the first time I've been shot. I can handle it."

This isn't the first time . . .

Doc shook her head, suddenly at a loss for words. She turned back to her black bag, withdrew a few packets, and said, "I'll check on that wound as soon as I can, but in the meantime, change that bandage if it gets dirty, and send someone to get me if that wound gets any heat in it. Otherwise, dissolve one of these packets in water and take it every few hours if the throbbing in your shoulder gets too bad. It'll keep any fever down and help you sleep."

Doc saw the smile that twitched at Taylor's lips in silent acknowledgment that his shoulder was bothering him more than he had let on.

Indulging a last glance at the big, handsome, but enigmatic fella now causing her so much consternation, Doc said, "I have to go. Sarah Collins's baby won't wait. Just remember, only a fool thinks he's invincible."

After hesitating a moment, Doc leaned down to press a kiss against Taylor's stubbled cheek. When he looked up at her, she said, "You scared the hell out of me, Taylor. Take care of yourself, you hear?"

Sniffing, Doc walked resolutely out the doorway.

Doc was right. He was weaker than he thought.

Taylor glanced at the bunkhouse window, noting that the light of day was beginning to go golden, indicating it was nearing late afternoon. He had taken Doc's powders and had slept despite the ache in his shoulder, but his effort to stand a few minutes ago had not proved successful. He was more thirsty than was natural, his shoulder would not quit throbbing, and the light-headedness that had struck him had been sufficient warning to keep him where he lay. Like Doc had said, only a fool thinks he's invincible.

Taylor remembered Doc's emotional farewell. Well, it had been emotional according to her standards, anyway. The truth was, he loved that old woman. She had been the only constant after the death of his ma, and he—

A sound at the door alerted Taylor the moment before it opened to reveal Buck standing unsteadily in the entrance. Despite his weakness, Taylor felt the urge to jump to his feet to steady the old man, but he knew intuitively that it would be a mistake. Buck would object, and the same war between them would start all over again.

Instead, Taylor waited. He did not have to wait long.

"How do you feel?" Buck's voice was strangely hoarse as he walked into the room. Taylor followed Buck's wavering progress across the floor to the bunk opposite his, where he sat with a grunt of relief he was unable to suppress.

Still shocked by the degree to which his once energetic, virile, handsome father had deteriorated, Taylor remained momentarily silent. The nagging thought that this sick, weak old man might be a vision of the future in store for him was sobering. "I'm all right," he finally responded. "I'll be on my feet tomorrow."

"I didn't come here to find out how soon you'd be ready to take up your chores." Buck paused, then said, "I figure I owe you an apology for what Celeste said. She was upset. I suppose she had a right to be, according to her thinking anyway, but that isn't the way family reacts when there's trouble."

"Oh, so we're family again?"

Buck's expression darkened as he said sharply,

"Maybe I made a mistake about that. Maybe you didn't come back to be a part of a family here, after all."

"That could be."

Halting Buck when he prepared to stand, Taylor said, "No, wait. I was just trying to be honest with you." Taylor continued, "I'd be lying if I said the thought of being a family with you and Celeste appeals to me. Celeste is right. I don't like her. I never will."

"She don't like you either, and that's not going to change. All the same," Buck continued, "that doesn't mean it sits right with me that Derek Beecher tried to shoot you. What did you do to that fella?"

"Nothing."

"Then why did he try to kill you?"

"I'm not sure. I thought maybe you could tell me."

"Me?" Buck's faded eyes widened. "You don't think I put him up to it?"

"No. But I thought you might be able to help me answer some questions." He asked abruptly, "Did you ever hear of a woman named Jeanette Borneau?"

The name temporarily halted the exchange between them. Taylor saw the confusion in Buck's expression as he searched his memory, then said abruptly, "Hell, I haven't heard that name in a dog's age. What's she got to do with all this?"

"I'm not sure. You knew her?"

"I knew her."

"How well?"

"That was years ago."

"I thought it might clear up some things for me."

Momentarily silent, Buck shrugged a bony shoulder and said, "I don't suppose it makes any difference now.

Your ma isn't around to suffer for the truth anymore."
Buck held Taylor's gaze with unexpected intensity as
he added, "That's one thing I never wanted, you
know . . . to hurt your ma."

Taylor's throat went tight. He did not respond.

"I knew Jeanette in New Orleans. I had been away
from Emma for a while . . . far away, to my way of
thinking. Jeanette was a good-looking woman, and I
was randy as hell in those days. Women liked me, and I
liked them. I figured what Emma didn't know wouldn't
hurt her, and I had myself a good time wherever I
went."

"What about Jeanette?"

Buck frowned. "Jeanette was married, but everybody
knew she liked to play around, including her husband.
Jeanette and I had a steamy time of it until her husband
came to see me one afternoon. He was kind of civil
about the whole thing. He just said if I'd agree to go
back home to Texas, I wouldn't need to keep looking
for the loan I needed, that he'd see to it I had enough
money to cover any stock I needed to buy. When I saw
the figure on the bank note he was offering, I figured it
was a bargain. I knew your ma would never know how
I got the money. She was so busy with you kids and all.
Besides, she always trusted me to do right." Taylor
noted the unconscious shake of Buck's head before he
continued, "Anyways, I was getting ready to leave New
Orleans the next day when Jeanette came to my room.
She took it real hard that I was leaving. I told her it was
fun while it lasted, but her husband had made me an
offer I couldn't turn down, and I had a wife and family
to think about. She looked stunned. I figured she
needed to know the truth so she'd know it was over

with then and there. I figured it didn't make any difference anyway, because I was leaving."

"She killed herself."

"Yeah, I heard. I never could figure it."

"You couldn't, huh?"

"Hell, no! Jeanette had a long line of fellas waiting for me to step out of the picture so they could take my place."

"Maybe she didn't want the others. Maybe she wanted you."

"Well, if she did, she made a mistake. Emma was the only woman I ever really loved."

"*Ma* was the only woman?" Taylor felt his face harden. "What about Celeste?"

A pained expression flitted across Buck's face as he said, "Emma . . . your ma was different. There wasn't nobody in the world as important to her as me and you kids. Everything else came second to her, even herself."

"So why did you make a fool out of her, Pa?"

"I didn't!"

"Everybody knew about your women. Everybody was laughing behind her back."

"No, they wasn't! Besides, your ma never knew."

"Are you sure?"

"Sure I'm sure!"

Buck was trembling, but Taylor felt little compassion for his father's distress as the hurts and humiliations he had suffered for his mother returned vividly. He said, "You may be sure, but I'm not."

Buck's eyes went wide. He then shook his head. "No . . . she never knew. Never."

"What about Jeanette?"

Buck took a breath. "What about her?"

"She killed herself because of you."

"I don't think so, but if she did, that was her choice. She should've known better."

"What about her daughter?"

"Jeanette didn't care about her daughter. She was ready to leave the girl behind and run off with me. She told me so."

"That should've made you realize how she felt about you."

"You think so? All it made me think was that if she was ready to give up her daughter one day, she'd be ready to give me up the next."

"It never occurred to you that her feelings for you were real?"

"Like I said, she should've known better . . . and to tell you the truth, it didn't much matter to me. I had what I went to New Orleans for."

"The money."

"Not just the money! I had what I needed to save the Texas Star and the life I had made for Emma and you kids. That's what was important to me."

"That's funny, Pa, but Cal and I never got that feeling. We always figured *you* came first with you, that you were getting *what* you could, *while* you could, and the hell with everybody else—Ma included."

"No, never your ma." His breath tight with emotion, Buck said, "Not her. I loved her. The problem was, I never realized how much until I lost her. I went kind of crazy then, especially after Bonnie . . ."

Buck could not continue.

Taylor's own head was aching and his stomach was turning, whether from his wound or from Buck's guiltless confession, he could not be sure.

Buck surprised him, ending their conversation abruptly by saying, "I'm done talking. I'm going back to the house. I'll see to it that Celeste sends you something to eat."

Celeste.

A slow rage built inside Taylor. He asked as Buck reached the door, "By the way, what was Jeanette's daughter's name?"

Buck appeared to search his memory, then said, "Jeanette told me once, but I don't remember. The truth is, I really didn't care enough to pay attention."

Taylor watched as Buck disappeared through the doorway.

His head pounded as his mind insisted, *Vida was right*. She had to be. But how could he make that stubborn old man believe him?

Chapter 11

Vida walked slowly down the boardwalk toward Trudy Bartlett's restaurant. She scanned the street around her, noting that the business of the day appeared to have barely begun. At the later hours when she normally emerged from her room, the traffic was much more brisk. She had retired as late as usual after a full night's work at the Last Chance, but she'd slept restlessly. The reason could be expressed in one word.

Taylor.

A familiar frustration gnawed at Vida's senses. Damn that Taylor! The hours had dragged as she had watched the saloon doorway, waiting for him to appear. She had been fairly certain the first thing on his agenda the previous morning would be to talk to his father. She had been just as certain that the second thing on his agenda would be to get back to her as soon as he was able, not only to report his findings, but to indulge in more of the heated lovemaking they had enjoyed the previous night.

A tremor of need moved down Vida's spine as the

memory of those hours again surfaced. Her heart fluttered, her body tingled, and the yearning to feel Taylor's arms around her was so strong that she ached physically. She had judged from the expression on Taylor's face when he left her that the same torment would drive him back to her before the day ended, but it had not.

So where was he?

The faded checked curtains hanging slightly askew in the restaurant windows were familiar to Vida. She nodded a flirting "good morning" to several cowpokes, declining invitations to join them as she went to sit at a table in a corner. Her only consolation the previous evening had been Derek's absence from the saloon. Considering her state of mind at the time, a few more hours of fending off his advances would have been more than she could endure.

The truth was, she was tired and not inclined to put much effort into the facade she had adopted. Silent testimony to that truth was the fact that she had come out on the street with her dark hair brushed simply over her shoulders, without any bright makeup and wearing a simple cotton instead of the gaudy satins that had become her trademark since arriving in town. It did not miss her notice that her appearance had turned several heads in her direction, but she didn't care. So much depended on Buck's responses to Taylor's questions—assuming Taylor had had the opportunity to ask them—that she couldn't seem to think of anything else.

Vida nodded when Trudy looked up from the stove, aware that a nod to Trudy would soon bring piping hot eggs, bacon, and coffee to her table even though her normally generous appetite had deserted her. She felt strangely unsettled, anxious, as if waiting for an unseen axe to fall.

True to her expectations, Trudy approached her table minutes later with a generously filled plate in one hand and a coffee cup in the other. Trudy's solemn expression nudged Vida's anxiety up a notch even before Trudy placed the plate down on the table and said, "Ain't it awful?"

Vida did not immediately respond.

"I'm talking about what happened yesterday." Trudy shook her head. "Randy Butler and Mitch from the Texas Star just dropped off Derek Beecher's body at the undertaker's a little while ago." At Vida's shocked silence, Trudy said, "You ain't heard about it, huh? I was wondering how come you looked so relaxed, considering . . . well, everybody knows about you and Taylor Star."

A sudden difficulty catching her breath choked Vida's voice into a hoarse croak as she asked, "What do you mean? What about Taylor?"

"Derek shot him."

Reality momentarily dimmed, but Vida forced herself to listen as Trudy continued, "Randy went to the sheriff's office to leave a full report, but folks are saying Taylor managed to finish Derek off and get back to the ranch before he collapsed. Folks are saying Doc Maggie said—"

Vida had reached the doorway before Trudy recovered enough to call out, "Where are you going? You didn't eat your breakfast."

Vida didn't hear a word.

* * *

Celeste's normally angelic countenance took on a flushed hue as Taylor walked in through the ranchhouse doorway and took his place beside Big John at the breakfast table.

The bastard! Derek, her only remaining ally, was dead. Plans for the vengeance she had sought so laboriously were falling down around her ears—all because of this man. He was pale, but appeared otherwise unaffected by the previous day's turmoil. The thought sent a fresh surge of heat into her face as she snapped, "What are you doing here?"

His gaze cold, Taylor responded, "I'm about to take my breakfast before I go to work, ma'am, just like I always do."

"What makes you think you're welcome at this table after the trouble you brought to this ranch yesterday?"

"Trouble *I* brought?"

"Shootings . . . dead bodies. It was shocking . . . unbearable!"

"It wasn't too pleasant for me, either."

"I don't believe you! You enjoyed every moment of the attention the bloody situation brought you. I won't stand for any more of it!"

Her eyes widening as Taylor took the platter Big John handed him and filled his plate as if she had not spoken, Celeste screeched, "What's the matter with you? Are you deaf? I've had enough of you. Get out! Get out of this house! You aren't wanted on this ranch!"

Taylor looked up at her coldly. "I'm just doing what my pa expects of me, *ma'am*."

"No, you're not. You're going to leave this ranch if I have to—"

"He's right, Celeste." Buck spoke up unexpectedly behind her. "Taylor and I talked yesterday. He's going to stay for a while."

Celeste turned, stunned at the sight of Buck standing in the kitchen doorway. The aging bastard was so waxen that he appeared lifeless, so thin that he was skeletal, but he was still giving orders—orders she had no intention of taking.

Celeste replied hotly, "You don't know what you're saying. You saw the commotion your son caused here yesterday . . . the death and destruction—"

"Derek Beecher tried to kill him."

"He must have had a reason!"

"There's no reason good enough for that."

"Is that so?" Celeste trembled with wrath. "I'll bet you would be saying just the opposite if the situation was reversed, if it was Taylor who had lain in wait for Derek Beecher."

"But it wasn't. Taylor is pulling his weight on this ranch, and he's welcome to stay here as long as he does."

"But he isn't really pulling his weight, can't you see that? He's causing problems, disrupting the work flow." Suddenly aware that bad-mouthing Taylor was not having the effect she sought, Celeste forced back her anger and said more softly, "And things have changed between us, Buck, all because of him. I . . . I don't know what to do anymore."

Stunned when Buck did not rush to console her, Celeste employed an artifice that had never failed her. "I just don't know what to do!" she repeated and fled the kitchen in a burst of tears.

She pushed open her bedroom door, flung herself

Elaine Barbieri

down on the unmade bed, and waited, her body quivering with false sobs as she listened for the sound of Buck's step. Satisfaction surged when she heard Buck enter the room. She did not turn when he closed the door and approached her. Instead, she wept softly until he said, "I'm sorry, Celeste. I know this is hard for you, but Taylor is my son."

"Your son . . ." Celeste looked up at Buck. Wielding the appeal of her tears with practiced expertise, she whispered, "Your son ignored you for years. He forgot you were alive, while I loved you and patiently tended to you in your illnesses, hoping that one day you would again be the man I married."

Buck's expression grew strained as he sat down on the bed beside her and responded with difficulty, "I know that. I know all those things, but he's my son."

"Cal is your son, too!" she retorted. "Does that mean he'll soon be taking up residence here as well?"

"No. Not Cal. Bonnie's dead because of him."

"What about Honor? Will I be saddled with that outspoken wretch here, too, simply because her mother attempted to trap you with her body?"

"It wasn't like that with Betty."

"Wasn't it?"

"No, she . . . it was my fault, Celeste. I knew Betty loved me. I saw it in her eyes . . . and I took advantage of it. I didn't love her. I really didn't care about her one way or the other, but that's the way it was with me then."

Inwardly raging at his revelation, Celeste nudged, "I suppose there were other women you treated that way, too."

"Yes, there were. Too many for me to even remember all their names."

Hatred boiled hot and deep as Celeste pressed, "Is that the way it was with me, also?"

"No. It was different with you. After Emma died . . ." Buck paused for a breath, then continued, "After she died, I realized what I had lost. Then Bonnie . . . I thought it was over for me forever. When I met you, I figured I had a second chance. I promised myself it would be different. I'd change. I kept my promise."

The impact of Buck's words hit Celeste hard. The fool didn't even realize what he had said! It wasn't Buck's love for her that had allowed her to control him. Instead, it was his love for his dead wife and all the deep regrets accompanying his love that had held him faithful to her.

He had inadvertently admitted that he loved Emma still!

Celeste drew herself slowly to a seated position. Aware that however uncertain her control over Buck had become, it would never be stronger than at that moment, she said nobly, "I kept the promises I made when we were married, too, Buck, but I can't go on this way. Taylor hates me. I can't live on this ranch if he continues to live here. You have to make a choice— Taylor or me."

Celeste felt Buck's shock as she stood up and added tearfully, "But I want you to be sure, Buck. I don't want you to make a hasty decision that you may regret. I'll take Madalane's room. The cot in the room off the kitchen will do for her until tomorrow when you've had some time to think things over. If you decide you want Taylor to stay instead of me, I'll leave, taking nothing with me. The choice is yours."

Celeste steeled herself against the fury inside her. The touch of Buck's papery lips repulsed her as she kissed him, then left the room.

The well-worn trail . . . the dusty terrain . . . the unrelenting morning sun beating down on her head as her unbound hair streamed out behind her—Vida was unconscious of it all as she pressed her mount to an ever faster pace toward the Texas Star. Three words drummed through her mind, consuming all thought as they had since the moment Trudy had uttered them.

Derek shot him.

She had not bothered to stop for the details before going directly to the livery stable. It hadn't mattered to her that she wasn't dressed to ride or that she had shocked the proprietor of the livery stable by mounting up astride despite her attire. Taylor was wounded and lying unprotected at the Texas Star ranch, and only she knew the dire risk he faced there. She needed to go to him, to tend to him and remain beside him, to protect him when he could not protect himself.

Vida glanced down at the derringer in the holster on her thigh, exposed as her skirt flew briefly backward. As small as the gun was, she was well aware that one shot would accomplish her purpose if it was needed.

Vida blinked back sudden tears as she recalled her annoyance the previous evening when Taylor failed to appear at the Last Chance. Impatient, wanting him more than she had been prepared to admit, she had formulated angry rebukes in her mind which she intended to speak the moment she saw Taylor. Yet she had known even then that the moment she did see him, the second he touched her, the instant he whispered his first word, she would melt in his arms.

The love that had always been meant to be but had taken so long to come to fruition, had finally happened. Had it come too late?

No, she could not bear the thought!

Vida's eyes closed briefly as the tears she had withheld escaped to trail down her cheeks. She brushed them away, then gasped aloud as a horseman leaped out of concealment in the heavy foliage beside the trail.

Vida reined her mount back sharply, struggling to control the startled animal as it whinnied and floundered. She looked up at the horseman when she regained command of her mount, an angry protest dying on her lips when she met a familiar gaze that robbed her of speech as efficiently as the gun the rider aimed at her chest.

"Speechless?" Pierre said softly. "Is that possible . . . *Lisette?*"

Vida replied calmly despite the heavy pounding of her heart, "Don't pretend ignorance, Pierre. You know my name isn't Lisette."

"How lovely to hear you speak my name again, my darling."

All semblance of civility disappearing, Pierre continued, "But that's right. You aren't Lisette, and you aren't 'my darling,' either, are you? You are merely a lying whore who used me to gain her ends."

Vida responded, "Tit for tat, Pierre. You used your position to increase your wealth, ignoring the loss of lives that resulted."

"Loss of lives?" Pierre nudged his mount so close that his tightly muscled thigh brushed against hers. He had changed physically since the last time she had seen him. He was thinner, his taut physique even harder. His hair was spiked with a more generous sprinkling of gray and his narrow face was more deeply lined; yet even dressed as he was in common western wear, the arrogance so much a part of his makeup was apparent.

"Do you really think that concerned me? Those seamen's lives were common, useless, empty lives. They were of no particular loss to anyone at all."

"Only to themselves and to those who loved them."

"They were expendable! Yet I never believed that of you, Lisette."

"My name is—"

"I know what your name is!" Pierre leaned toward Vida menacingly as he rasped, "You did your work well, Lisette. You charmed me. You enthralled me. You even led me to consider ending my bachelorhood for what I believed would be a future only you could fill. You *deceived* me—you and your Pinkerton partner, Taylor Star."

"Taylor didn't—"

"Don't lie to me!" Pierre leaned closer still. His finger tightened on the trigger of the gun he held only inches from her breast as he said malevolently, "You left New Orleans while I languished in prison. You disappeared from sight, but I knew I would find you. I knew that when I did, I would seize the opportunity you just now afforded me by riding so heedlessly to your lover's side. You see, I have great plans for you, Lisette. It's my turn now."

"I don't know what you mea—"

A quick swipe of Pierre's gun butt struck Vida with an explosion of pain that ended her statement in darkness.

Still seated on the bed where Celeste had left him earlier, Buck stared at the door she had closed behind her. He could not seem to comprehend her words.

Taylor or me.

The choice is yours.

Tomorrow . . .

She had said she loved him, that she had honored her marital vows, but could not remain on the same ranch with Taylor because Taylor hated her.

She had kissed him, a gentle, loving kiss that had left him strangely cold, and had then left him with the echo of her ultimatum still ringing in his mind.

But the echo of another question rang there just as persistently, allowing him no peace.

By the way, what was Jeanette's daughter's name?

What was her name? He couldn't seem to remember.

Taylor drew a bucket of water from the trough and started toward the barn where Big John worked while waiting for Randy and Mitch to return. Big John had deliberately delayed riding out to start the day's work, and Taylor knew why. Randy and Mitch had left Big John at the ranch in the event that Taylor's injury proved to be more than he could handle. Celeste's livid declarations the previous day had not escaped them. They had known there would be no help forthcoming from that quarter if anything happened to Taylor, and they were silently determined to make sure he wouldn't need it.

They were family—each and every one of those

men—just as surely as if the same blood ran in all their veins. Taylor knew they would never turn on him. Nor would they ever turn on Buck—a commitment they had made years earlier. That commitment somehow comforted him.

Taylor stretched his aching shoulder and winced at the stab of pain. He felt good, but it was obvious that complete mobility would not immediately return. He'd be handicapped for a while, a handicap he could not really afford with the situation at the ranch coming to a head. He needed to ride into town to let Vida know that he was all right. The arrival of Derek's body was sure to have concerned her. He had told Randy to tell Vida he would come to town to see her as soon as the situation allowed. He knew she'd understand what he meant, even if Randy didn't.

Hoofbeats behind him turned Taylor toward the sound. He looked up as Mitch and Randy drew up alongside him. He frowned when Randy glanced around the yard and said, "Where is she?"

"She?"

"Vida. She's here, isn't she?"

Taylor went cold.

"She found out about the trouble with Derek before we could tell her you were all right. Trudy said she was out of the restaurant like a shot as soon as she heard. She didn't even go back to the hotel to change her clothes before getting a horse at the livery stable and heading out of town. We figured we'd find her here when we came."

"You're sure about all this?"

"Of course I'm sure. Young Elmer Harden said he never saw a woman ride like that."

The knot inside Taylor tightened. He knew for a fact that Vida could hold her own on a horse with any man. There was no way she would've gotten lost, either. Not Vida. Her sense of direction was legend at the agency.

Taylor turned toward the barn. He was leading his saddled mount out into the yard minutes later when Randy asked, "Where're you going?"

"I'm going to find her."

"Hell . . ." Flustered, Randy glanced at the other men. "How're you going to do that? She could be anywhere."

"You said she was riding a horse from the livery stable?"

"Yes, but—"

"I'll find her."

Hardly conscious of the pain stabbing his shoulder as he pulled himself into the saddle, Taylor turned his mount out of the yard.

Buck had not moved from the bed where Celeste had left him. The sound of a horse's hasty departure from the yard finally drew him to his feet. He walked to the window in time to see Taylor disappear around the curve of the trail, with Randy, Big John, and Mitch in pursuit. He scowled. They hadn't stopped back to report what had happened in town and were riding too hard to be heading out to the range to work. Something was wrong.

Buck stood staring at the empty trail for long moments. He remembered a time when he wouldn't have wasted a moment before grabbing a horse and following to find out what was going on. He also remembered when he wouldn't have wasted time standing at the window, mulling over an ultimatum a woman had given him, either. But he had been young, handsome, and independent then. He'd had the security of a woman who had proved her unselfish love for him in countless ways, not the least of which was by giving him two strong sons, and a daughter whom he had loved more than his own life.

Yet he had been determined not to allow his wife's precious love to weigh him down when he went carousing.

Hell, he remembered that time in New Orleans that Taylor had asked him about. Jeanette Borneau had been young and beautiful. She had not bothered to hide her attraction to him, despite the fact that she was married. She had been crazy about him from the first moment he touched her. He had been drunk with his power over her—a woman who had been rumored to grow so bored with her lovers that her husband felt safe in ignoring her straying.

But, for Jeanette, it had been different with Buck. Jeanette had actually wanted to run away with him, to leave her husband and her daughter, Celeste, who was—

Buck went momentarily cold.

Jeanette's daughter's name was . . . *Celeste*.

Taylor had known all along.

Briefly staggered by a reality that could not be ignored, Buck turned toward the hall. He did not bother to knock at Madalane's door but pushed it open to find his beautiful wife whispering to her servant.

Celeste turned toward him as he said flatly, "Tell me your mother's name wasn't Jeanette."

Celeste's sudden pallor was unspoken confirmation.

Belatedly regaining her voice, Celeste stuttered, "Jeanette? I . . . I don't know what you mean. My mother's name was Marie. She—"

"Do not deny your mother, Celeste!" Madalane interrupted harshly. She turned back from her dresser, her venomous gaze all the more potent for the gun she leveled at Buck's heaving chest as she continued hotly, "Speak her name proudly! Your mother's name was Jeanette Dulay Borneau. She was beautiful and kind— a woman whose soul was innocent and beautiful. She was a woman who deserved a far better fate than the one forced on her by this man!"

"Madalane . . ." Celeste cast her servant a warning glance. "I don't know what you're talking about. My mother—"

"He knows, Celeste."

"Think of what you're doing, Madalane."

"He knows!"

Unable to catch his breath, Buck said hoarsely, "Yes, I know who you are now, Celeste. But no matter what Madalane says, I didn't force Jeanette into any fate. She took her own life."

"Liar. Murderer!" Madalane advanced threateningly toward him. "I despise your denial because I know the truth. You left my dear Jeanette humiliated, bereft, with nothing to live for when she discovered you had a wife and several children you preferred to her."

"She had a husband and a child, too."

"Which she would have given up for you."

"My mother would not have given me up for *him!*" Celeste's face flamed. "She loved me."

Madalane responded heavily, "Jeanette loved you, but her intoxication with this man was so great that she

309

could not envision her life without him. She gave up her life for him—and it is now time to take payment in return."

Celeste said abruptly, "All right, shoot him if that's what you want. You've ruined everything for us now anyway, so get it over with. The ranch hands will be back soon."

"We will be gone by then."

"It will be impossible to get away if you wait too long."

Madalane said hoarsely, "Do you think I care? Do you think I will leave before my dear Jeanette has been fully avenged?" Not waiting for Celeste's response, Madalane instructed, "Tell him."

Celeste remained silent.

"Tell him! *Your husband* deserves to learn how carefully we planned and executed our revenge from the beginning—a beginning that began with Emma's death."

"Emma's death?" Buck addressed Madalane, demanding, "What are you talking about?"

Madalane answered him with evil relish. "When you returned to New Orleans the second time, your image and an article accompanying it appeared in a New Orleans newspaper, describing the successful Texas rancher who was visiting the city. You were easily recognizable. Jeanette was cold in her grave and Celeste was satisfactorily married by then, but our plan took shape the moment we saw the story. It went so smoothly. Celeste's husband was old. No one challenged Monsieur DuClair's sudden death . . . and Celeste was then free."

Madalane continued, "Your Emma was so young to die. She was such a good wife to you, and she wanted to please her family. She had no way of knowing how easily a heart attack can be fabricated when the proper powders are employed, or that the freshly canned peaches offered to her by a traveling vendor would be the last she would ever sample—and then you were free, too."

"No!" Buck gasped.

Buck's legs went out from under him and he sagged down into a chair as Madalane continued, "You were devastated and bereft. Bonnie was a dear child and so saddened by her mother's death. She was completely unsuspecting. She had no idea that she presented the perfect opportunity for revenge when she leaned down to draw water from that well. Even the Ackerman woman who discovered her body shortly afterwards paid no attention to the old Indian servant woman wrapped in a torn blanket who promptly disappeared with a medicine wagon and a driver who was also never seen again."

Buck made an inarticulate sound of stunned disbelief to which Madalane responded, "You need not concern yourself that your daughter was afraid. She never saw me approaching."

Appearing to gain strength from Buck's shocked immobility, Madalane continued, "You cooperated so well with our plan. Guilty fool that you were, you blamed Cal for Bonnie's death and drove him away. You alienated your remaining son when you could not face his grief. You were so ready for Celeste's arrival and the sympathy and escape only she could provide that you were no challenge at all! You buried your guilt in her body, and never had a suspicion when my powders began their attack on you."

"You were behind it all." Buck attempted to stand. When he was unable, he looked at Celeste and said, "You allowed her to do this to me?"

Finally shedding the mask she had worn for so long, Celeste replied, "I *allowed* her? I *begged* her to work my mother's vengeance!"

Celeste continued viciously, "You sicken me, *Buck, darling*. So much so, that I *beseeched* Madalane to hasten our plan, to bring it to a quick end, but she stubbornly clung to our original strategy. She would not be satisfied until the Texas Star and everything you had gained with the money tainted by my mother's blood was destroyed. Were it not for Cal and Taylor's return and your continuing hesitation to change your will, our vengeance would have been complete by now."

"The letters that brought Cal and Taylor home . . ." Buck asked confusedly. "Who sent them?"

Celeste scoffed, "You don't really believe those letters existed, do you? Because I don't. Your sons conspired to *pretend* they received letters telling them to return. It was their excuse so they could come back and claim a part of the Texas Star. Those letters never really existed!"

"Yes, they did."

Madalane's virulent gaze glittered as she proclaimed, "Those letters did exist. I know, because *I* sent them."

At the gaping silence her admission evoked, Madalane addressed Celeste coldly. "Guilt is an effective tool. I knew it would bring those two back more effectively than any other incentive, and I used it well."

"Fool!" Celeste gasped. "How could you endanger everything we had worked for?"

"I am not a fool! *Total* vengeance, Celeste—that was our vow. *Total* vengeance did not end with your husband's death, or with the destruction of the Texas Star. *Total* vengeance ended with the termination of the Star progeny—progeny whose lives were forever stained with your mother's blood. You lost track of that truth as your impatience grew, Celeste, but I did not."

"Fool!" Celeste repeated. "The return of Buck's sons was the beginning of the end for us here!"

"Jeanette cried out to be avenged."

"Shoot Buck now if you want to avenge her!" Celeste raged, "You have ruined any attempt to gain further vengeance, just as you have endangered our chances to escape unscathed. Get it over with, dammit, or we won't be able to save our own lives!"

At Madalane's hesitation, Celeste demanded, "Shoot him, I said!"

Numbed by Madalane's shocking revelations, unable to think past the part he had played in the destruction of all he had loved, Buck did not react when Madalane leveled her gun in his direction. Nor did he cry out when the bullet struck him and he fell heavily to the floor.

Vida awakened slowly. Her head pounded as she breathed in the fragrance of a wooded glade, heard water flowing in the distance and birds chirping overhead, then the sound of footsteps approaching.

Footsteps.

Vida looked up as the footsteps stopped at her side. She was suddenly aware that her hands were bound behind her and her ankles were also tied. She squinted up at Pierre, her vision blurred as he crouched beside her and said, "Awake at last. But, *chérie*, you do not look so well."

Vida's head swam as she struggled to draw herself to a seated position. She felt the trickle of blood that trailed down her temple as Pierre explained, "I regret the need for such a despicable blow, Lisette, but it was necessary to my plan."

"Your plan?"

"Dear Lisette . . . you do not truly believe I came all the way to this wretched place without a purpose."

Vida struggled to clear her senses as she asked, "What are you talking about?"

"I was successful in arranging my release from the prison cell where I was sent due to your efficient work, but my lawyer explains that the deliverance is only temporary. As you know, the evidence against me is complete. I will be tried for the charges against me, and even should I escape confinement, once everything is learned about my participation in the shipping disasters, I will be ruined." Pierre added coldly, "To be succinct, I owe it all to you, *Lisette*—you and your Pinkerton lover—and I am determined to make you both pay."

"You are making a mistake, Pierre." Frantically searching her mind for a possible escape as she struggled to sit up, Vida continued, "Lowell is Taylor's home territory. Even if my death is overlooked, Taylor's will not be tolerated."

"I doubt it. Everyone believes Taylor is the drunken son of a man who is generally disliked, and you are just another saloon woman. You will both be easily forgotten."

Vida glanced down toward her thigh, and Pierre snapped, "The gun is gone, Lisette. Such a pretty weapon, and undoubtedly deadly as well, but you won't be bothered with it anymore. It's in my saddlebag—a souvenir. I hope you don't mind."

Refusing to allow Pierre the satisfaction he sought, Vida responded, "Even if you escape the law, Allan Pinkerton knows the truth, and he is a determined man. He will not allow the deaths of two of his best agents to go unpunished."

"You base your conclusions on a simple fact . . . that your bodies will be found." Vida felt the blood drain from her face as Pierre said softly, "That will not happen."

"Pierre . . ."

Producing a scarf from his pocket, Pierre tied it around Vida's mouth as he said softly, "I regret curtailing our conversation, but I can only assume your lover will be following sometime soon, and I want to be ready for him." At the widening of Vida's gaze, he laughed softly, "That's right. You don't know. Taylor escaped his attacker with a slight wound. If you had stopped to inquire, you would've heard that report, but you were so upset at the news, your only thought was to race to his side."

His expression darkening, Pierre rasped, "It would have been far better if you had shown that loyalty and affection for *me*, Lisette. The rewards would have been so much greater . . . in so many ways. Instead, you now hope in vain that your lover will rescue you, but he will not. I am prepared."

Pierre paused to regain his composure, then continued, "Look around you, Lisette. This is the perfect place, is it not? I chose it carefully after arriving in this godforsaken territory. There is a sheer incline behind us that guards our rear; a stream on one side, preventing unseen approach from that direction; on the other is terrain that is inaccessible on horseback. I left a very clear trail leading directly here and into the sights of my rifle."

Vida shook her head, then briefly closed her eyes against the pounding that resumed with greater vehemence.

"Don't bother to protest, Lisette. It will only cause you pain. Relax—we have some time yet. The Texas Star ranch hands will have returned to the ranch and Taylor will have concluded that something has happened to you because you didn't arrive ahead of them. It will take him some time to find our trail, but he will, and I'll be waiting." Pierre concluded more softly, "Don't bother to struggle, Lisette. It pains me to see the useless discomfort you cause yourself. My dear, the truth is, your fate is sealed."

With those final words, Pierre faded into the foliage behind them, leaving Vida with the echo of his deadly promise.

Celeste stared down at Buck's motionless body. It lay where it had fallen minutes earlier—a pale, faded skeleton of the man who even now threatened the future toward which she had so carefully planned.

Celeste glanced at Madalane, who stood stock-still, her gun still held tightly in her hand. Celeste said, "He's dead. Pack only the necessities. We have to get out of here quickly."

She had turned toward her room when she heard Madalane respond with a single word.

"No."

"What?"

"I said, no. I will not leave until Jeanette's vengeance is complete."

Astounded at Madalane's response, Celeste questioned, "What is that supposed to mean? We've accomplished all we can here."

"We have not! Taylor Star still lives, as does his brother. I will not leave this already bloodied soil until they share their father's fate. I will not be satisfied until this ranch house burns to the ground before my eyes!"

"Are you insane?" Celeste stared at Madalane incredulously. "The only way to do that will be to sacrifice our own lives."

"Do you think I care?" Obsession darkened Madalane's gaze as she rasped, "Only one thing is important to me—vengeance for my dear Jeanette, who has spent these many years in a cold grave only because she loved and was betrayed."

"My mother is dead." Pointing to Buck's motionless body, Celeste cried, "That is the man responsible for her death, and he has felt her vengeance. It is time for us to leave."

"I will not leave."

"You realize what you've done—what you intend to do." Rapidly losing control, Celeste raged, "You arranged for the failure of our plan by bringing Buck's sons home—for the collapse of my plans to return to New Orleans and the life I have so diligently earned."

"I do not care about the *life you have earned*." Her

dark eyes cold shards of ice, Madalane spat, "I care only for the life my dear Jeanette sacrificed. I will not allow her sacrifice to go unanswered."

"You are finally speaking the truth, aren't you, Madalane?" Celeste asked incredulously. "You didn't really care about me at all. My life . . . my happiness . . . were expendable. Even now, you disregard all thought of my safety while you pursue the vengeance you have sworn. Well, I will not stand for it!"

Celeste demanded, "Give me that gun."

"No."

"Give it to me! You've done enough damage with your insane obsession."

Madalane took a backward step.

"I said . . . give it to me!"

Celeste attempted to wrest the gun from Madalane's hand. The strength of the Negress's resistance widened Celeste's eyes. Infuriated, she shoved the woman hard, her hand still on the muzzle of the gun as she attempted to pull it from her hand, but Madalane would not surrender. Actively struggling, fighting the woman's unexpected defiance, Celeste twisted Madalane's arm, jerking her in a sudden circle that left the woman staggering. Celeste felt victory within her grasp when Madalane's weakened leg collapsed underneath her and she slipped toward the floor. But Madalane's grip on the weapon did not lessen, and Celeste gave her a final shove.

The explosion of sound was deafening.

Momentarily frozen, Celeste was unable to move as Madalane's dark eyes widened and she slid slowly to the floor still gripping Celeste's hand on the gun.

Celeste saw the rapidly widening circle of blood on

Madalane's chest. She discerned the moment when Madalane's intense gaze began to falter. She felt Madalane's hand loosen as she relinquished the gun at last.

Celeste stared down at Madalane, her heart pounding. Madalane was dead—Celeste knew that instinctively. There was no other way the Negress would have given up the gun that represented the vengeance for which she had lived.

Fool!

Witch!

Traitoress!

Celeste took a shaky breath, then stepped over Buck's inert body without a thought and drew open the door. A few things in a suitcase, and she'd be on her way. She'd go to New Orleans. She'd get there any way she could. The first thing she would do would be to withdraw the sizable sum deposited there in her name, and then the future would be hers to do with as she pleased.

Her heart thundering with anticipation, Celeste glanced back in afterthought at the two lifeless bodies lying behind her.

And she'd forget they ever existed.

The sun was directly overhead as Taylor crouched by the trail, his brow knitted in a frown. Conscious of the three mounted men at his rear, he looked up as Randy said, "What's the matter, Taylor? It seems to me what happened is pretty clear. Vida was headed up the trail when somebody rode out in front of her and blocked her off. You can see where her horse was startled, and where she brought it under control again; then where the two horses rode off through the underbrush. The trail from then on looks to be clear enough, with all that broken foliage and such. What are we waiting for?"

"That's the trouble. It's *too* clear . . . too easy to follow."

"What do you mean?"

Taylor looked up at Randy, his expression troubled. "Somebody went to the trouble of surprising Vida, of struggling with her, and then abducting her. Whoever it was, he had to be smart enough to realize the kind of a trail he was leaving."

"Maybe he didn't figure anybody would come after Vida."

"Somebody was lying in wait for her. The person had to know her. Anybody knowing Vida would have to know that I'd go after her."

"Maybe it was somebody who didn't know her, just some no-good saddle bum who liked the way she looked, and . . . and figured he had a chance for some fun."

"It wasn't a stranger. Vida knew the person."

"How do you know that?"

"I know."

Randy studied Taylor's expression. He glanced back at Mitch and Big John, then said, "What choice do we have? It's the only trail we got."

Taylor's mouth tightened grimly. "It's a trap. I don't want you fellas taking any chances. I can handle it myself."

"No, you can't. We need to go with you."

"You can go to town for help."

"I'm thinking there ain't time for that."

"Randy—"

"We ain't discussing it no further."

Anxiety squeezed tight in Taylor's stomach as he said, "I don't have time to argue, you know."

"Let's go, then."

Taylor had turned into the foliage, with the men close behind, when he heard hoofbeats thundering up the trail toward them.

Her head aching, her muscles stiffening, Vida lay in the wooded glade where Pierre had left her. Her mind clouded by her head's incessant throbbing, she was uncertain how much time had elapsed—only that her throat was dry from the gag that Pierre had forced on her, and that her limbs were numb and cold despite the warmth of the day.

A tight knot of concern twisted ever tighter in her gut at the thought of Taylor. She despised her helplessness, which was compounded by the danger Taylor now faced because of her.

Suddenly alerted to a restless movement in the bushes, Vida scanned the heavy foliage surrounding her. She stilled. Her vision was blurred, but her hearing remained acute. Pierre had concealed himself in the bushes behind her, but the movement she'd heard had not come from that direction.

Vida began a furious struggling. She needed to warn whoever was approaching. She had to tell them—

Vida gasped as Pierre's voice rang out in the silent glade.

"I know you're there, Taylor Star. You've come to rescue my darling Lisette. No, wait . . . her name is Vida, isn't it?"

When there was no response, Pierre urged, "Speak up, Taylor. I've been waiting for you."

Vida could hear the agitation growing in Pierre's voice when there was again no reply and he warned, "You stand no chance of approaching me unexpectedly, you know. My position is impregnable. Show yourself, and we can talk."

Silence.

Unable to control his irritation any longer, Pierre called out, "I tire of this game, Taylor! I see it will be necessary to force your hand." He continued harshly, "I'll give you to the count of five to throw out your gun and show yourself. If you don't, I'll put a bullet in Vida's dainty right foot. With each successive count that you refuse to show yourself, another bullet, until—well, you may divine that yourself."

Vida struggled harder. She wanted to call out to Taylor and tell him Pierre intended to kill them both anyway, but she could not.

"One."

No response.

"Two."

Silence.

"Three."

Nothing.

"Four."

Vida steeled herself against the first shot.

"Wait!"

Taylor's deep voice shattered the silence. A few seconds elapsed before he said, "I'm coming out."

No! Vida struggled to voice her protest as the foliage moved, as Taylor threw out his gun and stepped into full view. Frustrated tears streaked her cheeks as he advanced slowly toward her.

"Stay where you are!" Pierre's command was cold. "You have others with you. Tell them to do the same."

Halting where he stood, Taylor responded, "I came alone."

"No, you didn't! I know better than that. There are three ranch hands on your father's ranch. They would not have allowed you to come after Lisette without them. Tell them to show themselves, one by one."

"I'm alone, I tell you."

"One . . . two . . . three . . ."

The bushes moved. Randy threw out his gun and stepped into view.

Pierre questioned tightly, "Must I start counting again?"

A second man—Mitch—then Big John tossed out their guns and stepped into sight."

"All of you are so noble." Pierre's tone was mocking. "Now move to the side, away from your guns . . . that's right. That's perfect."

Vida saw Taylor glance her way. She felt his anger at her plight, then saw rage nearly slip out of control when he spotted the blood that trailed down her temple. She saw his jaw harden, felt the tension in his powerful frame as he said, "You can see us now, but we can't see you. Afraid to show yourself, Pierre? Is there something you don't want us to see?"

Vida heard the brush behind her move. She felt the enmity that filled the small clearing as Pierre emerged to stand boldly in clear sight. His gun aimed at Taylor's chest, he replied, "No, Taylor, as a matter of fact, I'm very pleased to show myself. I want you to see that you haven't won the game you and your beautiful partner played with me in New Orleans. I want you to know that it is I who will be the ultimate victor."

"Think it over, Pierre. There are five of us here. You can't kill us all."

"Can't I?"

"Think what you're saying."

"I know exactly what I'm saying."

"You said we would talk."

"I've changed my mind. I'm tired of talking."

Explosive gunshots reverberated in the small clearing, sending shock waves of terror down Vida's spine. A muffled sob escaped her lips as the tableau momentarily froze. Then she gasped at the sight of the widening circles of blood that stained Pierre's shirtfront before he toppled stiffly to the ground.

Unable to fully comprehend the burst of action that followed, Vida saw Randy run forward to kneel beside Pierre, saw Big John and Mitch race for their discarded guns as Taylor dashed to her side. Vida took a deep breath as Taylor ripped away her gag. Still unable to speak, she watched as he released her hands and feet. He winced at the deep, chafing cuts the ropes had made before gathering her into his arms.

Crushing her close against him, Taylor asked, "Are you all right? What did that bastard do to you?"

"I'm fine . . . just a bump on the head."

Taylor's fingers moved against her scalp before he looked down at her. The incredible blue of his eyes was intensely clear despite her blurred vision.

"Dammit," he whispered. "You nearly got yourself killed . . . because of me! If that had happened . . . if I had lost you—"

"But you didn't."

"That's right, I didn't, and I'm going to make sure I never do. You're going to marry me, Vida."

"Oh, am I?" Vida responded weakly.

"That's right, you are . . . because I love you, and you love me."

A smile touched her lips. "True."

"Damned right, that's true. When I found out you were missing it almost drove me wild."

Her thinking still unclear, Vida said, "I thought Pierre had won when you all threw out your guns. How—?"

Cal stepped into sight beside them, answering her unfinished question. She said softly, "Cal . . . I should've known."

Cal replied, "That Pierre fella thought he had everything figured out, but he forgot one important thing. Taylor has a brother."

Taylor turned toward Randy as he approached. He asked, "Pierre?"

"He's dead."

"Leave him where he is, then. We'll come back for him."

Drawing Vida to her feet cautiously, Taylor slipped his arm around her. He looked back at Cal and continued gruffly, "We need to go back to the ranch now, to talk to Pa. I'm tired of playing games, too, Cal. It's time Pa found out the whole truth about Celeste, whether he wants to believe it or not."

Cal asked tentatively, "The *whole* truth?"

"I'll explain on the way."

Still woozy, Vida did not protest when she was lifted up onto the saddle and seated in front of Taylor. She released a silent sigh when his strong arms closed around her. Her head still throbbing, she leaned back against his chest and closed her eyes as Taylor nudged his mount into motion.

She was wrapped in Taylor's loving embrace—just where she wanted to be.

Taylor walked cautiously through the silent ranch house, with Cal beside him. They had arrived moments earlier, dismounting to an eerie silence. The sight of preparations for the evening meal lying abandoned on the kitchen table increased Taylor's concern, and he called out Buck's name.

Silence.

They entered the parlor. The room was empty.

Taylor paused beside Buck's bedroom door. He knocked. He pushed it open when he received no response. Inside, bedclothes and clothing had been strewn around the room as if by a hasty hand.

Taylor's heart thundered in his chest. A quick glance at Cal revealed that the soft gold of his brother's eyes had turned cold. Striding boldly toward Madalane's room, Taylor thrust open the bedroom door, then stood back.

Buck and Madalane lay in pools of blood, a few yards apart on the floor.

Taylor rushed to Buck's side. Incredulous, he saw Buck's body twitch with a breath!

Aware of the shuffling of footsteps behind him, Taylor grasped a cloth from the bed and pressed it tight to the wound in Buck's chest, stanching the flow as he gasped, "He's alive! Get Doc Maggie."

Buck's eyelids moved spasmodically at the sound of Taylor's voice. Taylor held his breath as his father's eyes opened with excruciating slowness to focus on his face. Taylor asked softly, "What happened here, Pa? Where's Celeste?"

"She got away."

"What?"

"Go . . . get her."

Taylor glanced back to the door where Vida stood with Big John's brawny arm steadying her, then at Randy, who crouched beside Madalane and confirmed with a nod that she was dead.

Noting that Cal hung back, Taylor motioned him forward. He saw his brother's light eyes grow moist like his own when Buck rasped, "Cal . . . I'm sorry . . . sorry."

Taylor whispered, "Who did this to you, Pa?"

Buck took a gasping breath. "Celeste and Madalane . . . they killed . . ." He strained to breathe. "Getting away . . ."

At their side, Randy said hoarsely, "Mitch already went for the doc. I'll take care of your pa until she gets here, and Big John will take care of Vida. Do what your pa said, boys. Go after Celeste and don't let her get away. She's got a lot of explaining to do."

Taylor said softly, "Pa?"

"Hurry."

On his feet, Taylor glanced at Vida, then at Cal, who stood beside him. He said, "Let's go."

* * *

Everything was going wrong!

Celeste gripped the buggy's reins tightly, then slapped them sharply against the laboring bay's back as she urged the horse to a faster pace on the rutted trail. Still incredulous over the rapid progress of events in Madalane's room and the fiasco that had resulted, she had thrown a few essentials into her suitcase and had hastened to escape. She knew where she was heading. If she could just make it to the rail line in the next town before anyone became aware of her purpose, she would be able to catch the train and she'd be on her way. Once she reached New Orleans and picked up her money, she would disappear into the vast frontier and no one would ever find her.

Excitement charged through Celeste at the thought. She had been making good time, no one was following, and she had actually begun feeling confident that all would be well—when she noticed that something was wrong with the buggy. It began riding poorly, dipping and swaying with an unnatural rhythm. Her horse had begun reacting to the problem, upsetting her by whinnying and tossing its head. The rocking had become so bad that her suitcase had bounced off the rear of the conveyance, and she'd been forced to stop the buggy and go back to collect her few essential belongings, which were strewn all over the road.

She had glimpsed the lopsided rear wheel then, but she'd had no choice except to go on. But the rocking was now so severe that she was uncertain—

Celeste gasped as the buggy abruptly flopped to the side at a tilt so extreme that it almost dislodged her from her seat. Drawing back on the reins as the foolish horse attempted to drag the vehicle forward, she looked back in time to see the buggy's rear wheel roll off into the brush beside the road.

Celeste's fair face flamed. It was Madalane's fault! Even from the grave, that damned voodoo woman was using her black magic on her!

Hatred boiled hot and deep within Celeste as she stepped down from the buggy and stood staring at the empty rear axle. She couldn't go any further this way, and she didn't dare go back to the ranch. In retrospect, she realized she shouldn't have left. She should've claimed that Madalane went crazy, that she had been struggling with Madalane after the crazed servant shot Buck, and that the gun then discharged and killed Madalane, too. No one would have dared contradict her story. Everyone knew how much she *loved* her husband—but it was too late now. She had panicked and had tried to get away, and the opportunity was lost.

Her anxiety expanding, Celeste looked at the wheel where it had come to rest at the side of the trail. She had to get to the next town, and she'd seen the men fix a wheel often enough. With some ingenuity, she might be able to fix it so it would last a little while, at least.

Celeste strode toward the brush lining the trail. She couldn't give up. She was only a few miles from the kind of freedom she'd always dreamed of. There were countless opportunities for a beautiful woman in California . . . so many men with money to spend on a woman. Possibly she'd even start a House of Pleasure of her own! She'd put Miss Ruby to shame and become so wealthy that she'd be able to pick and choose from a full stable of men waiting at her beck and call.

Celeste knelt at the roadside where the wheel lay. A little effort now, and all her dreams would come true.

But—what was that strange sound?

Celeste turned, then gasped at the sight of the rattler coiled behind her. Frozen into immobility, she watched, mesmerized, as it seemed to suspend itself in midair. It struck in a blur of movement too quick for her eye to follow.

But she felt the pain.

Celeste stared at her arm as the snake slithered away, at the twin pinpoints of blood seeping from her white skin. Her heart pounded and she gasped with fear. She sank to her knees on the dusty trail, the thunder of her heartbeat growing louder in her ears as the pain rapidly spread. There was no one to help her . . . not her mother, who had long ago deserted her; not Henri, with his hot, sweaty hands; not Derek, with his lascivious appetite; not Madalane, with her crazed obsession for vengeance; and not Buck, who had never really loved her at all.

She cursed each and every one of them with her failing breath . . . even though she knew she would meet them all again very soon.

Chapter 12

Taylor was perspiring heavily. He needed some air.

Not bothering to glance back at the parlor of the Texas Star, crowded to the maximum with smiling family and friends, he walked out into the sun-baked yard and took a deep breath. He moved restlessly in the dark suitcoat he wore. His trousers were pressed, his linen shirt starched and buttoned up to the neck, and his tie was secure. He was suffocating. He had worn similar attire with ease during his days working as a Pinkerton in many of the country's largest cities—days which now seemed distant to his mind.

But Vida didn't seem distant.

Taylor felt a leap of excitement at the thought of her. In a few minutes she would be his wife—and she would belong to him forever.

Taylor's mind swiftly negated that thought. Vida would never *belong* to anyone. She was too independent, too secure in what she had to offer, too smart. No, in a few minutes she would enter the parlor where he and the wedding guests awaited her, and she would *join* him in a union presided over by the Reverend Aims that would bind them together forever . . . a union of equal, loving partners . . . partners who had passionately consummated their love the previous night, and many nights before.

Taylor's unconscious smile faded. Vida was well now, but the impact of Pierre's blow had been long-lasting. Doc Maggie said Pierre had struck Vida so hard that he had made her brain suffer temporarily, causing her blurred vision and weakness. Doc had also cautioned that if Vida did not allow herself the time she needed to fully heal, the result might be disastrous.

That thought had panicked him. Life without Vida would be horribly flat and empty.

As it had been for Buck after Emma died.

Taylor knew he would never forget the determination with which Cal and he had raced to catch up to Celeste after finding Buck lying shot and abandoned on Madalane's bedroom floor. Nor would he ever forget the moment when they came upon the buggy with Celeste lying beside it.

Dying from a poisonous snakebite—it was a fitting end for a woman as venomous as she.

He had been surprised, however, when they returned to the ranch house with the buggy in tow, and Buck's only reaction to the news was . . . satisfaction.

The old man had somehow survived his wound with Doc Maggie's diligent care. Another day that was burned into Taylor's memory was the morning Buck called Cal and him to his room and related the full account of Celeste and Madalane's confessions that last day.

Shock . . . disbelief . . . despair.

Buck had gone silent at the conclusion of his recitation. As pale and skeletal as he had become, Buck was just a whisper of himself as he looked at them and said, "I'm sorry . . . more than you'll ever know. I'll never forgive myself for being so damned selfish and arrogant that Emma and Bonnie died because of me. And the years I lost with both you boys . . ." He had shaken his head, then said, "I won't forgive myself, neither, for the vanity that overwhelmed my common sense while I tolerated Madalane and told myself that Celeste really loved me—when all the while they were both doing their best to destroy everything and everybody connected to me."

His faded eyes bright, Buck then whispered, "You know the truth—why I turned away from you both after Emma and Bonnie died, don't you? Because I knew if I didn't, I'd have to admit all my shortcomings, if only to myself, and I didn't have the stomach for it. I blamed you for Bonnie's death, Cal, and I stuck to that thought because I knew I'd done wrong—that I should've thought more about easing Bonnie's grief than indulging my own. Then Celeste showed up, Taylor, and she gave me the perfect escape from the accusation I saw in your eyes. The hard truth is, your ma believed in me . . . but I never stepped up to being worthy of her. Hell, I don't even know why she kept on loving me. All I do know is that when she was gone, I knew I'd never love anybody the way I had loved her."

Aroused from his thoughts by a burst of laughter from the house, Taylor glanced back, then wandered toward the barn as memories took over again.

It had been strange, with Pa and Vida both recuperating at the Star ranch. Aware there was no woman on the place to act as nurse, Doc had taken care of Buck by making the ranch her base until he was out of danger.

As for Vida, Taylor had returned "tit for tat," a favorite of Vida's sayings, by taking care of her just as she had taken care of him—moments he treasured more than she knew.

The "family" had gathered around, too: Honor, all blunt honesty and gentle heart; Jace Rule, her husband, the soft-spoken sheriff who had no need to raise his voice to be heard; Cal, Pru, and Jeremy, the newest offshoot of the Star family; and Randy, Big John, and Mitch, always dependable, truly family in spirit.

Of course, there were also Vida's steadfast admirers at the Last Chance Saloon, who had made sure she knew they missed her and wondered when she was coming back.

Taylor had a message for them. She wasn't.

With the exception of the Last Chance customers, everyone was inside, waiting for the ceremony to begin. *Everyone* included Larry, Josh, and Winston, the three ranch hands who had remained faithful to Cal and had helped pull him through tough times. Those tough times had finally come to an end for Cal when Buck revealed the truth of Madalane's horrific act at the well. However vile, the revelation that she had killed Bonnie had finally freed Cal from his lingering guilt.

Silent amidst all the frivolity at the house, Buck sat in a corner with Doc Maggie watchful nearby. Doc Maggie had informed Cal and Taylor that Buck wouldn't last much longer. Celeste's malevolence would soon reap its final reward.

Yet, in spite of her, it appeared the family had survived, closer to each other and stronger than ever—a blessing in disguise, to hear Doc Maggie describe it.

Taylor entered the barn and paused in the cool interior, seeking a moment to come to terms with the thoughts inundating his mind. He wished—

A sound in the shadows at the rear of the barn caught Taylor's attention, and he went still. Silently cursing the fact that his derringer was not a part of his matrimonial attire, he took a few more cautious steps before coming to a surprised halt.

He asked, "What are you doing here?"

Vida replied, "I suppose I could ask the same."

"I needed some air."

"So did I."

Spontaneous emotion clenched Taylor's stomach when he looked at Vida. She was wearing her wedding dress, a simple gown of red taffeta. Yes, *red*, her favorite color—a shade that never failed to imbue her upswept hair with the shimmering depth of dark silk, and her eyes with the look of black velvet—a color which brought into sharper contrast flawless skin so smooth and white that he longed to feel it again under his lips. He had not blinked an eye when she informed him of her color choice. Vida was never one to surrender to conformity.

Taylor said, "You came out here because . . . ?"

Closing the distance between them in a few steps, Vida slid her arms around Taylor's neck and said softly, "I slipped in through the back door of the barn because I knew you'd be here, and I needed to say something to you privately before we spoke our vows."

Her eyes growing suddenly moist, Vida whispered, "I suppose it's strange to say this now, but I always knew I loved you, Taylor . . . *always*. But I never realized how much that love had become a part of me. I guess it took your sudden disappearance after that evening in New Orleans to stir my first realization; and every day since, after coming to Lowell and watching the intrigues that still threatened your life, for that realization to grow to fruition. It's a wonder to me now, that I could be so quick of mind and so intuitive, yet despite all the time we spent together, that basic truth escaped me."

Vida whispered, "It's important for me to say these things to you now, Taylor. I want you to know that from this day forward, wherever we are, whatever we do, I'll always love you." Momentarily unable to voice a response, Taylor gathered Vida close. Experiencing the sheer joy of her, he felt familiar passions heating— passions that halted when he drew back abruptly and said, "All right . . . so tell me the rest."

"The rest?"

"Vida . . ."

Hesitating only a moment longer, Vida said, "After you left me this morning, a telegram was delivered from Allan."

"Allan—"

"He says the agency has just gotten a case that he wants us to start working on. He says it's tailor made for us."

Taylor studied Vida's expression as he inquired, "Where?"

"New York City."

"When?"

"Right away."

"What did you wire back?"

"I didn't."

"What do you *want* to tell him?"

Vida hesitated again. Her beautiful face solemn, she whispered, "I want to tell him that you came back to Lowell to face your past, and you made me a part of everything that's good in it. I want to tell him that you've found your family again, that your family is now my family, and that it's all too precious and new, and there are too many things for us to do here—together—for us to put it all aside right now. I want to tell him that the best part of it all is what we've found in each other's arms . . . something that we need time to explore and indulge."

"And indulge—"

"And I want to tell him I've discovered how very much I love you, Taylor."

"It's not as much as I love you."

"No, huh?"

Steeling himself as heated emotions again began rising, Taylor whispered against her lips, "Just for the record—I love you, Vida. Everything you said is multiplied a hundred and ten times or more for me. As far as I'm concerned, we can respond to Allan's telegram in two words."

" 'Not now.' "

"That sounds right."

" 'And maybe never.' "

"That sounds right, too."

Taylor crushed Vida close. Vida . . . all woman and more, she fulfilled every need and desire he had ever experienced. She challenged him with her wit and intelligence; she raised his hunger for her in so many ways, with such a myriad of loving emotions that she left no fantasy unfulfilled. She was all he had ever wanted, all he had aspired to hold, yet she still remained a mystery he could never quite resolve. They were soul mates, lovers, partners for life—all and everything to each other.

Separating himself from her as his emotions threatened to slip beyond control, Taylor whispered, "I suppose they're waiting for us inside."

"They've been waiting a long time, too."

His arm around her, Taylor drew Vida back out into the yard. He glanced down at her when they stopped at the ranch-house door. He loved her.

She loved him.

There could be no more perfect ending.

Taylor paused a moment longer, suddenly realizing he was wrong.

There could be no more perfect . . . beginning.

TEXAS STAR

ELAINE BARBIERI

Buck Star is a handsome cad with a love-'em-and-leave-'em attitude that broke more than one heart. But when he walks out on a beautiful New Orleans socialite, he sets into motion a chain of treachery and deceit that threatens to destroy the ranching empire he'd built and even the children he'd once hoped would inherit it. . . .

A mysterious message compels Caldwell Star to return to Lowell, Texas, after a nine-year absence. Back in Lowell, he meets a stubborn young widow who refuses his help, but needs it more than she can know. Her gentle touch and proud spirit give Cal strength to face the demons of the past, to reach out for a love that would heal his wounded soul.

Renegade Moon

Elaine Barbieri

Somewhere in the lush grasslands of the Texas hill country, three brothers and a sister fight to hold their family together, struggle to keep their ranch solvent, while they await the return of the one person who can shed light on the secrets of the past.

No sooner has he rescued spitfire Glory Townsend from deadly quicksand than Quince finds himself trapped in a quagmire of emotions far more difficult to escape. Every time he looks into her flashing green eyes he feels himself sinking deeper. Maybe it is time to stop struggling and admit that only her love can save him.

BETH HENDERSON
AT TWILIGHT

When Louisa Burgess awakes to find a handsome stranger has come to her rescue, she thinks it is just another of the many daydreams she's indulged in since the death of her lying, cheating husband. But in the tattered remains of his Union Army uniform, this dark and brooding knight in shining armor is a waking fantasy. J. W. Walford is the answer to all her problems—her ticket away from hardship; away from the greedy eyes of banker Titus Gillette.

With Louisa's infant in tow, the pair set off toward an unknown future. But neither is intimidated, for under the grand expanse of the velvety Texas sky, J. W. and Louisa find solace in each other's arms, every evening...*AT TWILIGHT*.

The TROUBLE With HARRY
KATIE MACALISTER

1. He is Plum's new husband. Not normally a problem, but when you consider that Harry advertised for a wife, and Plum was set to marry his secretary, there was cause for a bit of confusion.

2. He has a title. Plum has spent the last twenty years hiding from the *ton*, and now Harry wants her to shine in society? Horrors!

3. He doesn't know about her shocking secret. How is she going to explain about the dead husband who isn't a husband . . . and who now seems to be alive again?

4. He's fallen in love with her. And yet, the maddening man refuses to confide in her. For Plum knows the real trouble with Harry is that he's stolen her heart.

BRAZEN
BOBBI SMITH

Casey Turner can rope and ride like any man, but when she strides down the streets of Hard Luck, Texas, nobody takes her for anything but a beautiful woman. Working alongside her Pa to keep the bank from foreclosing on the Bar T, she has no time for romance. But all that is about to change....

Michael Donovan has had a burr under his saddle about Casey for years. The last thing he wants is to be forced into marrying the little hoyden, but it looks like he has no choice if he wants to safeguard the future of the Donovan ranch. He'll do his darndest, but he can never let on that underneath her pretty new dresses Casey is as wild as ever, and in his arms she is positively...*BRAZEN*.
